CHRISTOPHER BUSH
DANCING DEATH

CHRISTOPHER BUSH was born Charlie Christmas Bush in Norfolk in 1885. His father was a farm labourer and his mother a milliner. In the early years of his childhood he lived with his aunt and uncle in London before returning to Norfolk aged seven, later winning a scholarship to Thetford Grammar School.

As an adult, Bush worked as a schoolmaster for 27 years, pausing only to fight in World War One, until retiring aged 46 in 1931 to be a full-time novelist. His first novel featuring the eccentric Ludovic Travers was published in 1926, and was followed by 62 additional Travers mysteries. These are all to be republished by Dean Street Press.

Christopher Bush fought again in World War Two, and was elected a member of the prestigious Detection Club. He died in 1973.

D0878631

By Christopher Bush

The Plumley Inheritance
The Perfect Murder Case
Dead Man Twice
Murder at Fenwold
Dancing Death
Dead Man's Music
Cut Throat
The Case of the Unfortunate Village
The Case of the April Fools
The Case of the Three Strange Faces

CHRISTOPHER BUSH

DANCING DEATH

With an introduction
by Curtis Evans

DEAN STREET PRESS

To

Some other men's wives;

in other words

MY SISTERS

Every character in this story is utterly
fictitious—with one exception, Ho-Ping

INTRODUCTION

THAT ONCE vast and mighty legion of bright young (and youngish) British crime writers who began publishing their ingenious tales of mystery and imagination during what is known as the Golden Age of detective fiction (traditionally dated from 1920 to 1939) had greatly diminished by the iconoclastic decade of the Sixties, many of these writers having become casualties of time. Of the 38 authors who during the Golden Age had belonged to the Detection Club, a London-based group which included within its ranks many of the finest writers of detective fiction then plying the craft in the United Kingdom, just over a third remained among the living by the second half of the 1960s, while merely seven—Agatha Christie, Anthony Gilbert, Gladys Mitchell, Margery Allingham, John Dickson Carr, Nicholas Blake and Christopher Bush—were still penning crime fiction.

In 1966--a year that saw the sad demise, at the too young age of 62, of Margery Allingham--an executive with the English book publishing firm Macdonald reflected on the continued popularity of the author who today is the least well known among this tiny but accomplished crime writing cohort: Christopher Bush (1885-1973), whose first of his three score and three series detective novels, *The Plumley Inheritance*, had appeared fully four decades earlier, in 1926. "He has a considerable public, a 'steady Bush public,' a public that has endured through many years," the executive boasted of Bush. "He never presents any problem to his publisher, who knows exactly how many copies of a title may be safely printed for the loyal Bush fans; the number is a healthy one too." Yet in 1968, just a couple of years after the Macdonald editor's affirmation of Bush's notable popular duration as a crime writer, the author, now in his 83rd year, bade farewell to mystery fiction with a final detective novel, *The Case of the Prodigal Daughter*, in which, like in Agatha Christie's *Third Girl* (1966), copious references are made, none too favorably, to youthful sex, drugs and rock and roll. Afterwards, outside of the reprinting in the UK in the early 1970s of a scattering of classic Bush titles from the Golden Age, Bush's books, in contrast with those of Christie, Carr, Allingham and Blake, disappeared from mass circulation in both the UK and the US, becoming fervently sought (and ever more unobtainable) treasures by collectors and connoisseurs of classic crime fiction. Now, in one of the signal developments in vintage mystery publishing, Dean Street Press is reprinting all 63 Christopher Bush detective novels. These will be published over a period of months, beginning with the release of books 1 to 10 in the series.

Few Golden Age British mystery writers had backgrounds as humble yet simultaneously mysterious, dotted with omissions and evasions, as Christopher Bush, who was born Charlie Christmas Bush on the day of the Nativity in 1885 in the Norfolk village of Great Hockham, to Charles Walter Bush and his second wife, Eva Margaret Long. While the father of Christopher Bush's Detection Club colleague and near exact contemporary Henry Wade (the pseudonym of Henry Lancelot Aubrey-Fletcher) was a baronet who lived in an elegant Georgian mansion and claimed extensive ownership of fertile English fields, Christopher's father resided in a cramped cottage and toiled in fields as a farm laborer, a term that in the late Victorian and Edwardian era, his son lamented many years afterward, "had in it something of contempt....There was something almost of serfdom about it."

Charles Walter Bush was a canny though mercurial individual, his only learning, his son recalled, having been "acquired at the Sunday school." A man of parts, Charles was a tenant farmer of three acres, a thatcher, bricklayer and carpenter (fittingly for the father of a detective novelist, coffins were his specialty), a village radical and a most adept poacher. After a flight from Great Hockham, possibly on account of his poaching activities, Charles, a widower with a baby son whom he had left in the care of his mother, resided in London, where he worked for a firm of spice importers. At a dance in the city, Charles met Christopher's mother, Eva Long, a lovely and sweet-natured young milliner and bonnet maker, sweeping her off her feet with a combination of "good looks and a certain plausibility." After their marriage the couple left London to live in a tiny rented cottage in Great Hockham, where Eva over the next eighteen years gave birth to three sons and five daughters and perforce learned the challenging ways of rural domestic economy.

Decades later an octogenarian Christopher Bush, in his memoir *Winter Harvest: A Norfolk Boyhood* (1967), characterized Great Hockham as a rustic rural redoubt where many of the words that fell from the tongues of the native inhabitants "were those of Shakespeare, Milton and the Authorised Version....Still in general use were words that were standard in Chaucer's time, but had since lost a certain respectability." Christopher amusingly recalled as a young boy telling his mother that a respectable neighbor woman had used profanity, explaining that in his hearing she had told her husband, "George, wipe you that shit off that pig's arse, do you'll datty your trousers," to which his mother had responded that although that particular usage of a four-letter word had not really been *swearing*, he was not to give vent to such language himself.

Great Hockham, which in Christopher Bush's youth had a population of about four hundred souls, was composed of a score or so of cottages, three public houses, a post-office, five shops, a couple of forges and a pair of churches, All Saint's and the Primitive Methodist Chapel, where the Bush family rather vocally worshipped. "The village lived by farming, and most of its men were labourers," Christopher recollected. "Most of the children left school as soon as the law permitted: boys to be absorbed somehow into the land and the girls to go into domestic service." There were three large farms and four smaller ones, and, in something of an anomaly, not one but two squires--the original squire, dubbed "Finch" by Christopher, having let the shooting rights at Little Hockham Hall to one "Green," a wealthy international banker, making the latter man a squire by courtesy. Finch owned most of the local houses and farms, in traditional form receiving rents for them personally on Michaelmas; and when Christopher's father fell out with Green, "a red-faced, pompous, blustering man," over a political election, he lost all of the banker's business, much to his mother's distress. Yet against all odds and adversities, Christopher's life greatly diverged from settled norms in Great Hockham, incidentally producing one of the most distinguished detective novelists from the Golden Age of detective fiction.

Although Christopher Bush was born in Great Hockham, he spent his earliest years in London living with his mother's much older sister, Elizabeth, and her husband, a fur dealer by the name of James Streeter, the couple having no children of their own. Almost certainly of illegitimate birth, Eva had been raised by the Long family from her infancy. She once told her youngest daughter how she recalled the Longs being visited, when she was a child, by a "fine lady in a carriage," whom she believed was her birth mother. Or is it possible that the "fine lady in a carriage" was simply an imaginary figment, like the aristocratic fantasies of Philippa Palfrey in P.D. James's *Innocent Blood* (1980), and that Eva's "sister" Elizabeth was in fact her mother?

The Streeters were a comfortably circumstanced couple at the time they took custody of Christopher. Their household included two maids and a governess for the young boy, whose doting but dutiful "Aunt Lizzie" devoted much of her time to the performance of "good works among the East End poor." When Christopher was seven years old, however, drastically straightened financial circumstances compelled the Streeters to leave London for Norfolk, by the way returning the boy to his birth parents in Great Hockham.

Fortunately the cause of the education of Christopher, who was not only a capable village cricketer but a precocious reader and scholar, was taken up both by his determined and devoted mother and an idealistic local elementary school headmaster. In his teens Christopher secured a scholarship to Norfolk's Thetford Grammar School, one of England's oldest educational institutions, where Thomas Paine had studied a century-and-a-half earlier. He left Thetford in 1904 to take a position as a junior schoolmaster, missing a chance to go to Cambridge

University on yet another scholarship. (Later he proclaimed himself thankful for this turn of events, sardonically speculating that had he received a Cambridge degree he "might have become an exceedingly minor don or something as staid and static and respectable as a publisher.") Christopher would teach in English schools for the next twenty-seven years, retiring at the age of 46 in 1931, after he had established a successful career as a detective novelist.

Christopher's romantic relationships proved far rockier than his career path, not to mention every bit as murky as his mother's familial antecedents. In 1911, when Christopher was teaching in Wood Green School, a co-educational institution in Oxfordshire, he wed county council schoolteacher Ella Maria Pinner, a daughter of a baker neighbor of the Bushes in Great Hockham. The two appear never actually to have lived together, however, and in 1914, when Christopher at the age of 29 headed to war in the 16th (Public Schools) Battalion of the Middlesex Regiment, he falsely claimed in his attestation papers, under penalty of two years' imprisonment with hard labor, to be unmarried.

After four years of service in the Great War, including a year-long stint in Egypt, Christopher returned in 1919 to his position at Wood Green School, where he became involved in another romantic relationship, from which he soon desired to extricate himself. (A photo of the future author, taken at this time in Egypt, shows a rather dashing, thin-mustached man in uniform and is signed "Chris," suggesting that he had dispensed with "Charlie" and taken in its place a diminutive drawn from his middle name.) The next year Winifred Chart, a mathematics teacher at Wood Green, gave birth to a son, whom she named Geoffrey Bush. Christopher was the father of Geoffrey, who later in life became a noted English composer, though for reasons best known to himself Christopher never acknowledged his son. (A letter Geoffrey once sent him was returned unopened.) Winifred claimed that she and Christopher had married but separated, but she refused to speak of her purported spouse forever after and she destroyed all of his letters and other mementos, with the exception of a book of poetry that he had written for her during what she termed their engagement.

Christopher's true mate in life, though with her he had no children, was Florence Marjorie Barclay, the daughter of a draper from Ballymena, Northern Ireland, and, like Ella Pinner and Winifred Chart, a schoolteacher. Christopher and Marjorie likely had become romantically involved by 1929, when Christopher dedicated to her his second detective novel, *The Perfect Murder Case*; and they lived together as man and wife from the 1930s until her death in 1968 (after which, probably not coincidentally, Christopher stopped publishing novels). Christopher returned with Marjorie to the vicinity of Great Hockham when his writing career took flight, purchasing two adjoining cottages and commissioning his father and a stepbrother to build an extension consisting of a kitchen, two bedrooms and a new staircase. (The now sprawling structure, which Christopher called "Home Cottage," is now a bed and breakfast grandiloquently dubbed "Home Hall.") After a falling-out with his father, presumably over the conduct of Christopher's personal life, he and Marjorie in 1932 moved to Beckley, Sussex, where they purchased Horsepen, a lovely Tudor plaster and timber-framed house. In 1953 the couple settled at their final home, The Great House, a centuries-old structure (now a boutique hotel) in Lavenham, Suffolk.

From these three houses Christopher maintained a lucrative and critically esteemed career as a novelist, publishing both detective novels as Christopher Bush and, commencing in 1933 with the acclaimed book *Return* (in the UK, *God and the Rabbit*, 1934), regional novels purposefully drawing on his own life experience, under the pen name Michael Home. (During the 1940s he also published espionage novels under the Michael Home pseudonym.) Although his first detective novel, *The Plumley Inheritance*, made a limited impact, with his second, *The Perfect Murder Case*, Christopher struck gold. The latter novel, a big seller in both the UK and the US, was published in the former country by the prestigious Heinemann, soon to become the publisher of the detective novels of Margery

Allingham and Carter Dickson (John Dickson Carr), and in the latter country by the Crime Club imprint of Doubleday, Doran, one of the most important publishers of mystery fiction in the United States.

Over the decade of the 1930s Christopher Bush published, in both the UK and the US as well as other countries around the world, some of the finest detective fiction of the Golden Age, prompting the brilliant Thirties crime fiction reviewer, author and Oxford University Press editor Charles Williams to avow: "Mr. Bush writes of as thoroughly enjoyable murders as any I know." (More recently, mystery genre authority B.A. Pike dubbed these novels by Bush, whom he praised as "one of the most reliable and resourceful of true detective writers"; "Golden Age baroque, rendered remarkable by some extraordinary flights of fancy.") In 1937 Christopher Bush became, along with Nicholas Blake, E.C.R. Lorac and Newton Gayle (the writing team of Muna Lee and Maurice West Guinness), one of the final authors initiated into the Detection Club before the outbreak of the Second World War and with it the demise of the Golden Age. Afterward he continued publishing a detective novel or more a year, with his final book in 1968 reaching a total of 63, all of them detailing the investigative adventures of lanky and bespectacled gentleman amateur detective Ludovic Travers. Concurring as I do with the encomia of Charles Williams and B.A. Pike, I will end this introduction by thanking Avril MacArthur for providing invaluable biographical information on her great uncle, and simply wishing fans of classic crime fiction good times as they discover (or rediscover), with this latest splendid series of Dean Street Press classic crime fiction reissues, Christopher Bush's Ludovic Travers detective novels. May a new "Bush public" yet arise!

Curtis Evans

Dancing Death (1931)

"Thank you, Pollock. What's the weather like? More snow coming?"

"Bound to come, sir. The sky's very bad."

FOR MANY devotees of vintage British mystery, there is nothing quite like a murder for Christmas, especially when that murder takes place in a snowbound country mansion during a violently acrimonious house party, as frosty wind makes moan. ('Tis the season!) Certainly Christopher Bush included all of fans' most desired Christmas murder trimmings in his deliciously devious mystery *Dancing Death* (1931), the fifth in the Ludovic Travers series of detective novels and one of the finest British Christmas crime tales published during the Golden Age of detective fiction. The roster of such novels, enough to stock the twelve days of Christmas, includes Molly Thynne's *The Crime at the Noah's Ark* (1931), C.H.B. Kitchin's *Crime at Christmas* (1934), Mavis Doriel Hay's *The Santa Claus Murder* (1936), Jefferson Farjeon's *Mystery in White* (1937), Agatha Christie's *Hercule Poirot's Christmas* (1938), Michael Innes's *There Came Both Mist and Snow* (1940), Nicholas Blake's *The Case of the Abominable Snowman* (1941), Georgette Heyer's *Envious Casca* (1941), John Dickson Carr's *The Gilded Man* (1942), and, if we stretch the traditionally accepted temporal limit of the Golden Age yet more, Gladys Mitchell's *Groaning Spinney* (1950) and Cyril Hare's *An English Murder* (1951). Dean Street Press's new edition of Christopher Bush's *Dancing Death*, the first in nearly ninety years, is a most welcome addition to this charming company of Christmas country house (in one case country inn) mysteries.

Little Levington Hall, the site of the seasonal house party in *Dancing Death*, is owned by Martin Braishe, inventor of a gas in which the War Office has taken a great interest, on account of its "amazingly lethal properties." Unfortunately for Braishe and his houseguests, however, the fancy-dress ball that

Braishe hosts at Little Levington Hall might more accurately be described as a fancy-death ball. After the formal festivities have taken place, nine guests remain at the Hall, along with a retinue of servants, including the butler, Pollock; the housekeeper, Mrs. Cairns; a lady's maid named Ransome; and a footman named William. It is at this point that dead bodies most inconveniently begin to turn up at Little Levington Hall, like so many unwanted Christmas presents. (Sadly, it is hard to regift a corpse.)

The houseguests fated to stay--and in some cases pass away --at Little Levington Hall are George Paradine, medico in high places, and Celia Paradine, his formidable wife; mercurial stage actress Mirabel Quest and her lofty sister, Brenda Fewne, vicar's daughters of rather different hues (Recalling the celebrated lines from the 2005 film *Capote*—"It's as if Perry and I grew up in the same house. He stood up and went out the back door, while I went out the front.—Bush writes of the sisters, "Brenda seemed to have left the vicarial nest by crossing the lawn to the duke's castle; Mirabel to have eloped from a back window with the frowsy leader of a pierrot troupe."); Brenda's husband, Denis, a novelist; Tommy Wildernesse, young man-about-town; stage producer Wyndham Challis, dismissed as a "cheap little vulgarian" by Brenda; and, last but certainly not least, our old friends Ludovic "Ludo" Travers, amiable, horn-rimmed author of *Economics of a Spendthrift* and something of a gentleman amateur detective, and Ludo's colleague John Franklin, still head of the Enquiry Agency at Durangos Limited. (It might be remiss of me not to give brief mention as well to Ho-Ping, Celia Paradine's huffing and puffing Peke —the only character in the novel who is not "utterly fictitious" according to the author.)

On the morning after the ball, an unexpected guest turns up at the breakfast table, cheerfully consuming toast and marmalade: one Crashaw, a schoolmaster at Westover, "the most expensive prep school in England," who explains that his car "conked out altogether in a drift," forcing him to seek shelter at the Hall. Soon afterward, many an unsettling thing is discovered at Little Levington Hall. Two of the guests are found dead, one of them in the house, still in the previous night's costume, and the other in a pagoda on the lawn, "contorted in the midst of a lot of exploded toy balloons," as one delighted book reviewer, a connoisseur of the fantastical in murder, put it. Additionally, some of the guests' rooms have been burgled and a cylinder of Braishe's incredibly lethal gas has gone missing. The Hall having become enshrouded in snow overnight and the telephone lines having been cut, John Franklin treks overland to reach the police on foot, leaving Travers on the scene of the crimes, free to indulge his penchant for amateur detection. Despite Travers' best efforts, however, a third death takes place at the Hall before the police finally put in an appearance, two-thirds of the way into the novel.

The police contingent at Little Levington Hall is led by another personage who by now was familiar to Bush fans: Superintendent Wharton, one of the Yard's Big Five, who with his "old-fashioned glasses" and drooping moustache looks like a "burlier Chester Conklin" (this a reference to a film comedian who had been extremely popular in the recent pre-talkie era). However, in marked contrast with many of the frequently brusque and bumbling police detectives of Golden Age detective fiction, Wharton is a smoothly astute professional and most decidedly nobody's fool (unless he decides deliberately to play one):

> He was so quietly paternal in appearance, so disarmingly jovial, so obviously understanding and sympathetic, that he might have been a popular medical practitioner. As to his colossal patience, his tenacious memory, and his occasional outbursts of perfectly terrifying and snarling indignation, these were sides that the unwary never expected. And he was a good mixer. He could be deferential, suave, retiring; even a damn fool, if circumstances demanded it.

With the belated appearance of the police, Ludo Travers is able to perform some longer-distance detection, and from there events move swiftly to a smash climax. Modern fans of classic crime fiction should be impressed indeed when they see just how dexterously Bush has managed his fiendishly complex plot, which includes a floor plan (relevant), a ground plan (including the fatal pagoda) and an illustration of the last scrawled words of one of the murder victims. As in Bush's *The Perfect Murder Case*, the first chapter is "by way of a prologue," and is constituted of a series of vignettes, drawn by Travers himself, of the case's "high lights and solutions and straight dope". It concludes with a cryptic parable, drawn by an author who was well-churched in his youth: a challenge to the reader, if you will, done in the best baroque Golden Age manner. Make of it what you can, dear readers:

> There were two men in one city; the one rich and the other poor.
> The rich man had exceeding many flocks and herds;
> But the poor man had nothing, save one little ewe lamb...it did eat of his own meat, and drink of his own cup, and lay in his bosom.

For many years, when the Queen of Crime Agatha Christie was still alive, fans of classic mystery intensely looked forward to reading their annual "Christie for Christmas." Let us hope they did not forget to include a Bush for Boxing Day.

CHAPTER I
TRAVERS DRAWS THE CURTAIN

Ludovic Travers refused immediately and absolutely to have anything to do with the writing of this account. The very first hints were enough to produce the refusal, and after that there was no particular point in marshalling arguments, of which the first would certainly have been that thanks to the circumstances in which he found himself, the case had been his from start to finish. Then might have come a short dissertation on the refreshingly original methods of an amateur when left to his own devices and resources.

All that, however, was unsaid. Travers must have seen something of the disappointment his refusal was causing, because in addition to the diffidence of his manner when it was made, he threw out a palliative hint in another direction—half an hour later, at tea.

"Things seem very different when you look back on them," he said suddenly. "Don't you think so?"

"What things?"

"Well—er—murder cases. Take that perfectly horrible affair at Levington. At first thought you'd say the—er—high lights were the events themselves—a knife thrust, a sudden gripping of a neck, a man in ghastly convulsions with the light full on, waiting for death and not knowing it. As a matter of fact, from the angle of this armchair they seem disproportionately unimportant."

I caught a smile which seemed helpful, if not generous. At any rate, it gave me my idea.

"Do you know, Ludo," I said; "I think you're wise not to tackle the whole book. There *are* people who might accuse you of prejudice or personal interest. But there *is* something you might do for us instead. Just a brief account of those things you do think important: you know—the kind of thing you did for us once before!"

He gave me a shrewd look. "Don't you think people would rather find the high lights for themselves?"

"Not in the least!" I assured him. "Just hint at what led up to everything. Tell us the things you wished you had known. Let the solution stare people clean in the eye, if they'd like to find it."

"Exactly!" His face showed he was amused at something. "I rather thought of offering you something of the sort—if you cared to have it! I don't mind owning up that I've interviewed Clerke—Wharton dug him up for me."

"Clerke! Who on earth's he?"

He smiled again. "But I thought you knew the case from A to Z!"

"Well, I thought I did."

"Hm! And I've also seen Reid."

That was really too much. "Here, I say, Ludo! What's the idea?"

He shrugged his shoulders humorously. "You mean to say you don't know Reid?"

"I certainly don't—not by name."

He laughed. "Capital! Then you'll do to practise on! I suppose, by the way, you don't want the reader led up the orchard, so to speak?"

"Heavens, no! That'd be unpardonable! You've got to write perfectly straight dope."

"I see." Then he gave me one of his old whimsical looks. "Of course you realize, as I did when I first thought about it, that you're asking me to exhibit myself as a first-class idiot!"

"Heaven forbid!" said I hastily. "But how do you mean, precisely?"

"Well, looking at these things in cold blood, in conjunction with what happened in the house, anybody could see that only a fool could have missed 'em. People don't get flurried, you see, in cold blood. Now, I *was* flurried. I don't mind telling you I was scared—badly scared. I missed everything. Even when Wharton gave me the tip that morning when I set off to Folkestone, I couldn't see it!"

"I don't think I'd worry about that if I were you," I consoled him, though I rather guessed there was more leg-pulling in it than apprehension. "What about that epigram of yours that

I always enjoy so much—'It's only the fools who never make mistakes'?"

So much for that. As for Ludovic Travers's ideas of high lights and solutions and straight dope, well, here they are; just as they were copied from his manuscript.

A

Chief Detective Inspector Clerke was most unlike a detective in those leisure moments of his that came immediately after an evening meal. Within five minutes of swallowing the last mouthful, he would have his pipe alight, and having put on an old blazer and got into his favourite chair, with slippered feet on a hassock, he would reach for the detective story he or his wife had got from the local circulating library and settle down to an evening's criticism. At his elbow would be his notebook.

Occasionally, of course, he was disappointed. There were rare evenings when a book either satisfied his professional judgment or proved so holding that errors of fact were never jotted down. Generally, however, there would be a grunt or a snort, and his wife knew what was coming. That was what happened that December night—with important variations.

Mrs. Clerke had looked hastily through the pair of novels her husband had brought in, to see if either contained a love interest, however fleeting. One did —*Murder at Murforde*. The other—*The Shot in the Night*—was apparently as bare of females as Crusoe's island; that was why she put it at her husband's hand and left the other for herself. But something unforeseen happened. She had read half a chapter when there came from the other side of the fireplace a snort of unusual violence. *The Shot in the Night* went flying across the room and landed against the couch.

There was a mild expostulation. "Whatever *are* you doing!"

"Doing! Hm!" He sat up and scowled. *"That* damn book's the limit!" He got to his feet angrily, fetched the offending volume, and with thrust-out finger indicated the final straw.

"Look at that! A detective asks for a warrant to arrest a man for murder! A warrant!"

His wife took refuge in generalities. "I don't know why they write such things!"

"Damned ignorance! or laziness! That's what it is! They think if they put in a detective the public'll swallow anything!"

He got into his seat again, threw the book contemptuously on the floor, and sat scowling over his pipe. *Murder at Murforde* was laid aside in sympathy, and the knitting was got out. A quarter of an hour of that, and her husband got to his feet and drew a bentwood chair up to the small bureau.

"What is it, dear? Going to work?"

"No! Going to write to *The Times*."

"Oh, but they'll never print it!"

"I don't know so much about that!"

The event was one that left her speechless. She knitted and watched. An hour went by before the letter was copied out from the much corrected original. Then he handed it over with the air of a man who thinks a job well done.

To the Editor of *The Times*.

DEAR SIR:

I have been very much struck and annoyed recently by the inaccuracies and absurdities which are occurring with monotonous regularity in the numerous detective novels which are being published.

In fiction, the professional detective is supposed to obtain ideas from the perusal of works of this kind. All I obtain, in nine cases out of ten, is exasperation at the stupidity or laziness of the author who will not trouble to verify his material. On the list enclosed with this letter I give the names of books and authors that have offended in this way; with comments on the points in question that must convince you of the truth of my statements.

There is one other important fact arising out of this question. If authors make these mistakes about the routine work of Scotland Yard and the police generally, must it not be a fact that they make precisely the same kind of mistakes over technicalities in other professions—the legal, the medical, and so on?

It is time that a public so well informed as that of today took the matter up. If every professional man who found in novels statements which are travesties of fact exposed the authors, I venture to think there would be very much more attention paid to the matter of local colour.

I enclose my card, and am, sir,

Yours faithfully,

CHIEF DETECTIVE INSPECTOR.

B

Walter Reid often looked back on that cold December Saturday as one of the luckiest in his life. From the very first, everything turned out so well that he was continually being startled. Moreover, the firm was extraordinarily pleased, and for a newcomer like himself that was decidedly cheering. Everything had gone with amazing smoothness. The suspect had never seemed to be alarmed. There had been no attempt at dodging; the man was plainly as unaware as a week-old kitten. The whole of that long journey to Finchley the taxi had gone direct, and, as far as he could see, never a soul had looked back from it to the car behind.

The first sight of the house, however, had given him a certain trepidation. It was a bare fifty yards back from the road—and a well lighted road at that, with trams clanking by, and a constant stream of cars. Then had come reassurance. The district was a high-class residential one, with neighbours reasonably separated. Round the approaches were shrubberies which a merciful providence had made evergreen. Then there was a side entrance to back door and garage, so there hadn't been much risk after all in getting right up to the window once the dusk fell and the light appeared in a downstairs room. And a window was open for ventilation! And one of the voices had been of that slow, drawling type that gives you time to think and memorize.

There had been only one real difficulty. The downstairs lights went out shortly after nine. A move was evidently about to be made, either upstairs or back to town. So he'd backed into the bushes in sight of the garage. Half an hour later there was still a light in the bedroom. In a few seconds it went out. A retirement, evidently, for the night. Fifteen feet above his head was an open window and no possibility of listening at it—and that was a pity! The night, and a situation so romantic, were certain to breed confidences. Everything overheard should be vital and intimate.

He'd tried to think of a solution. There wasn't one. Never a tree handy enough or an inch of foothold to climb up by. It was infuriating! There was the open window of a bedroom well sheltered from the road, and heaven knew what waiting to be heard. Out he'd moved again, over the sodden grass and round to the outhouses. If only, by some extraordinary chance, a shed could be broken into—and in that shed there should be a ladder!

Then he saw something that made him doubt his eyes. He felt it. It *was* a ladder, under the eaves! A gardening ladder, by the size of it, left there tucked away for the winter!

He took it down quietly, tested his weight on the rungs, then left it while he surveyed the ground to secure a hasty line of retreat. Next he sacrificed his muffler and, with a piece of string, wrapped it round the ends of the ladder to deaden the sound. Then, with infinite precaution, he got it round and, almost half an inch at a time, lowered it into position. Lastly came his own progress, deadly slow, up the ladder till his ear was level with the open window. The first words he heard were these.

"How *can* they suspect anything? We've only got to be reasonably careful!"

The other voice muttered drowsily.

C

Denis Fewne was restless. There he was, pacing up and down the small pagoda, hands deep in his coat pockets; pausing every now and then to look at the snow or lean back against the writing desk to speak to Braishe or answer his questions.

Martin Braishe was perfectly comfortable in the easy chair against the open fireplace. As Denis perambulated with his back towards him, he would give a puzzled look. Sometimes his eye seemed to dwell on the old camp bed that stood by the longer match-boarded wall, where the hectic stripes of Fewne's pajamas glared against the soberer colouring.

Fewne turned round and retraced his steps. Then he leaned against the desk.

"Do you know, Martin, you're an uncommonly good chap! I owe you a frightful lot!"

Braishe laughed. "Rubbish! You owe me nothing. This is your own home—you know that. And it's awful fun to have you here."

"You're too generous, Martin." He paused for a moment or two, then turned and looked out of the window. "How on earth am I ever going to repay you?"

Braishe looked distinctly bewildered. What was the matter with Denis? Getting nervy, or morbid, or what? He'd never talked all that drivel before.

"Repay me!" He laughed good-humouredly. "My dear old chap, there's no question of repayment between you and me! I mean—er—one's got to do something before one can be repaid, and all that sort of thing."

"Yes . . . I know. Still, I *shall* make it up to you. You can rely on me, Martin."

Braishe grunted, then, "Come and sit down. Never saw such a restless devil in all my life! What's the matter with you? Fed up with the book?"

"No . . . not really." He shivered slightly. "The room's rather cold, don't you think? Give the fire a stir, will you?"

The flames leaped up as they caught the dry side of the wood. Fewne watched them, made as if to come over, hesitated, then sat on the edge of the bed.

"Have a cigarette?" Braishe passed over his case.

"No, thanks . . . really. I think perhaps I've been smoking rather a lot."

"Shouldn't wonder!" He helped himself. "Tried on your costume yet?"

Fewne smiled. "Oh, rather!"

"Like it?"

"Splendidly! It's . . . I mean I think it's marvellous!"

The other smiled at his enthusiasm. "Glad you like it! Challis is a pretty shrewd chap when it comes to casting costumes!" He got to his feet. "Think I'd better push along now. See you as soon as . . . they arrive?"

"Oh, yes! . . . Give me a holler if I'm not there."

He smiled at Braishe as he left the room, then took the fireside chair. Outside, the sky was grey, and saturated as it were with snow, and the room was as dark as twilight. Then suddenly he sprang up and, standing by the side of the window, peered across the snow. Braishe could be seen passing the loggia, then disappearing into the front porch.

Fewne sank wearily into the chair again. For several minutes he sat looking into the fire, then all at once seemed to come to a decision. For five minutes he worked—and the things he did were curious ones. Then he gave another look towards the house. Even then he was not satisfied. He opened the door and peeped round the angle of the wall along the path. He re-entered the room, and when he emerged he was carrying something.

He halted at the edge of the veranda and, leaning on the pillar with his left hand, hurled that something into the air—a thin, dark object it seemed to be as it soared away over the snow towards the far lawn. Then it fell, thirty good yards away. From where he stood he could see nothing.

He turned back into the room. As he shut the door he was breathing hard, as if he had been running. Then he sank into the chair again.

D

There were two men in one city; the one rich and the other poor.

The rich man had exceeding many flocks and herds;

But the poor man had nothing, save one little ewe lamb . . . it did eat of his own meat, and drank of his own cup, and lay in his bosom.

L. T.

PART I
THE PROBLEM

CHAPTER II
ROADS OF DESTINY

WHEN MARTIN BRAISHE decided to give a house party at Little Levington Hall, his motives were decidedly mixed, as indeed the motives of all of us are, except in plain matters of eating and sleeping. Had he been asked, however, what his motives were, he might have given three excellent ones. In the first place, since he had come into the property on the death of his father the previous summer, he had done no entertaining whatever, and a house party was therefore indicated; moreover, as Celia Paradine was available as hostess, the occasion was too good to be missed. Then some sort of celebration seemed overdue on account of that gas discovery of his. Not only had the War Office definitely taken it up, but if George Paradine was right, there seemed likely to be certain commercial uses to which it could be put, provided its amazingly lethal properties could be adequately harnessed. And lastly was the most obvious reason of all. There were people whom he liked and to whom he owed things. What more delightful than to give them the pleasure, in his own company, of knowing each other?

The fancy-dress ball was really Brenda Fewne's idea. Old Henry Braishe had made it an annual affair for New Year's Eve, and it did indeed seem rather a pity to drop an event to which so many of the most charming people in that corner of the county looked forward. Martin, indeed, needed little persuading. Many snows have melted since those days when your scientist was necessarily of mature age and monastic tastes. Braishe, just in the thirties, could shake as loose a hoof, as they put it, as the best of 'em.

As for those people who accepted the invitation to that small house party, their motives too were decidedly mixed. If one were fantastically minded or had a liking for high-flown imagery, one might say that all sorts of roads, during those twenty-four hours, led to Little Levington—as, for instance, The Street of Unlawful Delights, The Path of Prevarication, Hilarity Highway, and The Road to Dusty Death. Had you asked them what their motives were, their answers would certainly have been equivocal. In order to arrive at something like the truth, therefore, the best thing to do seems to be to use the available keyholes or to maintain a precarious hold on the luggage grids of a mixed assortment of cars.

George and Celia Paradine came down by road the previous afternoon. George was rather a quaint figure, on the short side and the least bit stout. The previous two years he had spent in Central Africa with the Pfeiffer Commission on Tropical Diseases, and his face still carried a dark tan that went very whimsically with his vast overhanging moustache. He was a good sort, was George. Ludovic Travers said he had the homeliest first-class brain in the Royal Society. What he was, was the chief authority on the fly areas of Africa; what he looked like was a benevolent uncle who was accustomed to act as horse in a series of nurseries.

Celia had the grand manner. She made no bones about acknowledging her remoteness from fifty—indeed, she made precious few bones about anything. She was accustomed to giving a withering look and then going straight on. You'd have sworn, after an hour in her company, that she carried a lorgnette, which she certainly didn't. Travers called her a maternal martinet. He also said that were she either, she'd be the world's best mother and its worst mother-in-law. But Travers had known her since he was a boy and knew how to approach on the leeward side.

"Hallo! Getting pretty near now," said George as the car lurched into the side road.

Ho-Ping, the Pekinese, almost rolled off his mistress's lap. Celia clicked her tongue.

"You must speak to Sheffield, George! His driving is getting positively reckless."

"Expect it's the camber," said her husband mildly. "Still, as you say, my dear."

She soothed the lump of fawn fur with words at which George had long ceased to wince: "There! Didum's auntie let little boy fall?" then, "Did you say Martin had got some of that dreadful gas in the house?"

George smiled. "Of course not! Besides, if he had, it'd be as safe as—safe as the Bank of England. You forget Martin's not a boy. He's a man and just as responsible as I am."

Her sniff made the obvious retort. She tickled the ears of the Peke. "Didums think he'd smell the horrid gas, then?" then, with her usual machine-gun manner, "Why is Ludovic Travers coming down to see you about it?"

"My dear, I've told you! Ludo's coming because he knows Martin, and Martin asked him. Then, sort of—er—to kill two birds with one stone, we thought Ludo could give us some idea of the financial side—company flotation, and so on—if we actually decide on anything."

For fifty yards nothing was said. Ho-Ping resumed his stertorous sleep; then, "I'm sure we should have come down yesterday. Martin can never fit all those people in."

"I thought you wrote."

"Wrote!" Another sniff. "Well, everything will probably have to be altered in any case." She thought of something else. "Who's that man Ludovic's bringing down?"

George shrugged his shoulders. "He'll be all right if Ludo's bringing him." He smiled. "All I hope is he doesn't cut me out by coming as a station master!"

"Why you indulged in that absurd fancy, I can't imagine!"

George chuckled. "Oh, yes, you can! I told you, my dear, I always wanted to be a railway porter when I was a boy. Now I've got the chance for the first time in my life, I'm jolly well not going to lose it. Besides," with extreme diplomacy, "think of the foil I shall be to you and Ho-Ping, straight from the Imperial Palace!"

"Don't they have Chinese porters?" asked Celia frigidly.

George was spared a reply. The car lurched again as it turned into the Hall drive, and as Ho-Ping woke up he had to be told all about it.

Mirabel Quest and her sister, Brenda Fewne, came down after lunch, in Mirabel's car, with Ransome, Mirabel's maid, inside with the smaller luggage. Physically the pair were alike as two peas; in most things else they were as unlike as a couple of women can be. Brenda was aloof. She seemed to be perpetually aware of the fact that other people knew her brow was like the snowdrift and her neck like the swan's. She seemed rather a Ruritanian alabaster princess than the product of a country vicarage—even taking into account the fact that her grandfather was a colonial bishop. She possessed a sort of devastating, married virginity; could refuse a cocktail with the divinest air of apology and swing into a dance with the same bored, apologetic sort of grace. You wondered what she would be like if she really laughed, but, as she never got beyond that wistful smile, you never knew.

Mirabel was a year older—twenty-eight, that is—and of the stage stagey. Her mouth was the tiniest bit larger and her lips the tiniest bit thinner than her sister's, and her moods were as many as expediency demanded. Sometimes, in repose, she looked as repulsively efficient as a bargain hunter; when she cared to be herself she could be calculatingly jolly. Her other poses—both a kind of second nature—were a Topsyish, gushing volubility and a raucous, slangy masculinity. Off the stage she was quite a good actress. On it she was a magnificent one, though the spiteful described her as a rhythmic recitation laboriously conned from Wyndham Challis. As for the pair of them, to use language purely figurative, Brenda seemed to have left the vicarial nest by crossing the lawn to the duke's castle; Mirabel, to have eloped from a back window with the frowsty leader of a pierrot troupe.

"What'll Denis make out of that last book?" she was asking. Denis was, of course, Brenda's husband, and the book his latest—*Tingling Symbols*.

"I don't know, really." She gave the faintest suggestion of a frown.

"You don't know! Well, I should jolly well know. Blue blood's all very well, old dear. Give me the boodle every time!"

"Don't be vulgar, Myra darling!"

"Vulgar be damned! What do you think Windy's coming down for, this week-end? Boodle! Wants Martin to put up the needful for the new show. *And* he'll get it!"

"I'm not quite so sure," said Brenda with rather exasperating indifference. The other flashed a quick look at her.

"How do you know what Martin'll do?"

"I don't. It's merely my opinion, darling."

The pair were silent for some time, then Brenda drawled out, "You're really so illogical you know, darling. You cling to this man Challis because he can keep you where you are. If you married Tommy Wildernesse you could snap your fingers at a cheap little vulgarian like Challis."

"You're jealous, old dear!"

"Now you're merely being absurd." Then her face showed a sudden interest. "If you must marry for that kind of thing, why not Ludovic Travers? He's simply rolling in money, and he's just been made a director of Durangos. And he knows everybody worth knowing."

"What've Durangos got to do with it?"

"Publicity, darling. They're the biggest people in the world. If you married Travers, he'd put your name on every hoarding in town."

Her sister laughed. "Why don't you get him for Denis? The poor mutt needs a little publicity—and so do you, for that matter, old dear."

Brenda was perfectly unruffled. "Well, darling, that's certainly better than notoriety!"

"You make me sick! You and your strait-laced tommyrot!" She scowled as she trod viciously on the accelerator. "What bought the car you're in? And the flat you weren't too strait-laced to sleep in?" She wrenched the car to the crown of the road. "You and your damn virtue! What good's it done you? Let you land a husband like yourself!" She mimicked Fewne's voice. "Er—how d' you do, Mirabel? . . . My God! you make me sick—the pair of you!"

Two minutes before, Ransome had shifted her seat, and with back to the wheel sat listening to the conversation.

Ludovic Travers was the next to arrive. He left his sister's place in Sussex just after lunch, Franklin in front with him, and his man, Palmer, behind till Tommy Wildernesse should be picked up at Tonbridge. Travers was mildly excited, chiefly about seeing George Paradine and Celia again after more than two years. Also, according to George's letter, that gas business of Braishe's might turn out a really big thing. George's name would carry tremendous weight with any administration in malarial or tsetse areas, and if Braishe had delivered the goods there looked like being a fortune for those who got in on the ground floor. That "if," of course, was everything. Braishe, for all his reputation and what he had undoubtedly accomplished, was just the least bit too suave, too persuasive for Travers's liking. His career was just a bit too meteoric; he lacked maturity.

Not that Travers was feeling at all apprehensive. All the apprehension he was feeling at the moment was for two vastly different things—the snow that had fallen that morning, and the sort of figure he'd cut at the dance. Ursula had been awfully decent: two days of gramophone and laborious steps; but somehow, just when he was hoofing it most smoothly, something or other would go wrong, and his feet would get all tangled up. Perhaps, in spite of what Ursula had said, he needn't dance after all. He might slightly sprain an ankle and then merely sit around in that Malvolio costume and watch the proceedings. Then, just a little later, perhaps, at the end of the evening, he might pick a partner of large forgiveness. He put the idea tentatively to John Franklin. Franklin laughed.

"You'll be all right! We'll have a rehearsal after tea. Don't give a damn if anything goes wrong. Just lug the girl round."

"Sounds easy at a distance," remarked Travers. "That looks rather like Tommy, by the way."

"Don't forget about not mentioning I'm a detective! I mean—well, you know!" said Franklin quickly. "I'm just a friend of yours, that's all."

Tommy Wildernesse, boisterous as ever, got in the rear of the Isotta with them, and Palmer took the wheel.

"What's the weather like, Tommy?" asked Travers.

"Oh, I rang 'em up about an hour ago. They've had the plough on the road as far as the drive, so we'll be all right. You got chains?"

"Oh, rather!" Travers had a look at his happy-go-lucky face. "You're a fortunate young devil, Tommy! Nothing to do but play golf and have your photo taken for the papers. By the way, haven't we got to congratulate you?"

Tommy looked blankly at the pair of them.

"Sorry if I've put my foot in it," said Travers, "but surely somebody—who was it, John?—told us you and—er—Mirabel had sort of—er—got engaged?"

"Gossip paragraph in the *Record*," said Franklin.

"Wish to hell they'd mind their own business!" exploded Tommy. "Sorry! I didn't mean you fellows."

"Then there's no truth in it?"

"No . . . and I'm damn glad there isn't!" Somehow the words rang none too true. Then the truth came out. "What's your opinion of that little squirt Challis?"

Travers smiled. "Well, I'm not an authority on squirts, Tommy. Do you mean as a squirt, as a super-Pellissier, or as a husband for Mirabel?"

Wildernesse grunted. "Damned if I know what I do mean. Let's talk of something more cheerful. What's your costume, Ludo?"

"Oh—er—Malvolio."

"Mal—who?"

"You're an ignorant swine, Tommy. He's a long-legged, Shakespearian sort of butler chap. Bat-eyed—and he can't dance."

"Hm! That'll suit you all right," said Tommy wholeheartedly. "What are you, Franklin?"

"An apache. Parisian burglar sort of bloke."

Tommy frowned. "Wish I'd got the brains to think of things like that. Me, I'm going to be a jolly old harlequin. Had it for the Faversham's' dance last week."

"I say! Martin'll be rather upset," said Travers. "He's a harlequin."

Tommy whistled. "Is he, by Jove! Then you fellers'd better keep quiet about it till I get it on. They can't make me take the damn thing off. By the way, I shouldn't be surprised if the whole thing's a washout. Martin said his phone'd been going all the morning with people ringing up to know if it was still on. He told 'em all it'd be on if nobody got there at all."

"How many'd he ask?"

"Forty, I think. That's all the floor holds with comfort. He says he's sure half of 'em'll risk it, even if it snows again. And he says there'll be plenty of girls."

The car skidded slightly. Palmer drew her up slowly to the side of the road where the snow lay piled up as the plough had left it.

Wyndham Challis came down by train, and Martin Braishe met him at Great Levington Station. If Braishe, with his blue-black jowl and dense black hair, looked like a toreador, then Challis, with wide felt hat, side whiskers, streak of moustache, and pasty complexion, resembled a matador off duty.

His volubility was not a love of words but merely an expression of an overwhelming self-assurance. As he walked along the platform with his host he was talking continuously and making little gestures with his hands. All the time he seemed to be wholly unaware of the actual bodily presence of anybody but himself; he floated, rather than passed, through the ticket barrier and handed over his ticket as part of a gesture.

"Hop in!" said Braishe, indicating the Daimler. "The luggage will come later."

Challis hopped in, still talking. "What are you going to do about the band, old boy? Do you know, I think that gramophone arrangement'll be perfectly efficient. I've brought some new records, by the way. We'll try 'em over after tea."

"The band have cried off in any case," said Braishe. "They say they daren't risk it with the weather as it is. They got rather badly snowed up once last year."

"Preposterous people—bands! Better get somebody to officiate at the gramophone. What's yours do, old boy? Fifty at a time?"

"Somewhere about that. We'll get the programme out after tea. Decided on your costume yet?"

"Chinaman, old boy. Mandarin. Pigtail and so on. You know, that stunt I'm doing at the show."

Braishe smiled. "You're the chap Aunt Celia's looking for. She's the Dowager Empress, or something like that. By the way, the balloons have come. Couple of hundred of 'em! Have you brought the cylinder for filling 'em?"

"I have, old boy. What I was thinking was, we'd try that big scene in the new show—kind of game plus dance sort of thing. Of course, we can't get the lighting effects. . . ."

The last member of that house party—Denis Fewne—was in the fortunate position of not having to travel. For the previous seven weeks he had been at Little Levington Hall, installed in the pagoda that fronted the old croquet lawn.

That needs explaining, unless you have discovered at once that temperament must have been the explanation. What had actually happened was that until Lady Barbara died, in April, the Fewnes had lived with her. Unfortunately her annuity died with her, and as his mother's house was too unwieldy, Denis and his wife—three years of marriage, by the way—made shift for a bit till something turned up within their means. Then the Fowlers had carted Brenda off to Switzerland for six weeks or so, and as her husband was wrestling with the final third of a new novel, he had fallen in with Martin Braishe's offer of quietude at Little Levington, where Brenda was to come for a short stay on her return from Switzerland.

Fewne was undoubtedly unfortunate. People interpreted his reticence as swollen-headedness or gratuitous superiority, instead of the natural timidity which it was. There were two things in life for which he had an intense passion—his wife and his work; the rest was something he did rather forlornly or clumsily or damned offhandedly, according to how you took it. As for the pagoda, old Henry Braishe had had it modernized—open fireplace put in, parquet flooring, and all the rest of it, and more than once when the house was chock-a-block it had been used as a spare bedroom. Fewne went one better—or Martin did for him. A recess was screened off for a bathing corner, a writing desk with typewriter well was installed, and altogether it was as cosy a den as a natural hermit might wish for.

And yet Fewne wasn't working. Five days before, three chapters had been left to do. Those chapters remained untouched, and yet, except for meals and two short trips to Folkestone, he had never left that workroom. On the bed, at the moment, lay the costume he was to wear that night as a street seller of toy balloons, and by it on the bed were a score of unfilled balloons in gaudy colours. Behind him on its special shelf above the low bed the acetylene lamp burned brightly. Outside the wind was getting up, and the air was bitingly cold.

Fewne sat in the easy chair before the fire, eyes scarcely flickering, his thin aesthetic face so expressionless, and his whole body so motionless, that he might have been asleep. Half an hour later he was still there. Had you been with him in the room, his stillness would have made you want to shriek, so unnatural it was. Half an hour later you would have wondered whether he was mad or sane. Pollock—Braishe's butler—wondered something of the sort as he peeped at him through the slit of the blind, before knocking at the door.

"Mr. Braishe's compliments, sir, and they'd like your help over the programme, sir. There's a meeting, sir."

Fewne looked round dreamily, then smiled.

"Thank you, Pollock. What's the weather like? More snow coming?"

"Bound to come, sir. The sky's very bad."

"Hm! Tell 'em I'll be over at once."

He stood for a moment thinking. Then his lips pursed to a smile that the shadows made almost evil in its deliberate irony. Pollock, who had heard him move, turned back and closed the door after him, then followed him along the paved path in the shelter of the box hedge.

CHAPTER III
AFTER THE BALL WAS OVER

THE ROOM LOOKED sadly empty as they trooped back from the entrance hall. Mirabel Quest gave a little shiver and a giggle and scurried to the fire to warm her hands. Brenda Fewne floated in her Pre-Raphaelite way to the cosiest chair and sat demurely regarding the fire while the others stood round idly. On the floor lay scores of the coloured balloons that a quarter of an hour before had been flicked and fisted and blown hilariously over the heads of the dancers. Palmer still sat on his chair where he had been superintending the gramophone, and he'd probably have gone on sitting if Travers hadn't caught sight of him.

"I'd go and get some supper, Palmer, if I were you," he told him. "You've done some very sound work."

Palmer was gratified. "Thank you, sir. And shall I be required again, sir?"

"Don't think so. I'd push off to bed if I were you."

It was about five minutes later when Braishe came back, presumably from seeing off the last of the guests from the front porch. He seemed rather worried.

"What do you feel about it, everybody? Think we did right?"

"Of course you did right!" snapped his aunt. "They never ought to have come. It was sheer lunacy."

Braishe laughed. "Well, we *are* lunatics, aren't we? Take a peep, Aunt Celia!" He looked round and explained. "You see, when Pollock told me it'd been snowing hard for a couple of hours, I didn't quite know what to do. It seemed pretty rotten, after those twenty sportsmen—and women—had rolled up, to hint they should kick 'emselves out before the show was over."

"The only thing to do, old boy." Challis patted him effusively on the back. "And they knew it."

"Jolly lucky they'd all got chains," said Travers.

"The Payne girls hadn't," said Braishe, "but Bewly's taken them in his saloon. And now, then. What are we going to do?"

"Sit round and have a yarn," suggested Franklin.

"Go on dancing!" gurgled Mirabel. "I'm like an icicle."

George Paradine started to speak, then caught his wife's eye. "What do you think, my dear?"

"Bed!" was the reply, and everybody laughed.

"I know," cut in Challis quickly. "Let Mirabel and Brenda do their stunt for us!" He twisted the pigtail round his neck, backed his way out and indicated a comparatively open space. "Just clear these balloons away, you fellows! Come on, girls! Tommy, you take the piano!"

"So sorry!" came Brenda's voice plaintively. "Really I'm most frightfully tired. I'd much rather sit and talk to Denis."

"How frightfully jolly!" drawled her sister, with such a perfect imitation of the voice that everybody laughed again. Except Fewne, that is. He sat in the Chesterfield corner by the door, quietly watching. Ho-Ping yapped, and his mistress soothed him. "There! Didums sit up too late, darling." Again everybody laughed. Perhaps all the odd drinks had something to do with it; perhaps the realization that everybody was looking so unusual, from George Paradine with his corduroys and brass buttons to Franklin with his appalling air of ferocity.

Mirabel leaned back in the chair, kicked her heels in the air, then sprang up.

"Sit down, folks! I'll do the show myself. Come on, Broody! Make 'em all gather round!" She bustled the men unceremoniously into chairs and took the floor. "Come on, Tommy! Hit 'em up! You know the tune."

Tommy, face all smiles, swayed at the piano to the tune of the latest fox trot. Mirabel gave a yell.

"Hold on a minute, Tommy, while I say my little piece! You see," she explained, "this is one of the impersonations I'm going to do in the new show. As you see by the costumes, my sister and I are featuring the Sally Sisters. She's Beauty and I'm Cutie—only, of course, in the show I'm doing both myself. Get ready, Tommy! Let her go!"

Whether Wyndham Challis had a hand in it or no, the turn was an uproarious success. If you knew the Sally Sisters you would have recognized with your eyes shut Beauty's affected little lisp and Cutie's nasal huskiness. Even when you opened your eyes you'd have sworn there were two dancers as Mirabel leaned forward, almost overbalanced by the monstrous feather headdress, fingers resting on the shoulders of her imaginary sister. The music was enough to set feet tapping and Ho-Ping yapping. Tommy swayed like one mesmerized as he pounded the ivories.

Another minute, and the men were joining in the chorus—except Denis, that is, who sat quietly smiling in his corner. When it was over there was a hurricane of applause. Challis poured Tommy a hasty drink.

"What about you, Myra?"

"Just a spot, old dear!" She looked round, face flushed with excitement.

Travers came over. "Extraordinarily good! Haven't laughed so much for years!"

"Jolly fine! Myra, you're a wonder!" That was Braishe. "And you, Tommy!" He turned to Challis. "Haven't you got room for Tommy in the show?"

Challis laughed. "Wait till you see *my* little turn!" He began a preparatory unwinding of his pigtail; then Celia's voice cut in with cold decision.

"No more shows to-night. Come and sit down, everybody! What time is it, George?"

"Just gone half-past."

In a couple of minutes the chairs were in a semicircle round the open fireplace. Franklin put another log on the fire.

"I say, do let's have the lights out. It's so romantic!"

"That's the idea, Mirabel!" Tommy hopped up and switched off the lights. With the flicker from the logs and the glow that reached the circle of chairs, the room looked deliciously cosy. Then Braishe spotted that something was missing.

"Hallo! Where's Denis?"

"Here I am." There was something curiously fine about the voice, after the noise of the last few minutes.

"What on earth are you doing over there? Come along, old chap! Open out the chairs, everybody!"

"No, really! I say . . . don't move. Do you know, I've got rather a headache. It's quite cool . . . and jolly over here."

You could just catch the colour of the yellowish scarf he was wearing, and above his head the mass of balloons, fastened to his coat, or the settee, by a string, looked like a futurist picture on the wall by the door.

"Poor darling!" Brenda's voice was like a caress. "You've been working much too hard."

Everybody suddenly realized that Fewne *had* been rather out of it that evening. True, he had danced once or twice, but generally he had sat watching the others or talking to Travers or Celia Paradine Poor old Denis! Quite a decent sort in his retiring way. Everybody felt an overwhelming itch to show him that he was really one of the party.

"How's the book going, old boy?" asked Challis.

"Not so bad," said Fewne very quietly. "Sorry to be such a—er—conspicuous—"

"That's all right, old boy!" Challis assured him. He looked round the circle. "We all know what work is and—er—inspiration and so on."

"What's the book about?" asked Travers quickly.

"The book? Well—er—the usual thing."

"What's the title?"

"Oh—er—*Distressful Virtue.* It's a sort of sequel to the other . . . you know."

"What, *Tingling Symbols?*"

"Far too gloomy for me!" broke in Celia. "Why don't you write something more cheerful, Denis?"

"Talking of cheerfulness, what are *we* going to do if we're snowed up?" asked Mirabel.

"Do!" Braishe laughed. "There's a bridge four and some over; and the billiard room—and the gramophone. Much better than a band, don't you think?"

"Oh, much better!"

"There's plenty of food in the house, that's more to the point!" said Celia Paradine decisively. Then everybody laughed again.

It was just over an hour later when Franklin and Travers with George and Celia Paradine reached the top of the stairs, where their ways separated. George gave a prodigious yawn.

"I don't know; I'm feeling uncommonly sleepy. Must be the air."

Travers laughed. "Air out of glasses, George!" Then he yawned.

Celia yawned too. "Do stop it. You're starting everybody off!"

Travers laughed again. "Well, good-night, Celia. Sleep well. Good-night, George, old chap. Jolly happy New Year to you both!"

Franklin said good-night too, and they moved off round the corridor.

"Damn glad we dodged that last drink!" whispered Franklin.

"What do you mean 'we'?"

"You and me. I saw you take a sip and tip yours into the log holder, so I did the same with mine."

Travers felt for the switch and turned on the light. "Do you realize we've probably put a hoodoo on this party? There's the final toast of ourselves and the New Year, and we go and libate the logs, so to speak." He had a look at himself in the glass. "My God! I look horrible!"

Franklin laughed. "You weren't so bad till you put your glasses on." He looked round the room as if he'd seen it for the first time. "Jolly decent of Mrs. Paradine fixing us up in a couple of beds here."

"Wasn't it! If Fewne hadn't stayed in the pagoda she'd have been in rather a hole. As it is, Brenda's got one of the small rooms."

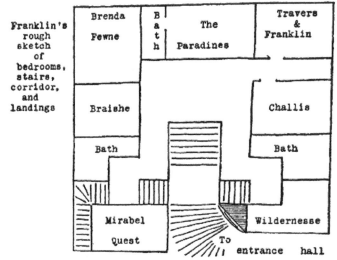

Franklin's rough sketch of bedrooms, stairs, corridor, and landings

Brenda Fewne · Bath · The Paradines · Travers & Franklin

Braishe · Challis

Bath · Bath

Mirabel Quest · To entrance hall · Wildernesse

Franklin removed his villainous scarf and the velveteen coat. "I say, that sister of hers is pretty hectic! What was all the row about after tea?"

Travers shrugged his shoulders. "Myra's a bit temperamental. She and Brenda don't hit it off very well. Challis had to pour oil on the waters."

"Curious!" said Franklin, "sisters being like that."

"One's such an absolute topper, and the other . . . phew!"

"Mirabel's all right, for what she is," protested Travers. "She's a darned attractive woman. The other one's too statuesque for my money. However, she and Fewne suit each other, so there we are."

"I rather like Fewne. Gloomy sort of cuss, but quite a good sort, if you know him, I should say. Delightful voice he's got!"

"Eton and Balliol!" grunted Travers. "Not much—"

Then the light went out. There was a second's silence.

"Hallo! What's up now?"

"Fuse, probably," suggested Franklin. They pottered round the room for a good minute till there was the sound of a voice outside, then another, and they moved gingerly across to the door and out to the corridor. Travers, in the darkness, hacked somebody's shins.

"Hallo! Who's that? Oh, sorry, Challis! What's gone wrong with the lights?"

"Damfino!" began Challis. Behind them there was the snapping of a blind as Franklin released it. The clear moonlight suddenly lighted up the corridor behind them, and outside his door they could see George Paradine, still in his costume. He came along to the corridor to where they stood by the twin doors.

"Any use going downstairs to see if Pollock's got any candles?"

"Probably be on again in a second," Travers told him.

"What about the women?" asked Franklin. "Won't they be alarmed?"

Challis sneered. "Take a bit more than darkness to scare women nowadays, old boy."

Paradine stifled a yawn. "Do you know, I haven't felt so sleepy for years!"

They stood there making conversation for a couple of minutes, then Franklin had an idea. Why not draw the curtains of the bedrooms? The others watched him while he tried the experiment on his own room. The effect was wonderful; one couldn't perhaps see much detail, but all the main objects in the room stood out clearly, as in an early twilight interior but more subdued and silvery.

"It's stopped snowing!" announced Franklin from the window, but Travers wasn't there. Challis and Paradine could be heard saying a further good-night, but it was a minute or so before Travers came in.

"Just went to tell Tommy to draw back his curtains, but he wasn't there. One of the women's just come up. Think it was Mirabel."

"I say—quick!" exclaimed Franklin. "Just look out there, Ludo! There—in the snow!"

Outside, on the path that led direct from the porch to the pagoda, a figure could be seen. When Franklin had first caught sight of it, it had made a wild rush as if to take the snow by storm. In the first few yards, where the house sheltered from the driving wind, the going had been fairly easy; then, as the drift gradually deepened towards the pagoda, it seemed incredible that a sane man should attempt it, especially in that incongruous garb, with the tails of that outlandish coat trailing in the snow where he stuck, and the mass of toy balloons dangling round his head. With the snow knee deep he floundered heavily and scrambled from step to step. The last few feet became a crawl, with hands pawing at the snow. A violent lurch, and he clutched a pillar of the veranda and drew himself to the platform. There he stood a second or two, then disappeared round the angle.

"My God!" said Franklin. "What is he? Mad or tight?"

"Why didn't he go round by the hedge?" asked Travers, as if reproaching himself. "It wouldn't have been deep there. That reminds me: You know when we all went out to the porch? I heard Pollock say, 'Shall I have the hedge path swept again?'

and Fewne said, 'Don't bother, Pollock. There won't be much snow there.'"

"I expect he was a bit tight," said Franklin. "Probably not used to taking much—and he's had a few this evening."

Travers shook his head. "Something's the matter with that chap. I've been thinking so all the evening. I'd say he's been doing a bit too much: heading for a breakdown, or I'm a Dutchman."

"You know him pretty well?"

"Fairly. He's a charming fellow, especially when he forgets things."

"Such as?"

"Well, that his father was an ambassador, that he failed himself for the Foreign Office, that he's got a sister-in-law . . . and that he's frightfully hard up. You ready for the bathroom?"

There was a tap on the door, and Pollock came in with a candle.

"Thank you, Pollock," said Travers. "What's happened to the light?"

"The master and William are trying to find out now, sir. We thought you could manage with this."

Travers assured him they could manage admirably and added a word or two of congratulation on the general management of the evening. Ten minutes later the room was quiet except for Franklin's steady breathing. Travers stirred restlessly.

"You asleep, old chap?"

Franklin muttered dreamily that he wasn't.

"Then if you don't mind, I'll lower the blind a little. The moonlight's clean in my eye. You don't want to wake up in the morning with a gibbering idiot."

Over at the window his voice came again.

"Fewne's not in bed yet. Must be working at that book of his. No, he isn't! There's his shadow! He's parading up and down!"

"The light's on again, then!"

"Not necessarily. He's got an acetylene lamp there—not electric. However, we might as well try our own while we're about it. . . . Hm! Still off!" and he got into bed again.

Franklin at the time thought it was much later, but it was barely half an hour after that when he woke—not with any sort of suddenness, but sleepily and dreamily. Then he slid slowly out of bed and blinked his way towards the door. Then there was a crash as he came a cropper over a chair. Travers got up on one elbow.

"Hallo! ... What's up?"

Franklin tried the switch. The light was on. Then he explained. "Do you know, I'd have sworn somebody flashed a light across my eyes!"

"You weren't dreaming?"

Then Travers sat up in bed and groped for his glasses.

"Who put that chair there? It wasn't there when I turned in."

He hopped out of bed and slipped into his dressing gown. Franklin rubbed his shins where the chair caught them.

"That restless devil Fewne's still up," remarked Travers from the window. "His light's still on. . . . Listen! . . . Wasn't that Ho-Ping?"

"Sounds like it." Franklin put on his dressing gown and opened the door quietly, then stood listening. Travers joined him. It might have been imagination, but from somewhere away in the darkness there seemed to be a sound.

Franklin nodded. "Come on!"

"What about a stick or something?"

"Sh! . . . Light the candle. We don't know where the switches are."

They moved quietly down the main staircase, round the bend, and into the entrance hall. In the short corridor that led to the lounge Franklin suddenly made a motion to stop. They listened. From somewhere close was the thud of a grandfather clock, its beat preposterously exaggerated in the quietness. Then something else was heard. Franklin nodded towards the staircase they'd just left. A couple of steps back and a figure—a footman, by the look of him—was seen at the foot of the stairs, carrying a lighted candle. He seemed to show no surprise whatever at the sight of them; he merely waited for them to come over.

"Who are you?" asked Travers, then, "Oh! It's Charles, isn't it?"

"Yes, sir."

"What are you doing down here at this unearthly hour?"

"There were noises, sir. I thought I would come and see what it was, sir."

"Hm! . . . See anything suspicious?"

"No, sir."

"Better have a look in the dining room," said Franklin. The footman moved forward at once, felt for the switch, and opened the door for them. Everything seemed to be perfectly normal inside. Franklin even drew back the curtains and examined the windows.

"What was the matter with the light?" asked Travers.

"The light, sir? It was—tempered with."

"Tempered? . . . Oh, I see! You mean *tampered* with?"

"Yes, sir. It was cut, sir, against the—where the meter is, sir."

"And where *is* the meter?" asked Franklin.

"This way, sir. Under the stairs, sir. . . . Just here, sir."

In the angle where the staircase curved to the entrance hall a tall screen hid the door of the cubbyhole—it was little more than that—where the meter stood. Franklin got inside and had a look round.

"Looks as if it's what Charles was saying. One of the cords has been cut. . . . Don't see how it could have broken itself. . . . It's been bound up with adhesive tape where it enters the metal sheath."

Travers had a look at the hall clock. "Half-past two. . . . You been in all the rooms, Charles?"

"All the downstairs ones, sir."

"Hm! Then you'd better push off to bed. If you hear anything else, tell Pollock ... or us. You know where we are."

He watched the footman move off in the direction of the kitchen, then turned to Franklin.

"What was his idea? Why didn't he warn Pollock or the other footman?"

"Sh! You'll rouse the whole house!"

"Another thing," whispered Travers. "He had crêpe soled shoes on . . . and they were done up!"

"You mean he didn't come down in a hurry?"

Travers nodded. "And did you notice his careful intonation? I believe he's a Swiss."

Franklin frowned, then smiled. "Hadn't we better push off to bed? We'll be waking everybody up."

They moved quietly up the stairs again. At the top of the main landing Travers touched Franklin on the arm.

"Why is it that we've been the only ones to hear any noise?"

It was just after eight when Franklin opened his eyes the following morning. He sat up and yawned then yawned again and woke Travers.

"When's Palmer bringing tea?"

"I told him to wait till we rang. Push the bell, since you're so energetic. . . . What's the weather like?"

Franklin had a look out.

"No more snow. . . . You can see Fewne's last night's traces perfectly clearly. . . . Sky looks pretty bad. ... Wonder what the time is?"

He went over to the dressing table, then to the chest of drawers, then fussed round anxiously.

"I say! My watch is gone!"

Travers laughed. Two minutes later he swore! Franklin's gold repeater *had* gone, and with it his own notecase with the better part of fifty pounds in it. Franklin's money was intact. More by luck than by design he had pushed it under a spare suit when he changed after dinner.

CHAPTER IV
ONE COMES—ONE GOES

"MR. BRAISHE will be down in a moment, sir," said Pollock.

"Good! What's your idea about it? Anything missing?"

"Two miniatures from the drawing room, sir—rather valuable I believe, sir. Nothing else we can—Ah! here is Mr. Braishe, sir."

Braishe, looking sleepy in spite of his hasty tub, hailed them before he reached the bottom of the stairs.

"Morning, Travers! Morning, Franklin! I say, this is a damn funny affair. What'd you say you lost?"

Travers told him. "You lost anything?"

"About a tenner altogether—and a signet ring. What'd we better do? Ring up the police?"

"Hadn't we better see everybody else and get a full list of what's missing?" suggested Franklin. "Mind you, he's probably miles away by now, in any case."

Braishe hesitated. Pollock took advantage of the short silence to come forward.

"Excuse me, sir, but there's a gentleman in the breakfast room, sir. A Mr. Crashaw, sir."

Braishe looked at him blankly. "Crashaw! Who's he?"

"Charles heard him knock, sir, just as it was getting light. It appears, sir, his car broke down in the snow near the drive early this morning, so he came here, sir, thinking he could get help. Nearly dead with cold he was, sir."

"Better go and have a look at him," began Braishe. Pollock followed, still explaining. "You see, sir, the breakfast room was warm, and I didn't expect anybody down at present."

"That's all right, Pollock. Come along, you fellows, and get some breakfast. Perfectly filthy taste in my mouth this morning. Feel as if I could drink a gallon." He stopped suddenly. "Good God! I wonder—" and sprinted across the parquet flooring towards the dining room.

"What's up now?" asked Travers quietly.

"Probably gone to see if something's been pinched," smiled Franklin.

They stood there watching the door. In less than a minute Braishe reappeared. He looked round to see if the coast was clear, then beckoned them over.

"I say, something pretty awful's happened! The safe's been opened!"

"Something important gone?" asked Franklin.

"Important! My God! It's awful! I had a siphon of gas in there! Got it down for you and George to see."

Travers whistled. "That's pretty bad! But—er—bit risky, wasn't it, having it in the house?"

"Good Lord, no! Come and have a look here!"

He went across to the far end of the room where a small, two-shelved bookcase stood on a mahogany side table. A touch of a concealed spring and books and all opened out, disclosing a safe built into the wall. He closed the shelves again, then turned to Travers.

"Now, you two open it!"

"That's just it!" he said, when both had made a hopeless hand of the job. "Here's the secret. I steady the bookcase with my right hand, thus; and with my left hand, which you watch, pretend to work the spring. But I don't! It's the right hand does that! . . . So! Now look at the safe. Absolutely empty. *And I found it with the combination set just as I left it!*"

"Good Lord! I say, that's extraordinary!" Franklin shook his head. "But—er—who knew about it—I mean, even that the safe existed?"

"As far as I know, only Pollock and—well, I might as well say—Denis." He grunted. "That's ridiculous, of course."

"Either know the combination?"

Braishe looked at him queerly. "Denis did—but don't mention the fact. It's absurd to—er—"

"Quite! By the way, had you anything else in it, besides the siphon? Notes or formula or anything like that?"

"Not a thing. Except in my own mind—and what the War Office have—there's no formula in existence. I had this siphon by special permission of the Colonial Office, by arrangement, in view of the possible developments we were going to discuss down here. I had it at the conference on Monday—you know, the one at Oxford."

"What was the siphon like?"

"Tiny cylindrical affair, holding the liquefied gas—under pressure. Eighth of a gill. The release plunger was sealed and fastened."

"Doesn't sound much—eighth of a gill!" remarked Franklin.

"Good God, man!" Braishe snapped out. "Don't you realize a single drop'd vapourize into enough to kill a man!" He looked helplessly at Travers. "What are we going to do?"

"Well—er—I don't think there's so much to worry about," said Travers hopefully. "It could only have been taken for a very definite purpose. Tell me, any foreign power likely to be interested?"

Braishe hesitated for a moment. "You're asking me to blow my own trumpet, but ... I should say *any* government might be interested."

Franklin broke in there. "I think Travers is right. If it was taken by someone of that kind, then the taker knows what it is, and it's away and gone by now without any danger to anybody in this house." He stopped suddenly. "But what about the robberies during the night? What was that? Camouflage—to conceal this?"

Neither could answer.

"Well, if I were you," went on Franklin, "I'd call up the special branch at Scotland Yard. There's one stroke of luck. We shall be able to follow up the fellow's footprints in the snow."

"I should say he couldn't get clear away," said Travers. "How deep'll the snow be in the drive? Best part of a couple of foot?"

"More!" said Braishe. "However, hold on for a minute." He went across by the door and opened the telephone cabinet. A blank look came over his face.

"I say, the telephone's gone!"

"Gone!" The others nipped across.

"Yes. Look there! The cord has been cut! The whole bag of tricks has gone!"

"Another phone in the house?"

"Afraid there isn't. Rather looks as if this chap—whoever he was—did the job pretty thoroughly." He stood there indecisively for a moment or two, then, "Tell you what I'll do! I'll have a spot of coffee and slip across to the Paynes' place. Let's go along. You fellows are probably a bit peckish."

"You two push on!" said Franklin. "I'm going to have a look at those footprints—where the chap got out," and he moved off to the hall. Braishe took Travers's arm.

"Wonder who this chap is Pollock let in," he whispered, with his hand on the knob of the breakfast-room door. Travers grimaced and shrugged his shoulders as the other motioned him in.

At the end of the long table a youngish man sat over his toast and marmalade. Pollock appeared to have been right for once in his use of the all-embracing term "gentleman": this fellow's face had character in it and a certain diffidence which the glasses made rather noticeable. Quiet sort of cove, by the look of him, thought Travers. Then, as the stranger dropped his napkin and got to his feet, a shy sort of smile made his face positively likable at first sight. It didn't need more than the "Good-morning! I'm— er—afraid I'm rather—er—" to tell where that accent came from.

"Good-morning! My name's Braishe. This is Travers. How're they doing you? All right?"

"Oh, marvellously, thanks! My name's Crashaw," and he waited with a shy hesitation.

"I say—do carry on!" said Braishe. "You must be frightfully hungry. What happened exactly?"

Crashaw sat down. "Well—er—you see, I was with some people at Tonbridge till about ten last night, then I pushed off in my little Morris to—er—get to Hythe—if I could; only it started snowing like blazes. They'd told me of a short cut—and then the carburettor went wrong and—er—the snow kept holding me up, and shortly after I got in the side road she conked out altogether in a drift . . . and there she is!" He smiled ruefully.

"But—I say! You haven't been out there all night!"

"I'm afraid I have—most of it. It wasn't bad—really—while the engine was warm. Then I had to empty the radiator in case she froze up. Of course, I had a rug or two. Er—then I thought I'd try to get down your drive for a bit of help. You see, there weren't any cars on the road."

"No need to apologize," smiled Braishe. "What was the snow like? Pretty deep?"

"Frightfully! I thought I'd never get here. Must be three foot in some places."

Braishe nodded. "That's because the plough didn't get along here yesterday—after the fall we had in the morning."

"And my legs are on the short side," smiled the other. He exhibited a pair of black trousers that went rather humorously with the grey sports coat. "Your man let me have these while mine are drying."

"Splendid! Well, you stay here as long as it suits you. Have some more coffee?"

"Thanks, I will."

Travers was already tackling his porridge. Braishe took some toast and marmalade.

"Hallo! What's up with you?" asked Travers. "Off your feed?"

Braishe frowned. "Damned if I know what *is* up! Something must have gone the wrong way last night." He explained to Crashaw. "We had a bit of a dance here last night. Quite cheerful—while it lasted."

"Oh! That was what the cars were I passed! About half-past eleven or so?"

"That's right," He finished off the breakfast cup of coffee. "By jove! That was good. Where's Franklin got to?"

"I shouldn't worry about him," smiled Travers. "He's a bit of a crank on finding things out." He turned to the stranger. "You know this part pretty well?"

"I can't say I do—really. I live in Oxford actually, but—er—I put in most of my time in Warwickshire."

"Really!"

"Yes. ... I'm a schoolmaster ... at the moment."

Travers laughed. "You needn't be so diffident about it! We've got to have 'em, you know. . . . . Pretty decent spot?"

"Er—yes . . . rather. Westover. Do you know it?"

Travers hesitated as if in thought. "I seem to know the name. If I remember rightly, they say it's the most expensive prep school in England."

Crashaw smiled modestly. "I'd hardly like to go so far as that . . . still, I suppose it's rather expensive."

Travers remembered something, or thought he did. "Oh, yes! Didn't your cadet people do frightfully well at Bisley last summer?"

The other smiled apologetically. "I'm afraid I'm not a very warlike person. . . . Still, they did do rather well ... I believe."

Just at that moment Franklin came in. "Nothing doing!" he began, then caught sight of the stranger. Braishe introduced him, then answered Franklin's look with an explanation.

"We had a burglary here during the night. Various things taken."

"I say! How exciting!"

"Isn't it! Tell Franklin so! He's lost the family watch. By the way, what did you find out?"

"Not a damn. I've been the whole way round the house, and there's only two lots of prints: where Mr. Crashaw here came in, and where Fewne went over to the pagoda. Pollock had a path cut to the outhouses, but that's a *cul de sac*. And there isn't a tree to get on, or a roof or anything!"

It was Crashaw who spoke, as if involuntarily. "Then your man must be in the house. ... I beg your pardon!"

"Don't worry," said Braishe. "It's a perfectly true observation." Then he frowned, got up, and pushed the bell. William was dispatched for Pollock and Charles.

"Look out there!" said Franklin. "Snow coming down in clouds. And it looks like keeping on."

Braishe had a look through the window, over towards the northeast. "I'll push off as soon as I've seen Pollock. . . . Oh, Pollock! Who locked up last night?"

"Charles took the front door, sir. I went round the house."

"And who unlocked this morning?"

"Charles, sir."

"I see. . . . Everything all right, Charles?"

"Yes, sir. Everything, sir." But he looked across to Travers.

Travers took the cue and told just what had happened during the small hours, but the inquiry that followed produced nothing. When the servants had gone Braishe gave his views.

"There was that electric light last night," he said. "That was pretty silly. Do you know I thought at first some idiot was playing a joke, only it happened long after they'd gone. Probably due to the same chap."

"The door was open, you know," Franklin reminded him. "Anybody with sufficient nerve could have slipped in."

Braishe nodded. Then, "What about leaving Franklin to feed alone? Crashaw might like a smoke."

"The others coming down?" asked Franklin. "It's best part of nine."

"Probably come in driblets. Aunt Celia'll hang on a bit . . . and the girls, probably. Tommy ought to be down."

"The unrising generation!" remarked Travers. Crashaw caught his eye and smiled.

Then something happened. As Travers opened the door and drew back to wave the others through there was a sudden shriek from somewhere upstairs. A second's silence as the four of them listened . . . then a second shriek. Then a perfectly uncanny one! Braishe and Travers bolted for the stairs. Franklin screwed up his napkin and followed with his mouth full. Crashaw stood perplexed by the door.

On the first landing, where the main staircase branched off left and right to two narrower stairways, Braishe pulled up short. As Travers halted behind him the first thing *he* saw was George Paradine's head come round his door. Then he saw the body of a woman, and nothing else for a second while Franklin moved quickly in front of him. Braishe's voice came nervously.

"What is it? Is she all right?"

"Just a faint," said Franklin. Travers, craning round, knew the woman for Ransome, Mirabel Quest's maid.

Franklin looked from her to the other two. "What's in there?" He took the lead in the short corridor, to where the bedroom door stood open. But the room was apparently empty. Then, just visible beneath the bed, he caught sight of a pair of shoes—those silver shoes with paste buckles which Cutie Sally had twirled so dexterously a few hours before. With a wave of his hand he motioned the others back, then knelt by the side of the bed and pulled up the valance. Underneath lay the body of Mirabel Quest, still in the jazz costume; the monstrous feather headdress all awry and just discernible in the uncertain light of the closed room.

He struck a match. On the bodice was a red stain; in the centre of the stain the brass handle of what looked like a dagger.

He slipped back to the corridor. "We'd better keep out of there. One of you go and fetch Mr. Paradine!"

CHAPTER V
THE MAN WHO WENT MAD

FRANKLIN STOOD just inside the room while Paradine was making his examination. The curtains had been drawn, but the snow from the blizzard which was now raging outside filmed the windows and gave the bedroom an ill lit, cheerless look.

Just behind in the corridor, Travers was whispering to Braishe. "I didn't mention it before, but Franklin's the head of our detective bureau. Take my advice and give him a free hand."

"I thought you said he was in the secret service!"

"So he was—during the war. You see, we guessed people mightn't be any too keen on—er—what one usually thinks a detective is."

It might have been Travers's imagination, but somehow Braishe didn't seem any too pleased with the disclosure. Then Mrs. Cairns, the housekeeper, coughed just behind them.

"Ransome is better, sir. Just a faint, it was."

"Thank you," said Braishe. "Mr. Paradine'll have a look at her as soon as he's finished here. Oh, and Mrs. Cairns—don't let the maids start panicking. Keep them going just as usual."

Inside the room George Paradine backed out carefully from under the bed. In spite of the pajamas and dressing gown, there was nothing humorous about him at the moment. A certain dignity, new to Franklin's experience of him, and an absolute absence of excitement, gave him an authority of which he appeared to be unconscious. He shook his head.

"A bad business! A bad business!"

"How long's she been dead?"

"Can't say exactly. Probably just after we got upstairs—judging by the clothes."

"Any deductions from the wound?"

"Can't tell—as she lies now."

Franklin glanced round. "I think we'd better lock up the room till the police get here." The other nodded and moved out. At the door Franklin stopped. "No use worrying about the knob now. The maid's already smudged it. Perhaps Travers might let Palmer come on duty outside as a precaution."

He handed the key over to Braishe. Travers was already on his way downstairs.

"What's happened to the other men?" Franklin asked.

"They'll be here in a minute," Braishe told him. "They were sleeping like logs, the pair of 'em—and they say their mouths taste like nothing on earth."

"Did you hear your dog yap about half-past two?" Franklin asked Paradine.

He thought for a moment. "I seem to have a faint idea, now you come to speak of it—but I don't remember Mrs. Paradine moving. Usually she pats him or something. He sleeps at the foot of the bed," he explained.

"Well, I don't want to talk rot," said Franklin, "but I can't help thinking that final drink we had was doped. Travers and I only sipped ours, and we slept normally. Who else didn't have it? Oh, Mrs. Fewne. She can be asked later."

He watched while Travers gave Palmer his instructions about the door, then, "Mr. Paradine, you might ask your wife and Mrs. Fewne how they slept, will you? And perhaps Mrs. Paradine would break the news to Mrs. Fewne. We'll go down now. Join us as soon as you can."

Little Crashaw was waiting in the hall. "Something happened?"

"Someone died . . . suddenly," said Franklin. "I'm just off to phone. Ours is out of order. What's the drive like?"

"Well, it was pretty bad for me, as I told you, but you see my legs are shorter than yours. Tell you what I'd do if I were you: I'd go through the wood at the back of the house—it's bound to be less thick there—then I'd keep under the hedges till I got to the road."

"That's a good idea," said Braishe.

"You see I thought of trying that way myself as soon as I could get a can of hot water. And I know what'd help. Put on some puttees!"

Franklin nodded. "Splendid! Only, if I were you, I'd stay here till I saw what happened to me." He glanced at the window. "Look at that! Coming down in a white sheet!"

In five minutes he had made his preparations, and the others followed him to the breakfast room, where the hedge sheltered the door from the northeast wind.

"I'll get back as soon as I can," he told Braishe. "And I'll do that other little job for you at the same time. Where do I find out about the snow plough? Great Levington?"

"That's right. And you're sure you won't wait till we search the house?"

Franklin shook his head. "By the way, if I'm late I should be inclined to let Travers keep an eye on things, if I were you. He knows the ropes. He and Mr. Paradine won't lead you far wrong. Oh, yes! Before I forget it." He pulled out a folded paper. "If it's any use to you I've just jotted down a few things you mustn't do—if you don't want to get into trouble with the police." He handed it to Travers. "Well, cheerio, everybody! See you later!"

From the north window they watched him disappear along the hedge and into the wild garden. It seemed to be something to do, something to relieve the tension. Even where the hedge sheltered from the blizzard, the going seemed very bad in places; what it would be like out in the open meadows would be hard to say. Travers expressed the general view when he remarked, "I wouldn't mind betting he'll be back again in five minutes. How far's he got to go when he reaches the main road?"

"Best part of another half mile before he gets to the vicarage. That's the first house—but only on the bye road. Your car'll be in a pretty bad way, Crashaw!"

Crashaw smiled good-humouredly. "It will . . . rather. But weren't one or two cars completely snowed up last year?"

"One or two! The place was littered with 'em. Hallo! Here's George!"

As the other two turned away, Travers flashed a look at the note Franklin had handed him. What he read gave him a sudden start. He looked round quickly, then screwed the paper into a ball. Over at the fire, where he stooped and chafed his hands, he deposited the paper dexterously in the flames. Just then the last couple arrived, Challis's pasty face looking perfectly ghastly; Wildernesse, rosy as ever, but nervous and very badly rattled.

"I say, this is absolutely horrible!" Challis began, then caught sight of the stranger.

"No use arguing about it," snapped Braishe with that rather pompous voice of his. He introduced Crashaw and pointed vaguely to the fireside chairs. "Best thing to do is to talk things over properly. What do you say, Travers? You see the police'll be here at any minute."

Travers nodded. "That's the best thing to do . . . when we're all here."

There was a sudden silence, then Braishe laughed feebly. "Good Lord, yes! We've forgotten Denis!"

As he pushed the bell an unusual restraint fell on the room. "Excuse me," came Crashaw's voice timidly, "but—er—don't you think I'm rather out of it? I mean I—"

"Not at all!" said Travers sharply. "We want all the cool heads we can find, for this business. A schoolmaster's the very chap!"

Pollock came in: rotund, fleshy faced, head bald as a rook's, and his hands shaking.

"Mr. Fewne been called yet, Pollock?"

"Not yet, sir. William's just swept the path by the hedge. He said not to disturb him before ten, sir."

"I see. Well, give him my compliments and ask him to come over at once—in his dressing gown, if necessary."

Pollock flustered off. Braishe turned to Challis and Wildernesse. "Either of you two lose anything last night?"

"Yes! I did." Wildernesse answered at once. "About fifteen quid in notes—off the dressing table."

"Bad luck, old boy," commiserated Challis. "He got about a tenner of mine, out of my trousers pocket."

"What about the women, George?"

"We lost nothing at all. The dog'd probably scare him off. And Brenda says she's lost nothing—and she left a couple of rings and a bracelet on the table."

"Hm! And how's she bearing up?"

"Pretty well—on the whole. You know what an icicle she is. Celia had a good cry."

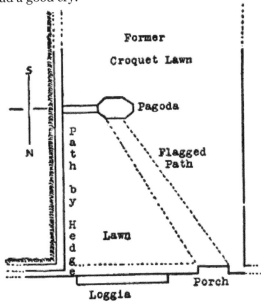

Challis fidgeted nervously and moistened his lips. "She was a good old scout, was Mirabel."

"Do be quiet!" snapped Braishe, whose nerves seemed to be going to pieces. Then there was a patter of feet in the outside corridor. The door was flung open, and Pollock burst in, overcoat sprinkled with snow, his breath coming in short gasps.

"The pagoda, sir!" He gasped again. "Mr. Fewne . . . dead, sir!"

"Oh, my God!" came from Braishe.

Travers went forward quickly.

"George, you come with me! Perhaps you'd better come too, Martin. You fellows stop there! And for God's sake, don't let the women know!"

The blinding snow had already covered the path by the hedge, although William had scarcely finished sweeping it. On the veranda they halted till Pollock came puffing along.

"What about the door? Was it open when you got here?"

"No, sir. Shut, sir."

The butler stood on the threshold, sheltered from the wind, rubbing his hands nervously while the others looked round from the doormat. Immediately to their right was the open fireplace; to their left, beneath the first window, a writing desk—opened—with typewriter well. By the opposite wall was a low, ancient-looking bed; on it, Fewne, lying face downward, legs upward so that the heels almost touched his back, and hands clutching his hair. To Travers he looked like an overgrown, sulky boy who had thrown himself down in a fit of temper.

"Have a look at him!" he whispered to Paradine, then wondered why he had whispered. With an eye on the floor for footmarks he moved along to the writing desk, then sniffed.

"Extraordinary smell of acetylene here!"

Paradine turned from the bed. "Been dead some hours. Looks like heart failure." He broke off. "What's that you were saying about acetylene?" He sniffed. "The lamp was acetylene, wasn't it, Pollock?"

Pollock stepped gingerly onto the mat. "Beg your pardon, sir?"

"The lamp there—above the bed. What happened when it went out?"

"I think I can explain that," said Braishe. "You turned the water off first, before you wanted to put it out; then, when it burned low, you blew it out and put it out of that special window there. There's a ledge outside for it. Then you closed the shutter again. Any spare gas simply blew away."

"How long would it burn?"

"Eight hours, sir," said Pollock. "It gave a very bright light, sir. William used to attend to it during the evening while Mr. Fewne was at dinner."

"Hm!" He looked at Braishe. "You can go back to the house now, Pollock—and don't say anything to a soul. Mr. Fewne's had a heart attack—that's all."

He pulled up the blinds, and the room took on a new aspect. The splashes of drab colour on the floor became the skeletons of toy balloons, each gashed and ripped and thrown about as if in a fit of furious temper!

"Don't move—either of you!" said Travers quickly. "Just in front of you, George, towards me. Isn't that a pen?"

Paradine picked it up. "The nib's been trodden on."

"Bring it over here, will you? Don't tread on those balloons! . . . Now, let's have a look at it."

He took it to the window and peered at it. "Don't think it's been trodden on. . . . Shall I tell you what I *do* think? For some reason or other—heaven knows what!—he suddenly went stark mad at the sight of those balloons. They infuriated him. There's the main string—look! tied to the end of the bed, and the knot's tight as blazes. What he did was to cut and slash at them with this pen, using it like a dagger. Then he wrenched them off and threw them about the room. Here's one he stamped on; look at the heel mark . . . slipper probably. Then he threw himself on the bed and lashed out with his heels like a boy in a fit of temper."

Paradine grunted—and said nothing.

"Anything in the fireplace?" asked Braishe.

The other two looked round. There didn't seem anything except ashes. "We can have an examination of that afterwards to—" He broke off suddenly as he caught sight of Braishe.

"I say, you must put that balloon back again!" he said sharply. "Nothing's to be touched here."

"Sorry!" said Braishe and smiled foolishly. He dropped the orange-coloured skeleton on the floor by the bed. "But I thought it was merely suicide?"

"That doesn't matter a damn. There'll have to be an inquest. And—er—don't think I'm being awkward, but we're rather crowded in here. Would you mind pushing off back? I'll stand on the mat till George has finished. Sure you don't mind?"

"Mind!" He grunted. "I think I'd faint if I stopped here much longer." He was certainly looking pretty ghastly himself, and Travers watched him from the veranda as he went slowly along through the blinding snow by the hedge.

"How'd he get in that extraordinary position?" Paradine was asking as Travers re-entered the room.

"Don't know. There's a lot of things in this room I don't know much about."

Paradine gave him a queer look. "Why did you get rid of Martin?"

"We didn't want him here while you were telling me it *wasn't* heart failure after all."

"Hm! And what leads you to that conclusion?"

Travers smiled. "Look at that body! It's a photographic pose. I'm no medical man, but I'd swear every muscle was instantaneously paralyzed. I admit that if the left foot weren't touching the wall the whole body'd topple over. Still, that doesn't affect the argument. Am I right or wrong?"

The other looked away for a moment, then pursed his lips.

"I'm not prepared to say ... at the moment. I *will* say it's a case new to my experience."

"It's not new to mine," said Travers bluntly. "I took over some trenches one day and came across a chap almost like that—on his belly, writing a letter. Concussion had killed him—what I called photographically. You'd have sworn he was alive." He shook his head. "Still, there's no point in you and me having a dogfight, George. The thing is, what'd we better do? Give it out as heart and leave it at that . . . till the police get here?"

The other frowned. "I think . . . perhaps . . . yes. You see, I'm in an awkward position. I daren't touch the body . . . yet."

"I realize that." He peered once more round the room. "Suppose that curtained-off space *is* the bathroom?" He moved over and verified it. "Cold tub every morning, by the look of it. By the way, I wonder where the manuscript of his new book is."

Paradine had already begun a search of the dead man's pockets. It was on the writing desk, however, that he found the keys. Travers tried the drawers. In the second was what he was

looking for—a neatly stacked pile of papers, typed in separately
fastened chapters.

"Hm! No title to it."

"I say; this is decidedly queer!" Paradine was holding a sheet
of quarto paper on which was a series of really extraordinary
scrawls. Travers had a look at it, then whistled dolefully.

"'To the Editor of *The Times*. Dear Sir:' That's it—don't you
think so?" He shook his head perplexedly. "He *was* mad, George;
that was what was the matter with him! Look here! He manages
to get a certain amount of coherence into the first line—then the
control gets less and less. Look where the pen's been pressed
on hard. The poor devil was trying to write . . . and he couldn't!
At the end he tries merely the form of address—and he couldn't
manage that. I say, where's that pen?"

He had a look at the ruined nib. "It's a J. The one he wrote it
with; don't you think so? If so, he tried to write *before* he went

quite mad and destroyed those balloons. . . . Better get back to the house, hadn't we?"

He looked round again and shook his head, then took the key from the inside and locked the door. "I'll keep this key, George. If there's a duplicate at the house I'll take that too." He halted for a moment in the shelter of the door. "Something I want you to do. When we have a powwow indoors, propose me as the one to take charge till the police come. Then I'll accept on condition that you're with me. If you want a reason, say that I and Franklin and you and Celia are the only ones with a first-class alibi... for that business indoors. What do you say?"

"Well, I don't know quite what you're driving at, but—er—I've no doubt you've a perfectly good reason." He turned up his coat collar and looked at the blinding snow. "Between ourselves— What's that over there in the snow? Broken branch, probably," and he started off.

Travers seized him by his coat tail. "Just a minute, George! How'd a branch get there? A branch'd be *under* the snow." He hesitated for the briefest instant, then stepped off the veranda. For the first yard or so, in the shelter of the pagoda, the snow was no more than a foot deep; after that, like Fewne on the previous night, he dragged his way through. But it was worth it. Lying there with mouthpiece just above the main surface of the snow was the missing telephone!

"What is it?" hollered Paradine.

Travers waved it at him, then took a few floundering steps farther into the croquet court, his long fingers combing the surface of the snow. Then he found the receiver he was looking for and, the snow blinding his glasses, struggled back. Paradine came to meet him and lent a helping hand, the pair looking like blurred figures in an ancient film. Travers shook himself like a borzoi and hooked the snow out of his turn-ups. Back in the entrance hall William was sent to find Charles.

"When you started to sweep that path round to the pagoda, William, did you see any sign of footprints?" Travers asked.

"No, sir."

"Absolutely sure of that?"

"Absolutely, sir!"

"Right! Go up to my bedroom where you can overlook the pagoda. Stay there and watch it till I tell you to go. Charles, you tell Mr. Pollock where William has gone."

He whispered something to Paradine as they moved away. As they entered the breakfast room, Braishe came to meet them. The others got up from their seats. Braishe's face still looked almost livid.

"Anything new?"

"No. . . . Just heart," said Paradine with a shake of the head. "He's been overdoing it a bit lately," and he sank heavily into a chair by the fire.

Nobody said a word. Even Challis seemed too appalled to make one of his usual trite remarks. Travers broke the silence.

"I think the house ought to be searched at once—and the outbuildings. If I were you, Martin, I'd get every man and do the job thoroughly. Any gardeners available?"

"Two—just cleared a path. And there's my chauffeur."

"Good! The first thing the police'll ask when they get here is whether we've searched the place. . . . Oh, and you might be interested to know we've found the telephone ... in the snow by the pagoda."

"What!" He looked flabbergasted. "How on earth did it get there?"

"Lord knows! Who's your handy man?—because he might as well get it put right. It's on the table outside."

"Right! We'll get going straightaway. Come on, you fellows! We'll make a start from the kitchen."

Paradine got up at once. "Count Travers out, Martin. He'll be in for a chill if he isn't careful. His legs are soaking."

"Nonsense!" began Travers.

"You stop there!" Paradine spoke sharply. "I'll send you in a tot of hot whisky."

Travers shrugged his shoulders resignedly and watched the party file out. For ten minutes or so he sat over the fire with his hot drink, then, in his favourite pose, stretched out his long legs and settled into the depths of the chair. Now and again he took off his glasses and polished them nervously. Then he strolled along to the dining room where the chauffeur had just completed the joining of the severed wires. He tried the phone. Still stone dead.

"There's a break outside somewhere, sir," the man said. "Probably a tree's been brought down by the blizzard last night."

Travers nodded. "And the devil of it is they won't be able to repair it in this weather."

He listened at the foot of the stairs and noted the progress of the search. Then he put on coat and hat and went out by the front door, hugging the wall. He circled the twelve-foot boundary that enclosed the outhouses and garage, came out again at the north of the house, and so round by the east end to the front porch again. Everywhere was the narrow trench that Franklin had made in the snow with his feet, still clear as a depression in spite of the snow that covered it. A minute to remove the traces of the expedition, and he went up to his bedroom. William had seen nothing.

A few minutes later the others returned to the breakfast room, trooping in quietly like people coming back from a dinner appointment which they'd kept on the wrong night.

"Anything happen?" asked Travers.

Braishe shook his head. "He's bolted long ago."

"Not long ago," remonstrated Travers with a dry sort of smile. "He hadn't gone ten minutes ago." He took off his glasses again, blinking round nervously as he polished them with the silk handkerchief. "Now, what about this—er—general meeting?"

CHAPTER VI
TRAVERS MAKES A START

TRAVERS HAD EXPECTED that meeting to be a simple affair. In one thing only, he was right. Everybody did indeed seem faced by a situation with which in his wildest dreams he would never have attempted to cope. But instead of being tongue-tied, people were quite the opposite. The meeting appeared to give them the chance to express emotions and feelings that had been bottled up. After half an hour of aimless talk and wordy suggestions Travers got rather restless. Each speaker seemed to imagine himself as the only one who realized the horror of the situation; and each, while anxious about his own exoneration, was elaborately careful about the susceptibilities of the rest.

"Look here!" he said, in practically the only pause there had been up to that moment. "What really is the use of theorizing? Admit anything you like—that the last drink we had was doped, that there was a burglary, that there's been a murder at any hour you choose to name. All that doesn't alter the one fact: We've no right to argue. We're all possible burglars and murderers in the eyes of the law—every man jack of us except Crashaw."

He waited till everybody had had his say to that.

"You noticed that I included myself. Who can really prove that I didn't burgle the rooms last night? Everything that was taken could go into my pockets, and I might have secreted it in a safe place long ago. And it would be a pretty difficult job to prove that I didn't do the murder—in spite of what George has been good enough to tell you. Now *he* might be vouched for by his wife. But what about the rest of you? Where's your alibi, Tommy? Yours, Martin? Yours, Challis?"

Challis got to his feet with a rare assumption of dignity. "If you think I'm going to stay here to be insulted, you're vastly mistaken."

"Oh, no, I'm not!" said Travers quietly. "You're going to stay here whether you like it or not, and I'll tell you why. If you're afraid to have—"

"Afraid! Who's afraid?"

"Let me finish. If you're shirking an inquiry into your alibi, you've got something to cover up—and that applies to all of us. Not only that. An inquiry's our best friend. When the police get here we want to be ready with a clean bill of health. Personally, I don't mind who inquires into my doings or affairs. I'd welcome it. Surely that's how we all feel?"

"Perfectly right!" said Braishe.

"If it comes to that, old boy, I see Travers's point: not that I've any use for snooping round. And who's going to do all this Nosey Parker business?"

Paradine cut in there. "That depends on ourselves. It might be you."

"Precisely!" added Travers. He looked round the meeting. "Somebody suggest a name, please. What powers he has can be decided on later."

"I refuse to stand," said Braishe firmly. "I'd much rather be inquired into; that's how strongly I feel about it. But may I ask a question? Why the urgency? Won't the police be here at any minute?"

"More likely they won't be here this time to-morrow. If this blizzard keeps up, they mayn't be here for days. And when they do get here, they'll expect us to have done something. We're responsible men—not children."

"May I ask something?" said Wildernesse.

"Why not?" smiled Travers.

"Well, then, we know there was a burglary. I say the burglar did the murder. Now, we know the burglar's gone. Then what is there to inquire into?"

"I think you're wrong," said Travers. "I may say I know you're wrong. There never was a footmark where he left the house. There isn't one now. He didn't dissolve into air."

"Don't be clever, old boy!" Challis's tone was decidedly nasty.

"Sorry!" said Travers imperturbably. "What I'm getting at is this: however thorough your search was, I'm convinced the murderer, or the burglar—call him what you will—is still in the house. Murderers are most unpleasant people. Isn't that an urgent reason for an inquiry, if only as a measure of protection for those of us who're *not* murderers?"

"That's sheer horse sense!" said Paradine, getting to his feet. In a couple of minutes the dictatorship of two was appointed.

"I'm not going to thank you," said Travers, "because it's going to be a most unpleasant job. But I would like to say that there should be no more ideas about what Challis called 'snooping.' Discipline is discipline, and there's the end of it. If anybody deliberately refuses to answer a question or hedges or lies, then he'll have to reconcile that with what the police are bound to find out. And you can bet your life they'll give him the hell of a time."

"I don't think you need worry about that," said Braishe drily. "Speaking as—er—for what I am, the house is yours to do as you like with. And you can't start inquiring too soon for *me*. You'll want some sort of headquarters, by the way. Where'd you like to be?"

"Here, I think. It's out of the way. And it leaves the dining room free for meals. What do you think, George?"

George nodded. Then came Crashaw's excessively timid voice. "Where do I come in, in—er—all this?"

"Don't know yet," smiled Travers. "You may be on duty at the telephone when it starts working again."

"I'm glad that question was raised," said Paradine. "My idea is that all of us—Travers and myself, for instance, when we're not what might be called 'on duty'—should be as normal as we can. We'll get the women down. And we'll keep off all morbid talk at meals or while they're present. There's nothing hypocritical about that."

That was voted a first-class suggestion. Travers had the last word.

"Don't forget we're the servants of this meeting—not its masters. You've three votes—four, if you count Crashaw's—so you can kick us out of office when you like. What's the time, somebody?"

"Just gone eleven."

"Good! Then if you fellows don't mind, George and I will have a committee meeting. And if there's any hot coffee going you might send me in a breakfast cup."

"Make it two!" said George.

It was a quarter of an hour later when Challis entered the room. He gave a wary look round, and his face assumed an expression of such extreme suspicion that Travers had to laugh.

"Come along in, Challis! You're not going to be executed!" He drew up a chair. "Sit down and be friendly!"

Challis permitted himself an inscrutable smile. "Rather like going to the dentist's, old boy, what?"

"Not at all," said Paradine stiffly. For the first time in twenty-four hours he was looking the heavy professional man, inclined to be obstinate and certainly not to be trifled with. "What it amounts to is this: we want to call you in as a witness and assistant."

"Better see if he can do the job," smiled Travers. "Did you design those Sally Sisters costumes?"

Challis looked mystified. "No, old boy; just copied 'em."

"But you do design costumes and sets and so on?"

"Well, yes—after a fashion, old boy, I do."

"Good enough!" Paradine took up the tale. "The situation's this. We're certain the police can't get here for some time—unless they get a rotary plough from God knows where—so whether we get into trouble or not, we've decided to move the bodies. It doesn't seem decent, as things are. We're going to bring poor Fewne over here and lay the bodies out decently—reverently, as it were. Now, we can't do that unless you help us—by making drawings of where the bodies are, and so on, in case the police want details. The thing is, will you do it?"

In Travers's opinion, Challis looked mightily relieved. He was certainly gratified. Then, as soon as he'd expressed himself as satisfied with what paper and pencils they could muster, they set about the job.

"If you don't mind getting on your hands and knees," Travers told him, when the bedroom door was open, "we'll move all round the bed to see if Franklin missed anything."

"What sort of things, old boy?"

"A hair—the mark of a foot on the carpet. Imagine somebody came in with snow on his boots, for instance."

Ten good minutes of that produced nothing.

"Ask Palmer to fetch that maid, George, will you?" said Travers. He let the valance fall and draped it carefully to hide the shoes.

Ransome was looking in a bad way. Her naturally pinched features seemed more sharp than ever, and the thin, almost bloodless line of her lips was the only semblance of colour in her face. She gave Travers two impressions—that she might faint again at any moment, and that under normal circumstances she was a shrewd if not feline customer. Still, he gave her a friendly smile.

"Feeling better, young lady? Capital! Now, we're not going to ask you to come in. If you just tell us something, it'll be quite enough. . . . You put the tray on the side table as you came in this morning?"

"Yes, sir."

"Then you saw the bed hadn't been slept in?"

She moistened her lips. "Yes, sir."

"What did you see then?"

"The shoe, sir—the tip of the shoe."

"Was the valance up?"

"Oh, no, sir!"

"You pulled it up? You're sure of that?"

"Yes, sir."

He frowned at that. "I see. You lifted the valance. You didn't touch the shoes."

Her eyes opened wide. "No, sir. I leaned down and saw . . . her. Then I remember calling out. . . ."

Travers smiled reassuringly. "Then you fainted. . . . When did you tidy up this room, by the way? After your mistress changed?"

"Yes, sir. She was a bit late changing—"

"I know. We'll go into that later. But just for the moment. About nine o'clock, that'd be. You tidied up."

She nodded and moistened her lips again.

"And when Miss Quest sent you word not to wait up"—he turned to the others—"about half-past twelve, wasn't it?—you went straight to bed?"

"Yes, sir. I was very tired."

"I expect you were. Sleep alone?"

"No, sir. I shared a room with Ellen—the head housemaid."

"Good!" He made a sign to Palmer. "We may not need you again, but perhaps you'll stay there with Palmer for a minute or two." As she turned nervously away he whispered in Palmer's ear, then drew Paradine inside and closed the door.

"Strange about that valance! It was down, therefore the burglar didn't see the body. And if he had seen it he'd have bolted like blazes, snow or no snow. And as he didn't see the body, why didn't he ransack the room?" He indicated the drawer he had opened. "However, let's get on."

The course of procedure seemed to have been mapped out beforehand. The whiting marked the position of the walnut single bed before it was moved clear of the body. Then Travers made an outline on the floor while Paradine took notes. Then Challis got to work—at least, he made a start. Travers noticed his hand shaking and nodded to Paradine.

"Don't trouble too much about detail," George told him. "Just the general lie of the limbs." He peered over his shoulder. "I say, that's awfully good!" and so on, till it was finished and the three of them had signed it.

"And you'll lend us a hand in the pagoda after lunch?" asked Paradine.

"And would you mind, on your way down, telling that maid she can go?" added Travers.

With Challis out of the way the work became more gruesome. The body was placed on the bed, and the bed itself moved to its original position. The ghastly headdress was put carefully aside. With his scissors Paradine cut clean through frock, slip, and vest from the low neck opening to the waist. While Travers steadied the body he got the pliers to the cross of the dagger and drew it slowly out. Still holding it by the pliers, he took it over to the window.

"Suppose *you* can't tell if there are prints on the handle?"

"Only a fool'd leave any!" grunted Travers. He had a good look at it, nevertheless. "Curious sort of affair, don't you think? Kind of Wardour Street look about it."

He slipped a miniature folding rule from his pocket.

"Blade eight inches. Handle five. Where'd it come from, George? Off that appalling display board in the hall? ... Drop it in the box, will you? I'll take it down and see."

That display board, as he called it, was some six feet deep by ten wide, covered with red baize that went badly with the wall paper. As Travers stood looking at it, his eyes—best part of six feet from the ground—were on a level with its bottom edge. The stout nails that held it to the wall were very necessary: that miscellaneous collection of swords, pistols, and daggers must have weighed well over a couple of hundredweight. But what his eye was following was the semicircle of daggers—twenty-six of them, he counted—held in position by a band of thick red braid through which they were threaded. One or two seemed to have blades of the kind he wanted, but the handles were all different. There were handles in steel and white metal; handles in bone, handles in wood reinforced with metal bands, but not a single one in brass.

Pollock emerged from the kitchen corridor, and Travers called him over. He waved his hand at the collection of junk.

"How did all this get here originally, Pollock?"

"The—er—weapons, sir? The late master bought them at a sale, sir . . . and rather fancied them here." He evidently gathered from the expression on Travers's face the opinion *he* had of them. "Mr. Braishe doesn't care for them, sir. He talks of having them moved."

"I see. But tell me. There are far more loops than weapons. Was that so when they came?"

"Yes, sir. We thought they'd been stolen from the sale room, sir."

"Well, have a look at 'em now! Any missing since yesterday?"

The butler put himself into an attitude of examination, solemnly ran his eyes over the lot, then shook his head. "To tell you the truth, sir, I never look at them—not purposely, sir."

"Don't blame you! But who cleans 'em?"

"The housemaids dust them, sir. And they were all cleaned in the spring."

That was more like it. Travers covered up the blade and gave the butler a good look at the handle. Everybody in the kitchen was to be questioned forthwith, and a report was to be ready as soon as possible.

"Don't forget: brass handle with spiral design curling round it!" Travers called from the staircase. Up in the bedroom Paradine had uncovered the wound and washed it. As Travers entered, he was completing his notes.

"Anything special about the wound—how it was done?"

The other went on writing. "If you mean, was it done with left or right hand, I can't tell you. ... I never could get the hang of those arguments. . . . Depends on the relative positions of the two people."

"Would right hand be more natural?"

"Might be."

"Much strength required?"

"Can't say till after the post-mortem." He closed the notebook and put it away. "The rib might have been struck first. Otherwise there'd have been nothing to prevent anybody doing it. Nothing to cut through but flesh—none of those corsets they used to wear years ago. Help me with the hair, will you?"

Between them they made Mirabel Quest's last toilet, then drew a rug over the body to the neck. As she lay there with eyes closed and lips slightly parted she might have been asleep. "If Brenda wants to see her now, it won't be so much of a shock," mumbled Paradine apologetically.

Travers nodded. Then, before they went, the wardrobe and the drawers were looked through. In the one Travers had previously opened was a small jewel case, and in the handbag its key on a bunch. Inside the jewel case were a short pearl necklace, a square emerald ring, a turquoise and diamond ring, and three empty boxes.

"There's one ring missing," said Paradine. "She's only two on her fingers."

"I noticed that. Nothing else missing, apparently. Just over six pounds in the bag. No correspondence. . . . Leave them here, shall we? And we might as well leave the door unlocked with the key outside. The dagger can be locked in the safe."

"All right, Palmer, you can go now!" said Travers. He let Paradine move off to the landing, then, "Get anything out of her?"

"She knows something, sir! She spoke very disrespectfully of Mrs. Fewne!"

"Right! Get her to talk—but go steady!" He raised his voice for Paradine's benefit. "You'd better bring that chair with you. The door's not locked now."

In the hall was Pollock, with two of the maids and the housekeeper, who scurried away at the sight of the two men. Pollock came to meet them.

"Sorry we can't help you, sir. We've asked everybody concerned, sir, and they all disagree about the number."

"Yes, but they remember the one with the brass handle? There *was* only one!"

"Pardon me, sir!" Pollock spoke with a respectful firmness. "There never was a brass-handled one, sir. Mrs. Cairns and Ellen are prepared to swear to that."

Travers gave Paradine a look. "Thank you, Pollock. Very good of you."

They had another look at the semicircle of daggers. "Take off that third one, will you?" said Paradine ". . . . Try its length. . . . Good God! It's the very spit of it!"

Travers agreed; moreover, two others were found that resembled the bloodstained specimen in the box. Still, Pollock had been so certain, that any further argument would have been time wasted. The box was locked in the safe, and with it each felt in some vague way the tragedy for a moment or two to be set aside. Paradine pointed out of the window.

"Look at that snow! Perfectly awful!"

"Wonder where Franklin is?" asked Travers.

"Wherever he is, he'll stop—if he's got any sense. Still, it's worrying."

Travers nodded. "I haven't owned up, George, but I'd give the devil of a lot to be well out of this business. However . . . we'll knock off for this morning. What about your seeing Celia and finding out how poor Brenda is bearing up? Be about lunchtime then."

CHAPTER VII
IN THE PAGODA

IT WAS CRASHAW who was the success at lunch. It is true that things were easier than most of them anticipated—Brenda Fewne was too distressed to come down, and Celia Paradine stayed with her—but all the same, the little schoolmaster revealed unexpected gifts of conversation. He was rather like a late autumn robin, piping in the absence of more popular songbirds and beneath skies less blue. Outside, the snow was still blinding down, and the wind kept up an eerie howl like the drone of a lathe, but somehow Crashaw kept insinuating himself deftly and inevitably into the conversation—keeping things going and raising a laugh at which he himself seemed timidly surprised. There was that discourse on nicknames, for instance.

"Well, I don't agree with you, Ludo," George Paradine had said.

"Pardon me," put in Crashaw. "But is that 'Ludo' a nickname? Anything to do with the game?"

"You're a bit benighted, old boy," laughed Challis. "Short for Ludovic. Famous author and all that!"

Crashaw's eyes opened. "I say—really? It was you who wrote *The Economics of a Spendthrift?*"

Travers admitted it. Crashaw definitely blushed.

"I say, I seem to be the only nonentity in a house full of celebrities! Too—er—"

"Don't worry!" Wildernesse told him. "I'm with you. But what was that you were saying about nicknames?"

"Well—er—you see, I'm rather interested in nicknames—sort of make a hobby of collecting them, so I wondered whether Mr. Travers's name was one—or not. What do you think *my* nickname is, for instance?"

Even Braishe smiled at that.

"Do you want the truth, old boy, or is this a riddle?" asked Challis.

"Give it up," said Travers.

"Well, it's 'Neddy'!" He looked round expectantly.

"The higher the fewer!" said Braishe. "Don't see it—unless your name's Edward."

Crashaw smiled. "Not at all. You see the name's Crashaw—that became 'Hee-haw' . . . and so to Neddy!"

"Ha! ha! Damn good!" said Challis. "Know any more?"

"Well, I knew a chap at school whose name was Miles, and his nickname, Andy. Do you see that?"

Nobody did.

"Well, it's rather silly, but it shows a perverse kind of logic. Miles *and* Miles . . . hence, Andy!"

Then Tommy Wildernesse thought of one, and George Paradine gave a contribution in Swahili. "Rather a jolly idea, don't you think," said Crashaw, "guessing the nicknames of complete strangers? Don't think I'm being personal, but what's yours, Mr. Paradine?"

"Lugs!" said George. "Look at 'em!" Everybody roared at that. They did stick out a bit.

"Martin there's got a good 'un," said Tommy. "He doesn't like it in the least, but I'll tell it. Broody. Now, then, how'd he get it?"

"Sleepy at school, perhaps."

"You're wrong. When he was at prep school, he and another bloke thought they'd have a regular supply of fresh eggs, so they bought—at least they *said* they bought—a hen, and kept it in the pavilion till they got found out."

"I say, that's awfully good!" Crashaw seemed really delighted. "If you don't mind, I'll jot that down. Might come in useful. No names, of course."

Though Travers had been contemplating the scene with a quiet amusement, he remembered afterwards every word that was said. And he had a contribution to make.

"Your kids pretty ingenious at that sort of thing?"

"Well, I suppose all kids are—really."

Travers nodded. "What particular line do you do with 'em yourself?"

Crashaw retreated forthwith into his shell. "I say, don't let's talk about me!" He gave a deprecatory smile which seemed perfectly unaffected. "I mean—er—you're not likely to want my signature for your autograph albums." He looked up quickly as if the thought was of tremendous moment. "By the way, what's it feel like to be famous?"

Travers gave him a dry look. "'Famous' is a very relative term, young fellow." He shook his head. "Present company excepted, as they say in polite circles; the only one of us who might have been so qualified . . . well, you'll never meet him."

There was an intense silence for some seconds, then Crashaw coughed nervously.

"Frightful bad luck—heart conking out and all that. . . . And you really think *Tingling Symbols* was—er—so very good?"

"I thought it extraordinarily good," said Braishe.

"Just a bit macabre," said Travers. "At least, I thought so. But it was good—damn good. I'm looking forward to reading that new manuscript of his—unless there's an injunction. That reminds me. Tell me, Martin. When did he last mention the manuscript?"

"Hm! When would it be? Saturday—on the way to town. I asked him how it was coming along, and he seemed extraordinarily pleased with it. He'd only three chapters to do—so he said."

"Suppose you don't know how many he'd done then?"

"But I do! Twenty-one, he'd done. I don't know why I know it, but I do. Suppose he must have said something about it."

"But he's—" began Paradine.

"Just a second, George," Travers cut in quickly. "We're just going over to the pagoda again, and as we're all here there's something George and I have to say. We're proposing to have Denis's body brought over to the house and laid out properly in the same room as Mirabel. It seems too callous—too awful generally—to leave him over there. Do all you fellows agree?—I mean, to share the responsibility if there's a row?"

Braishe scowled belligerently. "I'd like to hear anybody start a row!" Wildernesse and Challis nodded.

"That's all right, then. I wonder, Martin, if you'd have a settee or something taken up there . . . and perhaps there might be some flowers or something. Brenda might rather like it. And if you'd tell somebody to sweep the path by the hedge . . ." He got to his feet. "When we're ready and George has got his report for the coroner, we'll give you a call to lend a hand. You ready, Challis, old chap? Then we'll make a start."

It was lucky that Travers had got those candles from Pollock, for the light in the pagoda was really bad. Challis hovered nervously inside the door as Travers and Paradine stood looking down at the body of the dead man, the maroon stripes of whose pajamas positively shrieked discordancy against the fawn of his dressing gown. But the whole sight was ghastly, as Paradine knew when he placed his own body between the dead man and Challis. Had the pose been placid it might have been merely pathetic; as it was, the body seemed that of a monstrosity; some horrible paralyzed abortion.

Paradine turned his back on it. He spoke very quietly—almost persuasively. "This isn't going to be a nice job for you, Challis. Heart attacks are terrible things—merciful too, sometimes. The body's convulsed"; he drew back and held the candle. "You see, he's drawn up his legs with the agony of it. Just forget that, if you can. Draw what's there. Travers'll hold the candle for you."

Challis was not so nervous this time. For one thing, he knew little of the dead man, and from Mirabel's chatter had rather despised him. There was annoyance that Fewne somehow eluded him; his isolation was an insult. To Challis he had been one of those aloof, aristocratic, supremely indifferent highbrows who miss the good things of life—the things which he himself found so accessible. Perhaps that was why his drawing was now more fluent. He even came forward and verified the position of the left foot against the wall. Travers congratulated him on the effort, and the three of them signed it.

"Don't talk about this over there," said Paradine. "We don't want to upset people too much. And he won't be like this when we bring him over."

"What are you going to do then, George?" asked Travers when Challis had gone.

"Move the body on its side so as to inspect the lips and mouth—and alter the position of the hands; move them to the front as if he were curled up asleep. . . . Hold the candle very steady, will you?"

The face, as Travers saw it by the light of the candle, was even more terrifying. Its colour was a leaden grey, though where the candlelight fell on it, it became as luminous as old parchment. The finely cut features seemed transformed by some incredible and malignant rage. The eyes were screwed up, the forehead puckered, and the lips parted as if in a paroxysm of uncontrollable temper—or was it pain?

"The light quite close," came Paradine's voice. "And perfectly steady. That's it!"

Travers closed his eyes for a moment or two, then kept them deliberately away—on the varnished match-boarding that lined the room from floor to ceiling, on the ceiling itself, on the grotesque shadow of George's head. Then Paradine straightened up, looked round, and let his eyes rest on the curtain of the recess.

"I'll just wash my fingers in there."

He took one of the candles and pulled back the curtain. Travers followed him inside. Nothing there but what one might expect. Take away the curtain, and the continuity of the room, with its match-boarding, would have remained unbroken.

"Can't make it out," said Paradine. "The face indicates angina—but the colouring's not right!"

Travers clicked his tongue—not with annoyance, because he shook his head perplexedly. "That's all right. You needn't go into that." He looked outside at the dull grey sky, seen as a gloomy background to the wildly driving snow. "If it hadn't been for this damn snow—" He broke off abruptly. "But that's nonsense. If there'd been no snow there'd be nothing to look for." Perhaps that horrible face had set his nerves on edge, for he changed the subject again with a suddenness that was rather trying to the listener. "If we pick up those balloons near the door we can make room for the—er—others to get in—and out. Or will you do it while I sprint over to the house?"

In a couple of minutes he was back with Braishe, Pollock, and the two footmen. Paradine covered the body gently as it lay on the top of the trestle table and put the cushion beneath the head. Pollock looked as if he were going to be ill; the footmen looked startled, and Braishe was as white as a sheet when he saw that awful face. Paradine got them out quickly.

"I'll be over in a minute or two. We must go over his effects—for official purposes."

As he came back from the door he saw on Travers's face an expression he'd never seen there before. He looked at him intently, and Travers caught his eye.

"George, that face terrifies me! Don't you see it expresses everything that's been happening here? Do you really think—tell me?—that because he slept here he was shut off from ... all that other business?"

Paradine shook his head. "I don't know. I hesitate to know."

"You mean you're terrified, too." He scowled. "You didn't see him make that mad rush into the snow last night; those damnable balloons flapping about his head. . . . Still, what's it matter? Where are the balloons you picked up? . . . Good! We'll put 'em on the table for a bit. Gather up the rest, will you?"

"You really think we ought to touch them?"

"Doesn't matter in the least. He threw 'em broadcast. We can do the same before the police arrive. As it is, we can't move about the room."

He tried the costume Fewne had removed the previous night but found nothing in the pockets. One thing only was peculiar—that a pocket of the coat, so high comparatively from the snow he'd struggled through, should be soaking wet, and the rest of the coat dry. Still, he thought no more about it as he checked the belongings from his ordinary clothes and put them away in one of the drawers of the desk.

Then for some minutes he stood contemplating that sheet of paper on which the dead man had striven, as it were, to express something he had intensely felt, though the pen had refused to register what the mind so urgently insisted. Then he looked at that neat pile of manuscript and, on a sudden impulse, lifted it out of its drawer and checked the chapters.

"This is the lot of 'em," said Paradine, who'd been patiently holding the heap of torn balloons. "Where do you want them put?"

"I think we'll sort 'em out first—trodden on and not."

There were four of the former, with marks clearly corresponding with the leather-heeled slippers the dead man had worn. One balloon seemed, however, different from the rest. They had all been cut and slashed; this was merely punctured in a couple of places.

"How'd that happen?" asked Travers.

"I should say the pen went clean through one of the others and just touched this. By the time he'd got to it, it was deflated already. He'd thrown them all over the room. One in the corner there, another right over there, absolutely indiscriminately. Clean off his head."

Travers nodded gloomily. "Pretty awful to see a chap go like that." He looked at the punctured balloon. "By the way, wasn't that orange one the one Martin handled?"

Paradine frowned. "I believe it was."

"Right-ho! We'll put 'em all in the drawer here with the pen and that sheet of paper he scrawled on. Those'll be the main exhibits." He locked the drawer, then had a look round. "Anything else you can think of?"

"Don't think so."

"Right-ho, then. I suppose, by the way, you won't mind my reading this manuscript through. Rather strange to hear he hasn't touched it for all these days. My experience is, the nearer the end, the keener the effort."

"Take it, by all means."

Travers paused in the act of wrapping it up. "I wonder if he really did write anything? I mean, did he burn anything last night—you know, dissatisfied with it, perhaps? Do you know, I think I'll go over those ashes carefully. Wood, principally, by the look of 'em." He locked the desk and pocketed the keys. "I say, don't you wait, George. It's frightfully chilly over here."

He drew the blinds carefully and watched George Paradine scurrying back to the shelter of the loggia, then to the porch. Then he stood frowning for a moment. Things were not working out quite as he expected. Why, for instance, had George so dexterously avoided any reference to that gas of Martin's? Was it that he felt in some intangible way that if Fewne had met his death by that gas—of his own volition or not—there might be complications for Braishe himself? Travers shook his head. Let a man be as good company as you like—George Paradine, for instance—but what guarantee was that that he'd accept without prejudice the least implication against one of his own, or his wife's, family? Besides, George Paradine could be mighty obstinate on occasions. Travers shook his head again. Nothing for it but to carry on and leave George as much in the dark as common courtesy allowed. In the meanwhile, what about those ashes?

He shivered slightly—then sneezed. As he blew his nose he sniffed. Strange smell somewhere—not the handkerchief: his hand it was—and a smell remarkably resembling whisky. He thought for a moment, then unlocked the drawer and felt that damp pocket in Fewne's costume. He nodded. That was it. Fewne had done as he and Franklin had—dodged that last drink, and, no receptacle being handy, had unceremoniously tipped it into his pocket. But why? Travers shrugged his shoulders. Why not? Only—that hardly bore out the theory that he'd been tight. And now Travers came to reckon them up, Fewne had had very few drinks—fewer than he himself, for example. However, what did it matter?

With a couple of candles on the floor of the open fireplace he set to work on those ashes, raking them aside with tongs and poker, and even using his fingers. There was no sign of burnt papers—at least, none that he could distinguish from the ordinary. One thing only seemed at all unusual—the metal tag end of a bootlace, or that was what it seemed to be. But why had Fewne been burning bootlaces? Travers smiled to himself. Because they—or it—had broken. And if so, one of his shoes would show a new lace. There, however, the logic failed. The boots had leather laces with wire tags; the shoes hadn't a single new lace among them.

Travers looked round the room again. Assume the death by the gas: then, where had it come from? Not from a balloon—that was a manifest absurdity. And for sanitation or lighting there was no connection with outside. With the candle he worked his way round the room, going over the junction of match-boarding and ceiling, then match-boarding and floor. As far as he could see, there wasn't a crack. Then he groped beneath the bed to inspect the junction there—at least, he pushed the candle underneath and followed it up with his head . . . then he stopped short!

Two minutes later he was over in the hall, talking to the housekeeper. The pagoda was going to be used as a bedroom again that night. Could she arrange for the bed to be made with clean clothes, the grate to be cleaned out, and the fire lighted? William would do all that, would he? Then would she arrange it at once with Pollock?

He moved off again to the door, then turned round. Tommy Wildernesse was coming down the stairs, looking as miserable as sin. Travers decided to take a risk.

"Busy, Tommy?"

The other looked round with a start. Travers had been invisible in the shadows of the huge, unlighted room.

"Can you spare a minute or two over in the pagoda? Don't bother about coat or anything. Just sprint!"

Wildernesse looked quite startled for a minute. "What's up? Something—er—"

"Nothing at all—really. Just something I thought you'd like to see."

Whatever it was that Wildernesse was anticipating during that short sprint, it was worlds away from what he actually saw. To tell the truth, it was only after the most laborious of demonstrations that he saw anything at all—and when he did see it he could make nothing of it.

"Have a look under the bed," Travers told him. "Just where the boarding joins the skirting board. I'll hold the candle."

"Why not move the bed out?"

"Mustn't!" said Travers impressively. "The coroner'll expect everything as it was."

Thereupon Wildernesse had got down under the low bed, cursed when his skull had grated against the ancient mattress, then had gazed where Travers told him.

"Clean joint?"

"Absolutely!"

"Couldn't get a straw in between?"

"No. I don't think you could."

"Splendid! That's all, then, Tommy. Mind your head as you come out. I'd get on my back if I were you and come out face up."

Tommy rubbed his head. "Pretty Spartan affair, that bedstead!"

"Best for sleeping in," said Travers. "I never slept so well in my life as on an army mattress."

"So I've been told. And now—what was I to look at the joint for?"

"To see if it was practically airtight. However, never mind what it was for. All I want you to do is to remember it. And something else." He lowered his voice. "Don't think this is nonsense. I was never more serious in my life. Promise me you'll say nothing to a living soul about what we've done over here!"

"Yes—but why?"

"Because, if the wrong person knows what you've seen I wouldn't give twopence for your life!"

"Oh, I say!"

"Don't be a damn fool!" said Travers sharply. "Do you think Mirabel would have laughed if I'd told her the same thing last night?"

"You mean . . . you know who killed her?"

"I don't know anything, Tommy. All I'm saying is—a knife in the ribs is a damned unpleasant way of dying! . . . You give your word, then?"

The other's eyes fell. "Right-ho ... if you think it necessary."

"One other thing," said Travers. "You definitely refuse to sleep here to-night. You consider it unnecessary."

Tommy's eyes opened in astonishment.

"That's all right!" said Travers. "The thing's this: if you're asked what you've been doing over here, you can say I suggested you should have a look round with a view to sleeping here. I'll explain that later—to the others."

"Right-ho!" He was looking so unusually serious that Travers was enormously relieved.

"Just one thing, Tommy—something most damnably impertinent of me to say, even as we are now. . . . You thought a good deal of Mirabel?"

The other looked at him ... bit his lip . . . and nodded.

"That's all right, old chap. Then you'll be prepared to lend a hand to get the bloke who did her in. . . . I'd cut over now if I were you. And something you might do for me—purely a personal matter. Ask Pollock, if he has 'em, to put in my room all the back numbers of *The Times* from last Saturday inclusive."

When he'd gone, Travers looked suddenly very tired. And he was worried. If Tommy kept his word, he'd be all right. But what about himself? One thing only to do—to ape the cheerful idiot; to fuss round treading on nobody's toes; knowing nothing except what was likely to be farthest from the truth. Then William tapped at the door.

He watched the footmen enter with lamp, bedclothes, and firing; then, when Charles had gone, had a word with William.

"Charles been here long, William?"

"Just about a week, sir. I believe he came specially for the house party, sir."

"Really! Is he English?"

"I think he's Swiss, sir—least, he says he is; but he says he's spent most of his time in England."

"Hm! I guessed something of the kind. By the way, when you clean out the grate, see if you can find anything that Mr. Fewne might have thrown in."

"Something lost, sir?"

"Well, something I can't find. Do it carefully. It might be very small."

But whatever it was that Travers was looking for, it wasn't found. All that William ran across was a metal tag—the fellow of the one that Travers had in his pocket. Thereupon, as the cold was making his teeth chatter, he hurriedly put away in one of the large drawers the used bedclothes, then made his way back to the house, the bundle of manuscript under his coat. By this time the afternoon was nearly over. In the house, the lighted windows looked cheerily inviting. Above, the sky was a sullen grey, the wind cut like a knife, and the snow was blinding down harder than ever.

CHAPTER VIII
MORE COMPLICATIONS

CELIA PARADINE came down to tea after all: a can't-stay-more-than-a-minute visit that lasted twenty. Not that anybody wished it shorter. The men were beginning to get more than bored with their own company. That afternoon, with the funeral cortège from the pagoda, had, as Challis said, absolutely put the lid on it. All very well for Travers and Paradine, with a job of work to do; but to loaf round in a Sabbath atmosphere and feel every remark an indiscretion if not an indecency, well, wasn't any relief welcome?

It was George Paradine who accomplished it. Brenda, he said, would be all the better for a few minutes of her own company, and just then she was having a cup of tea upstairs. For the others, the change of room, the less sober atmosphere, the fire, even Ho-Ping, contributed to make things by comparison positively cheerful. Footmen and ceremonial were dispensed with. Travers, with a kind of subdued gaiety, fluttered round with cakes. Crashaw kept up a discreet chatter, and Challis ventured more than once on a guffaw.

"Don't you think it would be rather a good idea," Travers suggested, "if one of us—Martin really ought to be the chap—had a word with Brenda and—er—sort of said how sorry we all were; how we hoped she'd soon be down, and so on? I think, perhaps, she might appreciate it."

"That's a very sensible suggestion!" said Celia.

"Well—er—if everybody thinks so," said Braishe. "She's—er—quite presentable?"

"Of course she is!" snapped his aunt. "You don't think she's in sackcloth and ashes!"

Travers put a side table at her elbow. "What about Ho-Ping, Celia? Don't you think he might have a special éclair?—if he eats éclairs."

The point seemed to be missed. Travers explained.

"You see, if he hadn't been in your room you'd have lost the family jewels."

Celia gave a snort. "Murdered in our beds, more like it!" She glared at George; why, Travers didn't know. "What's been done about it? If I understand George's account, nothing's been done at all." She snorted again. "Why aren't the police here? What do we pay them for if it isn't to protect us?"

Travers smiled placatingly. "Look here, Celia; I'm not George, and you're not going to get round me. Don't let's talk about all this terrible business. We've agreed—"

Agreements to Celia Paradine were like ditches to a tank. "I don't care what you've agreed. I say I'm not going to let that poor girl be alone to-night! She's coming in with me!"

"Why not?" asked Travers mildly. "George can have Franklin's bed, and you can hammer on the wall if anything goes wrong—which it won't!"

Celia ignored that. "The sooner you get the police here, the better. Then *I'll* have something to say!" She glared at Tommy Wildernesse, who opened his mouth, then thought discretion the better part. "Didums feel frightened, then?" she asked the obese Ho-Ping. Nobody laughed.

Travers drew his chair up alongside hers and assumed his most ingratiating manner. In a couple of minutes he had her booming away, and things settled down again. That lasted till the end of the interlude, when Tommy Wildernesse started playing the piano—very quietly and rather well. Celia's voice came with disconcerting clearness.

"Do tell Mr. Wildernesse to stop playing—please! Most unsuitable!"

Travers raised his eyebrows. Wildernesse stopped abruptly, then, looking very confused, lighted a cigarette. Celia rose like a tragedy queen.

"I mustn't leave that poor girl any longer. Are you coming, George, or remaining here?"

"With you, my dear." He gave Travers a look. "Of course, you know, I shall have to be down again . . ."

The voices trailed away in the corridor. Challis looked round as if to sound the feelings of the meeting, then addressed himself to Wildernesse.

"Well, thank God she's not *my* aunt, old boy!"

For the first time since they'd been there Wildernesse looked at Challis as if he were a human being. But he said nothing.

"Celia's all right!" put in Travers, smiling. "We're all a bit on edge—and we do at least know something. She's been up there all day, having a perfectly filthy time—and knowing precious little."

"Well, we don't know so much, old boy, if it comes to that!"

"You may do in time!" said Travers, still smiling. Then Braishe came in with the news. Brenda was bearing up like a brick. Frightful shock, of course. And she'd been touched by the message they'd sent. Next day, perhaps, she'd be down. Company, according to Braishe, was what she wanted. Travers agreed, then announced that he had a rather important question to ask.

"I want someone to sleep over in the pagoda to-night. Fire's going strong, light's fixed up, and the bed's got newly aired sheets. Who's going to volunteer?"

"But—er—why?" asked Braishe. He seemed staggered at the suggestion and looked round helplessly.

"I'll tell you. Not that you'll agree. Poor Fewne went mad last night. You all noticed how uncannily quiet he was during the evening. When he got over to the pagoda he seems to have broken down pretty badly. He cut and slashed . . . things in the room, and threw himself on the bed like a lunatic. Whether that brought on the heart attack that killed him, I don't know. Still, there we are. What I suggest is that this must have been a cumulative process. He's been over there—introspective, worried, perhaps, and overworking—but is there anything else? Is there anything—don't laugh at me!—anything psychic, overwhelmingly depressing about that pagoda? Is there any noise you can hear that might torture one's nerves?—branch of a tree creaking or anything like that?" He looked round appealingly. "Did anything help to drive him mad? That's all I want to find out. And, if necessary, I'll sleep there myself."

"That's all right," said Braishe quickly. "I'll sleep there!" He laughed nervously. "I'm nervous enough at the moment—I mean I'm nervy enough to sense anything that's going."

"That's capital!" Travers appeared to be considerably relieved. "If you don't mind my suggesting it, Crashaw might have Brenda's room, and George might come in with me. Then we'll be all in a bunch together."

Braishe nodded. "Perhaps that would be better. I'll fix it up."

"Then, if you people don't mind," said Travers, "I'll push off to the breakfast room. Send George along when he comes." At the door he paused. "Why shouldn't you all lend a hand with the inquiry?" He came back and explained. "Why not find out where everybody was when the lights went out—servants and everybody—so as to see who really cut the cord? You might have a go at the same time at finding out when and how that burglar got in—assuming he *was* an intruder, as Tommy thinks."

The idea seemed well received.

"One thing I'd like to ask in that context," went on Travers. "That footman Charles. He brought in the special nightcap which everybody thinks was doped. Pretty certain about his references?"

Braishe's eyes opened. "That's an idea! I only really had him for this special show. If he turned out all right I'd thought of trying him out as a valet."

"Well, you make a few cautious inquiries!" said Travers from the door, and left them to it. As he stirred up the fire in the breakfast room he wondered just where Franklin was at that moment. He'd got through to the village, of course; there wasn't any doubt about that. The trouble was, when could he get back again? Travers was finding it hard work to keep his own counsel, and harder still to avoid criticism of his own efforts, and wondering what Franklin would do if he were there. And what *was* the best thing to do, now the ground had been roughly surveyed? Events in chronological order—say the doped drink, the cut cord, the burglary, and the murder? Or why not start at the murder and work back? Everything most damnably cautious, of course . . . then an idea! Why not play for safety and call in Palmer and hear if he'd got anything out of that maid? Just then George Paradine came in, and Travers drew him up a chair.

"Just wondering where we ought to start, George. And before I forget it—I'd rather like to read that manuscript to-night. You won't mind if I turn in early and make a start before you roll up?"

"I'm going to turn in early too," said Paradine firmly. "These late hours don't suit me. Only, you read as long as you like. You won't disturb me."

"Good!" He hooked off his glasses. "I'm probably talking rot, George, but what precisely did Celia mean when she said she'd start talking as soon as the police got here?"

George Paradine's head didn't move. He sat looking into the fire for several seconds while Travers polished the glasses and hooked them on again. His answer, when it came, was startling.

"You know when the lights went out . . . just as I came over to you and Challis and we stood talking? Well, Celia swears she saw Tommy Wildernesse come out of Mirabel's room, sort of furtively, and slip across to his own room!"

"But the light was too bad for that, surely!"

"That's what I thought at first. She says she heard a kind of click—that'd be when Franklin let the blind up—and just as I came over to you people she looked through our door . . . and saw Wildernesse. You see, that harlequin costume with its variegated colours was rather attracting."

"Hm!" Travers took off his glasses again. "Look here, George, we've got to look at this from every angle. Martin had a harlequin costume. How'd Celia know it wasn't he?"

Paradine hesitated again. "You and I know each other pretty well?"

"We should do, George!"

The other nodded. "Then, you trust me as I trust you. I don't care who's mixed up in this business—whether it's you or my wife's nephew or the man whose house I'm in. Nobody's going to keep my mouth shut! A square deal and no more. Now you know where we stand!"

As he scowled into the fire Travers felt a sudden glow of affection. "George, you're a bald-headed, bellicose old . . . sportsman! But, tell me. How'd Celia know it wasn't Martin?"

George turned and looked at him for the first time. "Think it out. Martin's costume was darker—green, black, and yellow; Tommy's two colours only—light and dark blue, and Celia says she caught a flash of the actual pattern. That window at the angle of the back staircase hasn't got a blind, by the way; therefore, what light there was'd be at his back. What she actually saw was this: The harlequin seemed to come quickly into sight. Then he halted at the top of the short staircase and drew his hand over his head as if he was smoothing his hair back. That's a trick of Wildernesse's, Celia says. Then the harlequin nipped like a streak across the landing and up the other short staircase."

"And Celia saw all that!"

"So she says. She's got amazingly good eyesight, you know!"

Travers nodded. "You realize that while all this was happening we were talking?"

"Talking? . . . I'm afraid I don't see—"

"All I meant was this, George. Why should the harlequin, after he'd murdered Mirabel, have risked being seen at all by the people whose voices he could hear? Why didn't he lie low? Or cut up the servants' staircase?"

"Because he wasn't aware that he *would* be seen. Everywhere was dark—except behind his back, and he couldn't see there!"

Travers thought it over for a minute. "I think there's only one thing to do, George. You and I have got to conduct this inquiry as openly as circumstances'll let us. We must see Celia and put it to the party or parties concerned. Do you mind if we have a word with Celia about it?"

"Now?"

"Well, yes ... if it's suitable. But what about Brenda?"

"Why not come in and have a word with Brenda yourself?"

Travers waited at the head of the stairs till George beckoned him in. There was a fire in the room, and Brenda, in a dressing gown, was lying back in an easy chair. Her face, all its rigidity of perfection and its aloof indifference gone, seemed to him then the loveliest thing he had ever seen. As she looked at him he seemed to catch for a moment something apprehensive and inquiring; then, as he smiled, there came a reaction—or a deliberate assumption of weariness.

"How're you feeling now, Brenda?"

"Better, thanks . . . Ludo." The voice had its old level tone.

"You must hurry up and get fit again—and come downstairs and join us." He hesitated, trying to find words. "We know just what it means to you ... or we try to." She gave him a wan smile as he patted her hand. Then he turned to Celia.

Outside, on the main landing, he listened without interrupting, while she gave her story in full detail. There seemed to be at least one flaw.

"You really mustn't say that, Celia," he told her patiently. "You didn't see him leaving Mirabel's room! You can't see the door at all from here. For all you know, the harlequin—whoever he was—was only coming down the stairs from the servants' quarters."

"What right had he got to be there?"

"Well, we might at least ask him. And if it *was* Wildernesse, he might have forgotten for a moment and mistaken the landing for his own. When you caught sight of him, he was merely rectifying the error."

"Rubbish! He'd been in the house long enough to know where his own room was!"

Travers smiled. "He was wool-gathering! However . . ." He turned to George. "What about putting out the light and then you coming down the stairs past the door with a handkerchief in your hand?"

Paradine carried out the instructions, then Travers changed places with him. Celia had certainly been right. Though the snow had stopped falling, the moon was not yet up; and in spite of that there was sufficient light from the window to make the handkerchief visible. Moreover, in spite of Celia's known tendency to welcome opposition and ride rough-shod over it, Travers was beginning to think it had really been Tommy Wildernesse she had seen; indeed, but for one thing he'd have needed no further convincing. He put it quietly to George as they made their way downstairs.

"I must say it, George, but that trick of smoothing the hair back is one that I've noticed much more in Martin than Tommy. However, we'll have it out with Tommy first, if you think fit."

"Best thing to do—then see Martin afterwards. Didn't you say he wasn't in his room when the lights went out, because you went to tell him about drawing his curtains?"

"That's right. See if he's in the drawing room, will you?—and bring him along."

In the drawing room the council of four was holding its first session, with Pollock giving evidence. Wildernesse seemed a trifle perturbed at being called away.

"Hallo! What's up now?" he asked, just a bit anxiously, it seemed to Travers.

"Just want to tell you something. Have a cigarette and make yourself at home!"

Paradine took over. "We're taking you completely into our confidence, Tommy, without any beating about the bush. To put the matter absolutely bluntly, we've a witness—whom you'll be allowed of course to confront—who says you came either out of or past Mirabel's room last night, shortly after the light went out—say, two minutes after."

"Good God! I say, what a damnable lie!"

"No need to get excited, Tommy!" said Travers. "Tell us, where were you precisely at that moment?"

"Hm! That's easy! I was—" He broke off abruptly. "Is all this without prejudice?"

Travers smiled. "Without prejudice to what?"

"Well, you're not going to rake up any private affairs of mine?"

"Don't be absurd!" said Paradine testily. "Everything here is confidential. All we want you to do is to clear yourself of what you evidently know to be a ridiculous charge."

"Charge! You don't mean to say you're accusing me of murdering—"

"Don't be a fool!" Travers told him. "We know you better than that. Come on! Cough it up, Tommy! Where were you?"

He gave the pair of them a damnably suspicious look. "If you insist on knowing, I was in the loggia—and I stayed there till just before Charles locked up."

"In the loggia!" Then Travers apologized. "Sorry! I'm not doubting your word, but what on earth were you doing out there in the cold?"

"Mirabel gave me a note—at least, she threw me a note—to meet me there after the show."

"Really! Did you keep the note, Tommy? I mean, the police might want to see it."

"As a matter of fact—I did!" This very deliberately. "It said I was to burn it, but... never mind the reason, I just kept it. Like to see it?"

In a couple of minutes he was back with it—a half sheet of writing paper, ordinary white parchment from the lounge desk, apparently. Travers smoothed out the creases.

See me in the loggia after the show. Most urgent. Burn this.

M.

Paradine had a look at it. "Suppose it's her writing, all right?"

"It's the first time she ever wrote me anything—that's one reason why I kept it. I tell you, I saw her flick it over. I was sitting down for a minute by the drinks table—you know, Travers; you must have seen me there; just before eleven, it was, soon after the balloons went up. She was dancing with Fewne, and then she flicked that over. I put my foot on it."

"Do you mind if George shows it to Brenda?" asked Travers.

"That's just as you like—except that I don't want it shouted all over the house!"

"You're a suspicious young devil, Tommy!" Travers shook his head at him. "Take it up, George! I've got a brain wave. Excuse me a moment, Tommy!"

When he came back Palmer was with him, looking, as usual, more like the family solicitor than a gentleman's general factotum. Travers whispered to Wildernesse, then began the questioning.

"Oh, Palmer! You were sitting by the electric gramophone all night?"

"Yes, sir, until you told me I might go, sir."

"Exactly! And all the time you were watching the dancers and so on?"

"Yes, sir . . . and very interesting it was, sir."

"Quite! Now, did you at any time during the evening see a note flicked across the room to anybody?"

Palmer gave a tentative cough. "Er—were you wanting names, sir?"

"Certainly!" blurted out Wildernesse. "Say what you saw—names and all!"

"Well, sir, Miss Quest was dancing with Mr. Fewne—I mean, he wasn't dancing very well, sir—"

"Keep to the point!"

"Very good, sir. Then, as they passed by Mr. Wildernesse, sir, I saw what I took to be a note, sir. Mr. Wildernesse put his foot on it, sir, and afterwards he picked it up . . . and then he went out of the room, sir."

"And you've not mentioned this to a soul?"

"Certainly not, sir!"

"All right, Palmer, thanks."

George Paradine had heard the last few sentences, and Travers filled in the gaps; moreover, he couldn't forbear the least bit of self-congratulation.

"There you are, Tommy! Great is truth, and all the rest of it!"

"Just a moment!" said Paradine. "This note isn't in Mirabel's writing. Brenda says it's nothing like it. And here's a letter Celia had from her a day or two ago. Compare them for yourselves!"

That, of course, upset everything. "If Mirabel didn't write it, who did?" asked Wildernesse, now rather alarmed.

"Are you sure it was she who flicked it over?" asked Travers.

"Well, she caught my eye at the same time—and gave me a sort of grin." Then he grunted. "What should Fewne want to do it for? Of course, he might have flicked it over because she asked him, but it doesn't look likely; I mean, the note says it's all secret. . . . And what should Fewne want to write it for? He wasn't so mad as all that!"

"Let's talk nonsense for a moment," said Travers. "Let's suppose Fewne wanted to murder her. Then why should he want to lure you away, Tommy? You had no assignation with her that he was likely to know about?"

"Had I, hell! I'd hardly spoken to her. She'd treated me just like dirt or tried to be funny at my expense all the time: as you know, if you think it over."

Travers nodded. "Then that isn't it. How long were you in the loggia?"

"How long! Long enough to freeze nearly stiff. It was as cold as hell in there."

"Anybody see you come back?"

He thought for a moment, then scowled. "Blast it, no! You see I didn't *want* anybody to see me. I just slipped into the hall and upstairs to my room. I was absolutely foaming at the mouth. I made up my mind I'd raise blue merry hell with her in the morning."

"You didn't tap at her door or anything?"

"No! I'll swear to God I didn't. I'll swear every word I've told you is true!"

"That's all right, Tommy. We believe you all right. It's just unfortunate, that's all. However," and he patted him paternally on the shoulder, "we'll be sure to find somebody who saw you come in."

"There was a light under the stairs, behind the screen; I know that. And I heard Martin say something!"

"Good! That's one up to you!" He turned to Paradine. "Now, what about asking the other harlequin to give *his* account?"

CHAPTER IX
EVERYBODY TALKS

As it happened, there was no need to look for Braishe. He came in while they were talking, holding a sheet of paper which appeared to be notes.

"Hope I'm not butting in, but I've got all those times you asked us to do—where people were when the light went out."

"Splendid!" said Travers. "Tell us all about 'em."

"Well, the female staff is all right—I mean to say they were all in bed and asleep; two in a room, except Mrs. Cairns. The sleeping two in a room is no actual guarantee, of course, though it's pretty strong evidence; also I should say there isn't one among 'em likely to burgle a room, let alone murder anybody. With regard to the men, I pushed the bell for Pollock just as we got up, you remember. He and William were just inside the hall as we came in. Charles says he was getting something from his room upstairs and just as he got down the light went out . . . but of course he can't prove it. The other two say Mirabel ran upstairs first, then you two and Franklin and Aunt Celia, then Challis and Brenda. Pollock says he doesn't know where Denis or Tommy was. He remembers Brenda stopped on the stairs and asked Challis if he knew where Denis was. Challis confirms that. With regard to myself, I was just behind the last pair and was actually talking to Pollock when the light went out. Tommy can probably account for himself, but we can't make out where Denis was. He spoke to William a few minutes later—just said good-night, or something like that—when William was in the meter cupboard. At that moment I was in the rooms, trying the switches to see if the breakdown was a local one."

"Now I come to think of it," said Travers, "I think I can explain where Denis was. When I came out of the room, I noticed those balloons of his still there—attached to the settee probably. I should say he suddenly remembered them, and by the time he'd gone back for them, the light went out. We know he took them over to the pagoda—heaven knows why!"

Braishe rubbed his chin and nodded thoughtfully.

"As you say, there wasn't any hurry. The balloons could have waited till the morning—or later. Still, they were part of the costume, as it were. Perhaps that's what he had in mind."

Travers might have added, "Then why did he take that trouble merely to slash them in pieces over in the pagoda?" What he did say was, "We know what happened to Tommy. He was in the loggia—for private and excellent reasons."

Braishe looked interested. "That explains it, then! Charles saw him come in again. He said you passed close to him, against the stairs; about a quarter of an hour later—would that be it?"

Wildernesse looked immensely pleased. "That was it!" He gave a nod of satisfaction. "That lets me out—thank God!"

Travers smiled. "Good for you, Tommy! But there's just one extra verification we can have of your being in the loggia. I looked out of my window and saw Denis go to the pagoda. You must have seen him too. Would you mind telling us exactly what you saw?"

"Would I! My dear chap, I saw the whole thing!" He gave an account that left no doubt whatever in Travers's mind; moreover, he added something that Travers couldn't possibly have known; something that fitted in with those amazing happenings in the pagoda and yet left them unexplained. "He was muttering to himself like blazes. Between ourselves, I thought he was tight. And my idea of where he was is that he went back to the room to have another tot. Perhaps he saw the balloons at the same time."

Travers nodded, then put a vital question. "I take it, Tommy, that when you said you were in the loggia when the light went out, you were talking—well, figuratively. I mean, you were there *while* they were out. Where were you when they *went* out?"

"I see." He shot a look at Travers. "Damn it all, Ludo; don't look at me like that! I slipped into the dining room till the coast should be clear. That's where I was."

Travers made a gesture of complete comprehension. "That's all right, Tommy. It's best for you to know the kind of question the police might ask."

"I shouldn't worry if I were you, Tommy," said Braishe. "Here's another confirmation he was in the loggia. He wasn't in his room when Pollock brought the candles up."

"Tommy's all right!" said Travers heartily. "The police'll get nothing on him!" He turned to Braishe. "How about Mirabel? Did she get a candle? There wasn't one in her room."

"No. She wasn't there."

Travers grunted, then frowned. "I say, that's bad! You see the point, George?"

Paradine hoisted himself up in the chair and looked round. "If Pollock looked in the room, then I do."

"He looked in all right," said Braishe. "He had a lighted candle."

"Exactly! She was under the bed—where we found her. That means she was definitely murdered when the lights were out—and before Pollock got there."

"And it may mean," Travers added quietly, "that the lights were put out so that she *could* be murdered! There was just the chance, of course, that she was elsewhere when Pollock looked in: the bathroom, for instance."

"She wasn't there. Pollock says it was empty."

They stood thinking that over for a minute, then Paradine cleared his throat. "There's something you ought to know, Martin. Your aunt says she distinctly saw a harlequin come down the side stairs past Mirabel's door, just after the light went out. Tommy proves it wasn't him; your aunt says it wasn't you!"

"Says she saw a harlequin. But it's—er—ridiculous! I was downstairs at the time!"

"Exactly. But she says she's certain. There weren't any other harlequins, were there?"

Braishe shook his head. Travers cut in quickly with a suggestion.

"This is what I think we ought to do—if only to satisfy Celia. George'll pardon my saying so, but she's bound to persist in her attitude if we don't make her prove herself wrong. Why shouldn't Martin and Tommy put on those costumes and let Celia have a look at 'em under the same conditions? We can use candlelight on the back staircase to represent moonlight—what little there was. You agree, Martin? You, Tommy? Then, if George'll tell Celia, we'll make a start."

In a quarter of an hour the stage was set. Most of the time was spent in approximating that light to the merest glimmer that had penetrated the narrow corridor from the staircase window. But as soon as Travers marshalled his two harlequins and put them through their paces across the landing something went wrong. Even when the motions as described by her were done with exaggerated slowness, she was wrong in her guesses.

"Who was that one?" Travers would sing out. Celia would have a shot, which might be right. The trouble was, it was just as often wrong. Moreover, as she finally had to confess, the lucky guesses were based rather on what might be called a fortuitous intuition than on a definite recognition of the patterns of the costumes. After that they switched on the light and held the inquest on the top landing.

Travers gave what he imagined was a roguish smile.

"Well, Celia, what about it now?"

Celia protested volubly. Whatever they said, she'd seen a man who'd worn a harlequin costume. She'd swear to that anywhere. She'd caught the lozenge pattern.

"Then there must have been heaps of white or yellow in it!"

"Perhaps there was. There must have been!" This very triumphantly.

"But there must have been some dark," went on Travers, "or you'd never have seen the pattern. You'd have thought it was a ghost!"

Celia was not amused. "I don't see there's any point in making a mock of tragic things."

"Sorry!" said Travers. "I simply meant it couldn't have been *all* white or yellow. But you're sure it wasn't Tommy—or his costume—you saw?"

"Well, apparently it couldn't have been!" Travers smiled to himself at the regret in her voice. "But he did smooth his hair back as Mr. Wildernesse does!"

There was a moment's silence, then Braishe saved Travers the trouble, by using the words he'd have used himself. "But that's something I do pretty frequently too!"

"That's right!" cut in Wildernesse, then, "I'm sorry! I didn't intend to—"

"What's it matter?" Travers laughed cheerfully. "It wasn't Tommy—and it wasn't Martin."

"It certainly wasn't!" added George bluntly. "We know where both of them were." He turned to Travers. "It was a burglar. That's who it was!"

"What was a burglar doing in Mr. Wildernesse's room?" Celia asked imperiously.

Tommy was as quiet as a pup that's had an unpleasant experience with a seasoned veteran of a cat. Braishe came to the rescue.

"He might have been doing anything, Aunt Celia. It's pretty dark in those corners, you know."

"Do you know," said Travers, "I'm inclined to think that burglar planned pretty well. All the district knew the dance was on, and there'd be plenty of local gossip about the house being full of people. So he came prepared. He wore a harlequin costume. You'll admit he had nothing to do but slip in the front door. He intended to go through the bedrooms while the dance was on; then, if he'd been seen by the servants, he'd have been unsuspected. That early breaking up of the party—before the official supper, when everybody'd have been downstairs—rather upset his plans. He couldn't get away because of the road, so he lay low."

"Yes—but why the *harlequin* costume?"

"Exactly!" Celia gave a nod of full agreement. "And why did he go to Mr. Wildernesse's room?"

Travers was enjoying it. "He chose a harlequin costume because he hoped he'd be right—and he *was* right. Whoever heard of a fancy-dress ball without a harlequin! We've even got a couple in the house—and we're only six men! I know what you're going to say—that none of the guests had them. That's because you didn't give me a chance to couple pierrots with harlequins. There were at least two pierrots, you know! But about going to Tommy's room—there I'm as much in the dark as everybody. He might have heard something upstairs and thought he'd shift his quarters."

He left them there, arguing it out, and made his way back to the breakfast room. In the hall he met Pollock.

"I've found those copies of *The Times* you were asking for, sir. They're on your dressing-room table, sir."

Travers thanked him and was passing on, then had an idea.

"Oh, Pollock! Ask Ransome—Miss Quest's maid—to come to the breakfast room, will you?"

He stoked the fire again and drew a chair up to the table. There was something distinctly unpleasant about that maid—not the fact that she was forty if a day and looked as if she were perpetually guarding a certain arid virginity, but some furtiveness of look that went badly with the smug servility which she cultivated. If his judgment were correct, she was about as much to be trusted as a female rattlesnake. For all that, he laid himself out to be pleasant.

"How're you feeling now, Ransome? Quite recovered?"

"Yes, sir . . . thank you."

"It must have been a pretty awful shock to you," he went on. "Had you been with Miss Quest very long?"

"Two years, sir. In *Parlour Tricks* at the Publicity was where I was with her first."

"I remember it—a very good show! But, tell me, now. Did she even hint to you this last day or two anything about this dreadful business? Was there anybody she was afraid of, for instance?"

"No, sir . . . not that I know of."

"Hm!" For all its patness, the answer didn't ring very true. Then he looked straight at her: six foot two down at five foot one. "Shall I tell you who I think *might* have killed her—if there'd been an opportunity?"

This time there wasn't any doubt in his mind. He saw the sudden start; he could almost see that cheap little brain of hers wondering just what he knew.

"Who do you think *that* was?"

She drew in a quick breath. "I don't . . . don't know, sir."

He smiled. "I was forgetting. You didn't see that show she did for us last night. If you had, you'd have said that Beauty Sally'd have murdered her with all the pleasure in the world!" He shook his head sadly. "Miss Quest was a marvellous mimic, don't you think so?"

"Yes . . . she was, sir."

He nodded again, somewhat pontifically. "I suppose she didn't by any chance ask you to scribble a note for her last night while she was dressing for the show?"

Her thin face coloured violently. "A note, sir?"

"Yes. We found a note she was supposed to have written to . . . somebody, but it wasn't in her handwriting. I wonder if you'd mind writing something for me on this sheet of paper." He passed over his pen. "Just write these words. Happy. Foggy. Burning. Urgent. Lodge. Meeting."

He took the sheet, then nodded pleasantly. "As you say, it's not your writing. Well, perhaps it wasn't *her* note after all."

He let her go at that and sat for some minutes before the fire, thinking things over, and the more he thought, the less he liked it. Take Tommy Wildernesse, for instance, congratulating himself on having a perfect alibi. If Mirabel Quest was murdered within a minute or two of the lights going out, then he had no alibi at all! The statement that he was in the dining room, dodging Pollock, might be a carefully thought out prevarication. The very note—presumably from Mirabel—he might have written for himself, and the fact that Palmer had seen a note flicked across the room was no guarantee that it was the same one that Wildernesse had produced for their inspection. As for the statement that he himself would be prepared to make to the police—that Tommy Wildernesse was incapable of killing anyone—that would cut precious little ice. Mirabel had infuriated him; she'd cut him; she'd sneered at him, and she'd possibly made a fool of him—and under such circumstances people do strange things.

As for Braishe, his alibi was worth precious little. When the lights went out he was on safe ground, and that gave him a start on Wildernesse. But after that his movements couldn't be verified. Still, in his favour was the apparent absence of motive. Braishe and Mirabel—an incongruous enough couple in all conscience!—had seemed to get on amazingly well together. Then another idea. Braishe was a high stepper, and heaven knew what entanglements he might have got into.

And lastly, with regard to those two harlequins, both had the best of all possible friends in Celia's temperamental obstinacy. Lord knows what she *had* seen! It might have been a harlequin—and it might not; the great thing was she could swear to neither Braishe nor Wildernesse, whatever her prejudice against the latter. But assuming Celia had seen what she claimed—seen it perhaps with senses suddenly acute—then why had that harlequin crossed the landing from staircase to staircase? Why had he halted to make that gesture—and halted in spite of the fact that voices were coming from a few feet away? And if he'd done the murder, why hadn't he bolted altogether while the darkness gave him a chance?

That led him to Fewne. Where had he been during that vital couple of minutes? To go back for those balloons, as he himself had suggested, was a matter of seconds—not minutes. Had he gone mad before he left the house? Was that why Tommy Wildernesse heard him muttering away to himself? And in the vital interval, had he been gibbering away in some corner?

Then he had another idea. Where had Fewne got that notion for a costume? Almost certainly he'd never chosen it for himself. Fewne's taking an interest in anything so mundane as a costume seemed absurd, and if he had been faced with the problem of getting one, he'd have chosen the easiest way out by placing himself in the hands of some firm or other. Perhaps Braishe could give some information.

The drawing room was deserted, and Travers retraced his steps to the dining room, where nobody but Charles was visible. The billiard room, perhaps—and he smiled to himself. Rather like Challis, that! At the top of the short staircase that led down to the basement room he heard the click of the balls. When he opened the door, there were Challis and Crashaw at it. Challis, in the act of striking, looked, for him, extraordinarily confused.

"You don't mind this, old boy?" he asked diffidently.

"Why should I?" smiled Travers. "You can't expect people to sit about all day like mutes. Only, if I were you—"

"I know what you were going to say! Don't let the old lady smell us out—what?"

Travers smiled again. "Well, perhaps it'd be as well."

There was something disarming about the buoyant vulgarity of Challis. Travers rather liked him in a queer sort of way. He was so cocksure, for instance; so utterly human and rather like a sparrow. Clever enough, too, in his own way, in spite of the fact that a saloon bar represented his spiritual home. As for Crashaw, he was looking like one of his own boys—caught red-handed—as he put away his cue. Travers put in a consoling word.

"Well, Crashaw, did you teach him how to play this game?"

Crashaw smiled modestly. Challis completed the answer.

"Tell you what, old boy: if I were this lad I'd give up school-mastering and take a pub!"

"Wouldn't mind a pub myself!" said Travers. "By the way, something I wanted to ask you. Do you happen to know why Fewne wore that balloon-seller costume? Simply a glorified hawker's get-up and a set of balloons, wasn't it?"

"Do I know, old boy? Do I not! You see, I thought it might be a good idea—one idea leading to another, as they say—to try out a little number we're probably putting on in the new show. The idea's this. There's a balloon seller standing at a corner. What corner? Any corner, old boy. Then a girl comes along and speaks, you know, 'Poor old man; have you no home?' and all that. Then enter Harlequin. He dances in the moonlight and sort of fascinates the girl; then they dance together with this melancholy-looking balloon seller in the background. Then the Harlequin gives the girl a wish—poorish sort of girl she is; down at heel, if you follow me, old boy—and she wishes she might be at a real ball—lights and music and so on. Then what happens, old boy, do you think?"

"Lord knows! . . . She dies to soft music!"

"You're pulling my leg, old boy. She doesn't die. She gets her wish. The lights dim out; the balloon seller's set of balloons gets enormous; he backs stage, and before you know where you are the lights are on, the dance is in full swing—crowded stage, everybody talking and laughing like hell; first-class band; everything, old boy, just as she'd wished, and in the middle of it the balloons float out over the room—hundreds of 'em—and the music gets faster; lights kaleidoscopic, and so on, and that leads back to where we started from: lights dim out—moonlight—balloon seller and the girl at the corner again. We're calling it 'Bubbles.' Damn good title, what? Rinnberg's doing the music. . . . What do you think of it, old boy?"

"Sounds rather original, don't you think so, Crashaw?"

"Yes . . . frightfully! Awfully ambitious, of course."

"Not for Challis!" smiled Travers. "He's an ambitious bloke. However, to be serious; your idea was to try this out without any possibility of lighting effects, just to see if you could get any fresh ideas. You were trying it out on the dog, if I may say so."

"That's right, old boy. The snow business rather put the lid on that. I'd thought of trying it out as a sort of grand finale, after the toast of the evening."

"You sent the costumes down?"

"I did, old boy. Got the measurements, and so on. Broody said he'd get Fewne in the mind. Chap with a face like that was too good to be missed. Alfred Lester type, old boy, don't you think so?—speaking well of the dead and all that."

"When did Fewne know about it all?"

"Oh—er—fortnight ago or so. I understood he was rather bucked at the idea—not having to think out one for himself and so on."

"Good!" said Travers. "You're an ingenious devil, you know, Challis. I shall have to come and see that show of yours." He took an arm of each. "Now you two young people had better get fit for dinner. The first gong went ten minutes ago!"

CHAPTER X
THE DEVIL TO PAY

DINNER WAS a quiet affair that night—just the five men to themselves, with an absence of tension but a strict avoidance of anything but the soberest geniality. The horrible novelty of the situation was wearing off and there were longer intervals between the sudden rememberings of what had happened a few hours before. Moreover, there was a further relief in prospect. The snow had definitely ceased, the wind had shifted slightly and Pollock—a reliable weather prophet, according to Paradine—was talking hopefully of rain. People were confidently thinking of town again in twenty-four hours, till Travers told them just how things stood.

"Now Franklin's got through to Great Levington, the police will rush a snow plough here in no time," Wildernesse had remarked.

"Don't you believe it!" Travers told him. "Excuse my being blunt, but because a murder's been done, that's no reason for clearing the road regardless. A murder, however callous the statement may seem to us, means a *dead* person. The authorities have to think about the *living:* clearing the roads for the doctors and so on."

"And when the police do get here," added Paradine, "they won't let a soul leave the house till they're satisfied. Then there'll be the inquests—and the funerals."

"Nothing you've forgotten, old boy?" asked Challis plaintively. That caused the first smile for some minutes.

Travers sat yarning till well after nine, then yawned and made his excuses. In the breakfast room Palmer was waiting, as arranged. Travers indicated a chair.

"Now, let's hear all about it. Keep your voice low. We don't want to be overheard!"

Palmer's voice became a hoarse, unnatural whisper. "Where do you want me to start, sir?"

"Anywhere you like. Say as soon as you got here. And for God's sake, don't bark!"

Palmer thought for a moment. "The first was that unpleasantness before dinner, sir."

"Unpleasantness! You mean between Mrs. Fewne and Miss Quest?"

"That's it, sir. You see, sir, I happened to be coming down the back staircase to your room, sir, when I heard it. Excuse me, sir, but I wrote down this morning what I heard, in case I might forget it." He produced a paper. "I was just turning the corner, sir, when I heard the first words, and it pulled me up short, sir, in a manner of speaking. It was Miss Quest's voice I heard, sir—very shrill it was, sir, and sneering like. She was saying, sir," Palmer consulted the paper, "And that's you, you smug-faced hypocrite!' Then she laughed, sir, very loud and spiteful; then she said, 'Oh, my God! Isn't it priceless!' Then she roared with laughter, sir; then she said something as if she was mad with temper. 'You cheap slut! You and your bloody sermons! Get out of here before I throw you out!' or words to that effect, sir. So, thinking someone was coming out, I went by quickly and entered your room, sir." Palmer drew a deep breath.

"Then what happened?"

"Well, sir, I was interested, in a manner of speaking, so I watched from the door, sir, and in a minute Mrs. Fewne came out and Miss Quest slammed the door behind her, sir. I watched Mrs. Fewne as she went along the corridor, sir . . . and her face—well, it absolutely shocked me, sir!" Travers looked suitably sympathetic. "It was awful, sir . . . like a devil, she looked . . . and I thought she was quite a lady, sir."

Travers grunted. What it all meant, he couldn't at the moment see. He knew, of course, the utter difference in temperament of the sisters, and he'd heard the current rumours of friction whenever they came in contact. But there his sympathies were wholly on Brenda's side. Life with Mirabel, for other than the briefest of moments, must have been an endless grating of nerves and a perpetual subordination of self.

"Just write that down for me, Palmer—word for word, as you've got it written there!" He watched his man as he made his transcript, and put an occasional question.

"That would be about half-past six?"

"That's right, sir."

"Where was the maid—Ransome?"

"In the servants' hall, sir. There's something I have to tell you about that, sir."

Travers ran his eye over the paper, pocketed it, and nodded to the other to resume.

"Later in the evening, sir—just after the house supper, I'm told, sir—Ransome showed everybody a ring, a valuable ring, by all accounts, sir, and she made a remark that I've since thought rather unusual. She said, sir, her mistress gave it her because of some good news, and when Mabel—she's the second house-maid, sir—said she'd like one like it, Ransome made the statement, 'You want to keep your eyes and ears open in this life, if you want to get on.'"

Travers grunted again. So that was where the missing ring had got to! "You say the remark was unusual. Why was that?"

"Well, sir, while I was sitting in charge of the gramophone last night it kept coming into my mind; and so it did again this morning, sir, when I was on duty outside the bedroom. I went over it again, sir, and if you'll pardon the remark, sir, I arrived at certain conclusions."

"Yes. Go on!"

"I thought, sir, that Ransome had been spying on Mrs. Fewne, and she'd seen something and told Miss Quest, and Miss Quest had given her the ring as a sort of present, sir. Mrs. Fewne is a lady—you can see that at first glance, sir—and keeps herself as she ought to be, whereas the other—well, she doesn't, sir, or she didn't."

"What do you mean by that, precisely?"

"Well, everybody in the kitchen was talking about it, sir. They say she and Mr. Challis weren't all they should be, sir, and they say everybody in London knew it."

"Don't go round in circles, Palmer. You won't shock me. Say straight out what you mean."

"Well then, sir, if you'll pardon the statement, sir, they say it's common knowledge that Mr. Challis used to keep her, sir, whatever he does now, and it was him that put her where she is now, or was, sir—I mean on the stage, sir."

"I see. And you've said nothing about this to anybody?"

"Most certainly not, sir!"

"There's no need to be indignant," said Travers curtly. "After all, however advantageous it may be to ultimate justice, the fact remains that you stuck your nose clean into what didn't concern you—an interest which I'm prepared to account for by your close contact with a person so curious as myself. And what happened this morning—with Ransome?"

"The first thing she said to me, sir, in that corridor upstairs, was, 'She did it, and I'm going to make her pay for it!' When I asked her who she meant, sort of persuasively, she closed up, sir. She said, 'Never mind who I mean. You'll know when the time comes!' Then, when you told me to find out what she knew, sir, I made one or two excuses to have a word with her, and I ventured to point out to her, sir, that if she approached you, you'd hear everything in strictest confidence—being a gentleman to be trusted, sir, as I told her."

"What'd she say to that damfool remark?"

"She seemed betwixt and between, sir. I saw her just now, sir, before I came in, and I got the impression that she was trying to put me off, sir. Earlier in the day she seemed the other way, sir."

"I see. And where's she now?"

"Just gone to bed, sir. You see, all the staff were up late last night, sir, and she and Ellen just went up, sir. Everybody's locking their doors—"

"Anybody else in the servants' hall know anything about this quarrel you—er—overheard?"

"I've heard no mention of it, sir. . . . Of course, there was a lot of talk about the changing the rooms, sir."

"Rooms! What rooms?"

"Miss Quest's and Mrs. Fewne's, sir."

"Yes. Go on! What about them?"

"Well, sir, the talk is that Miss Quest didn't like the room she was in originally—too far from the bathroom, she said it was, sir—and all I know is that sometime during the evening she and Mrs. Fewne changed rooms, sir." He nodded with sudden satisfaction. "I know when it was, sir. Ransome came into the servants' hall just as I was coming up to your room, as I told you, sir, and she said it'd just been done. She said—rather cheekily, I thought, sir—that Miss Quest had explained to Mrs. Paradine."

Travers stared into the fire more grimly than ever. "The fact is that Miss Quest and Mrs. Fewne changed rooms just before you heard that quarrel?"

"That's right, sir."

"Then there's the devil to pay! . . . All right, Palmer. You can go now. Bring me a thermos of coffee to the bedroom—and don't say another word to that maid till I tell you. You understand? That's an explicit order!"

Palmer backed nervously out. As for Travers, he was worried out of his wits. If Brenda Fewne had had anything to do with that murder it wouldn't do to give the slightest hint of suspicion before the police got there. It was incredible, of course, on the face of it—one sister killing another . . . but was it? What corner mightn't Brenda Fewne have been driven into? Had she got into the other's debt? Borrowed money on her husband's credit? He had a look at Palmer's evidence. "You smug-faced hypocrite!" That might be anything: merely vulgarity fingering its nose at respectability. "You cheap slut!" That rang different—and yet it might be simply the common vocabulary of an infuriated woman.

He scowled into the fire for a minute or two, then tried another tack. What was the sequence of events, according to Palmer's statements? Surely, to be logical, something like this:

Mirabel desires change of rooms. Brenda refuses.

Ransome tries to curry favour with her mistress by telling her something about B. F. which she can use as a lever.

Ransome is given the ring as a reward.

The rooms *are* changed.

M. Q. sends for B. F. to the new room and taunts her—or threatens her—as Palmer heard.

Then what had happened? At the scratch dinner, Brenda had been very *distraite* and had mentioned a headache. Mirabel had been uproarious. And then, while he'd been dressing—Franklin was in the bathroom—he'd heard words coming from the lower landing. Brenda it was. "Oh, don't, Myra! Please don't!" Then he'd closed his door, since the affair had been none of his. Later there must have been another scene, since Mirabel had refused point blank to come down to the dance; said she wasn't well; that Brenda hadn't learned her steps; that she wasn't going to wear the costume, and so on, till Challis went up and talked her round. Then there'd been various sneers during the evening, with Brenda making no retorts whatever.

But the really vital, the damning thing was, precisely who was aware of the change of rooms? He'd never for a moment believed that burglar-murderer theory. Whatever the provocation, a burglar would never have done a thing like that. If Mirabel had seen him in her room and had looked like screaming, he'd have bolted, or clapped his hand over her mouth, or threatened her. And above all, he'd never have carried a dagger—or have thrust the body beneath the bed. No! the murderer was an inmate of the house—and in the house at that very moment; and the problem should be solved from the two factors of motive and opportunity. Then who knew of the change of rooms? And that very question showed him something he'd not taken into account. The problem was twofold!

i. The murderer was ignorant of the change of rooms and therefore intended to kill Brenda Fewne.

ii. The murderer was aware of the change and therefore intended to kill Mirabel Quest.

Moreover, running right through the dual problem was the added complication of the identical costumes the sisters had worn, the startling similarity in face and build, and the fact that everything almost certainly occurred when the house was in darkness.

No wonder he whistled hopelessly. Brenda Fewne couldn't be questioned till the police got there—the men would never stand for that. In any case, what motive could there possibly have been for killing *her?* Or had the idea been even more hellish than common sanity suggested—a wiping out of both Denis Fewne and his wife at the same time? And if so—why? What, in God's name, was the motive? Travers shook his head. A thing like that was too awful to contemplate—and far too tremendous for him to tackle. The thing to do, till the police—or Franklin—arrived, was to walk warily; to keep a courteous distance and yet give no man offence; and as quietly as possible to go on working on the supposition that the murderer had intended to kill the one who *was* killed, and had therefore known of the change of rooms.

In the drawing room the men were still grouped round the fire.

"Hallo!" said George. "We thought you'd turned in!"

"Gone and quite forgotten, George!" He stoked up his pipe. "One last pipe, and I'm leaving you young people to it. Feeling nervous, Martin?"

Braishe looked startled for a moment, then smiled. "Oh—the pagoda! Good Lord, no! I've slept there heaps of times before to-day."

"By the way, I didn't know that Mirabel and Brenda swapped rooms last night! Did you people know?"

"I did," said Paradine. "I happened to be there when Mirabel told Celia."

"I thought everybody knew," said Braishe. "Celia mentioned it down here. Oh! but you and Franklin had gone up; I remember now."

"What was the idea, exactly?"

"Well—er—it's rather difficult to say. We don't want to rake up things—seems a pretty rotten thing to do, but—er—Mirabel was just a bit difficult at times. As a matter of fact, I think she rather resented Celia telling her one particular room was to be hers. She probably expected the choice of the house. Still, what's it matter . . . now?"

"It'll matter as far as the police are concerned," said Travers quietly. "They won't see things as we do. They may even assume that it wasn't Mirabel whom the murderer intended to kill. That'll mean they'll hunt for a different kind of motive."

"You're getting the wind up, old boy!" remarked Challis nervously.

"I think he's being unnecessarily alarmed," added Paradine.

"Perhaps I am rather rushing ahead." That remark was much more true than it sounded. "Still, there's one thing I would like to know—and it's going to be the rottenest thing that's been said during this business. What about Fewne? Did he know the rooms were changed? If I remember rightly, he didn't come in to dinner till late, and he left early; and he didn't come over in his costume till after everybody else."

"Oh! I expect Brenda told him!"

"Yes, but did anybody hear anything said? Sorry to be so pertinacious!"

"Why not ask her direct?" suggested Paradine. "All the same, I don't quite see the point. It's unthinkable that Fewne should have killed anybody. He was the most shy and retiring person I've ever known."

"Yes . . . but he *did* go mad, George. You'll admit that." He knocked out his pipe on the grate. "Still, as Martin said, what's it matter . . . now?" He looked round at Crashaw. "Rather rough on you, all this?"

Crashaw smiled gallantly. "Oh! I don't know. It's awfully good of everybody to put up with me. I only wish I could do something."

"Plenty of time for that! Well, I think I'll push off upstairs. Hope you all have a good night!"

"Same to you, old boy. Personally, I shall bolt the door and sleep with one eye open."

"Shrewd fellow! Well, cheerio, everybody! You coming, George?"

Outside the door Braishe joined them, and they stood for a moment at the foot of the stairs.

"I haven't been able to find anything out about . . . the one you suggested." He lowered his voice. "One thing might interest you: he slept last night in the butler's parlour, owing to a shortage of servants' rooms. That might account for his hearing the noise and telling nobody about it."

Travers nodded. "It does . . . in a way; except that we saw him coming *downstairs!*"

"What I'm more worried about is that siphon," went on Braishe. "Somebody's running round with enough gas to wipe out the house."

"I wouldn't worry," Travers told him. "I'll bet you a fiver that siphon's never seen again. And that reminds me: I forgot to tell you that I've locked up some things in the safe and reset the combination. And I spoke to Pollock about William sleeping in the dining room tonight. Hope you don't mind?"

Paradine was distinctly amused when Travers, having arranged the reading lamp and the thermos, began wading through an issue of *The Times*.

"Hallo! Thought you were going to read that manuscript!"

"So I am—later on. This is a preliminary idea. There must have been something he saw in *The Times* that made him feel as if he had to write that letter he began—that horrible scrawl on the sheet of paper."

The other settled into the bedclothes. "I don't know. Why *do* people write to the papers? He probably saw something he violently disagreed with, but outside the paper entirely. He was just writing to air his views."

"Maybe!" said Travers cheerfully. "Still, there's no harm in trying to see if it *was* in *The Times* itself he saw it."

A few minutes later George's voice came drowsily from the other end of the room.

"Something you ought to know. Martin thinks Denis did himself in with that gas. We were talking it over when you came in."

Travers grunted. "Was that why he was worried about the whereabouts of the siphon?"

"Probably."

"Hm! And if he did do himself in with the gas, where's the siphon now? You and I didn't see it!"

"I know. That's just what I told him!"

Travers muttered something under his breath, then settled to his search through those copies of *The Times*. But not steadily. More than once he broke off as certain incidents showed themselves in a new light or when he thought he was finding a road through the maze. Most of all, his mind would keep going back to what Paradine had reported after his good-night visit to the other bedroom. Brenda Fewne had *not* told her husband of the change of rooms. When she had halted on the stairs with Challis, it was because she was looking for her husband to let him know. Later on, just after the lights went out, she remembered she'd left her small bag in the downstairs room and had gone down to get it. At the foot of the stairs, on her way back, she had actually seen Denis and he'd seen her, but before she could speak, he'd uttered a curious sort of exclamation and had disappeared in the darkness, towards the outside door.

That, as Travers knew, must have been the immediate prelude to that mad rush through the snow. But why had Fewne not spoken to his wife? Possibly he hadn't really recognized her by the light of a candle that couldn't have been any too near. Or was he already mad at that moment?

CHAPTER XI
TRAVERS FEELS HIS WAY

PALMER HAD JUST left the room after drawing the curtains and depositing the early morning tea when there was a tap at the door, and Braishe looked in.

"Hallo! I see you're up! Had a good night?"

"Oh, rather! At least, I heard George having one! And you?"

"Pretty good, thanks . . . only something's happened!"

Travers rather guessed that, seeing that Braishe was shaved and dressed half an hour before the official breakfast time.

"Yes. I've found that siphon ... in the pagoda! Can't make out how you people missed it when you were looking."

The other two looked at each other. "We didn't look for it," said Travers. "Why should we? All the same, I ought to have seen it if it was there."

"Where was it exactly?" asked Paradine.

"You'd never guess. Remember how that fireplace is built? Sides made of ornamental brickwork—every other brick projecting slightly? Well, it was wedged between two projecting bricks, on the *inside* of the fireplace!"

"Good Lord! How the devil did it get there?"

Braishe was over at the window, looking gloomily at the snow, which in spite of Pollock's prediction was falling steadily again.

"There's only one way it could have got there. He must have put it there!"

"Just a minute, Martin," said Paradine rather bewilderedly. "Do I take it that you're definitely assuming that Denis committed suicide by means of that gas?"

"What else *can* I mean?"

"Yes, but if the gas was as lethal as all that, how could he place the siphon between the bricks and die on the bed?"

"It sounds silly; I know that. As soon as you're dressed, come over and see for yourselves—then you'll understand." He was looking terribly upset, and Travers wouldn't have been surprised if he'd broken down badly. "Do you know, I had it on my mind. I was thinking about it all night. It's been a nightmare to me ever since I saw his face . . . and knew what had killed him. I had a hunt last night and couldn't find anything, so I had another go this morning . . . and found it."

"Sit down, old chap. Have some tea!" Travers moved the wicker chair to the table. "We'll get a move on. George, you seize one bathroom and I'll collar the other!"

Braishe was still there when they got back. The cigarette he was smoking seemed to have steadied his nerves, but Travers kept chattering away while getting into his clothes.

"Why exactly did he persist in that pagoda idea, Martin?"

"Well, you know what he was like. He was the same when he was a boy; wasn't he, George? Never happy unless he got off somewhere by himself. You see, he couldn't bear being disturbed when he was working. When I was here—and that wasn't very often lately—he just used to come over after dinner, and we'd talk till I turned in. After that he'd often work till well into the morning."

"And how'd he come to know about the gas?"

"How'd he know! Good God! Weren't the papers full of it?"

"Yes—but to know the siphon was in the safe; to know its properties; to know the combination, and so on."

"Oh, that! Naturally, we talked about it. I regard Denis as my own brother. I'd trust him with anything. I showed him the siphon; told him everything—except the formula. He wouldn't have understood that if I'd told him."

"Quite! You see, I'm not asking questions for the sake of it. We're just having a dress rehearsal before the Scotland Yard person gets here. . . . Any row likely, do you think, because it's gone?"

Braishe grunted scornfully. "I don't give a damn if there is! I'd as much right to have that gas in my house—lethal or not—as you have to keep a pet cobra—provided it's under proper control. The gas was in a foolproof siphon, in a safe with a combination known only to two people."

The three of them scurried along by the hedge path. Travers deposited his parcel of manuscript on the desk and ran his eyes round the room. Braishe made straight for the fireplace.

"I'll strike a match, then you'll see it. Here we are! Wedged in between two bricks, with the plunger down."

"Gas all gone?"

"Gone twenty seconds after the plunger was depressed!" said Braishe bluntly.

Paradine said nothing. He merely shook his head and looked worried. Travers stepped back, ran his eyes round the room again, then frowned.

"It seems all so damn silly to me!"

"That's just it!" agreed Paradine. "It's unnecessary—except that mad people do mad things."

"There you have it!" Braishe cut in quickly. "Let me explain, and I think you'll see it. He was heading for a breakdown. Perhaps the book wasn't going any too well—or he imagined it wasn't. Am I right in saying that people who have lost control like that are apt to be . . . cunning?"

"Possible, of course," said Paradine.

"Well, during the evening—personally, I should say between the time we got up to go and the time he spoke to William—he took the gas and the phone—"

"Excuse me," interrupted Travers. "I don't yet get the hang of that phone business. Why should *he* take the phone? If it'd been the burglar who took it, I could have understood the motive."

"Well, as I see it, it was like this: He took the gas so as to have it by him. Probably he had fits of depression that terrified him, and rather than face another one, he'd decided to kill himself. When he took the phone away he had some crazy sort of idea that if the loss of the gas was discovered, the police couldn't be warned. ... Still, what's it matter? He did take it: we know that. Didn't you find it out there in the snow? Then, when he got inside here, he had a brainstorm and cut and threw all those balloons about. Then he did himself in. The little siphon's just two and three quarter inches by three quarters, with the plunger at safety, so he merely held his breath, pushed down the plunger, and wedged the whole thing between the two bricks. Then— *and this is the point*—he threw himself on the bed, face down, legs up, and his hands to his ears—perfectly natural attitude, under the circumstances—and waited for death. It probably caught him in a second or two. . . . Oh! and just one other thing in confirmation: Pollock says every window was shut—the first time that's happened since he slept here."

He looked at them inquiringly. Travers got his comments in first; it might have been said that he stampeded the meeting.

"That's all right. I don't think the authorities'll have anything to say to that. What do you think, George?"

"Of course, it's—er—"

"Of course it is! It's unusual, that's what you were going to say! But it's an unusual case!" He waved his hand airily round the room. "Everything's unusual. It's bound to be!" He went straight ahead without a pause. "About that siphon. Could you get it out without touching anything except the plunger?"

The merest depression of the plunger released it. Travers was amazed when he saw it at close quarters.

"Good Lord! It's like a tiny scent bottle!"

"It is rather. Just a cylinder with a siphon top. This plunger has to have two complete turns before it can be depressed: that constitutes the safety device. The apparent thickness of the glass is due to its really being a vacuum flask. I should also add that the plunger was sealed with wax."

"What happens when the plunger is depressed?"

"The gas emerges as a fine mist; in other words, it vaporizes, then diffuses and percolates. It's colourless, odourless, and heavier than air."

"The very thing I wanted to ask!" said Travers. "I'm probably speaking with all the ignorance of the layman, but if the gas was heavier than air, why didn't it sink to the floor and stay there? I mean, how did it get as high as his mouth?"

Braishe smiled faintly. "Density has nothing to do with it. It doesn't matter how heavy it is! It'll diffuse in any case, only, the heavier the gas, the slower the diffusion. The molecular motion within the gas itself would cause diffusion to every part of an enclosed space, however small the amount of gas and wherever released."

"That's good enough for me!" said Travers. "I'll put it back myself, if you'll indicate exactly where. His prints are sure to be on it."

"What's to be done now?" Braishe asked as he wiped his fingers on his handkerchief.

"Well, George and I'll have to put everything as it was yesterday morning; then we'll lock the place up till the police come."

Braishe showed no particular inclination to move. Even when Travers backed to the door and Paradine prepared to replace the balloons, he still hugged the mat.

"Sorry we must kick you out," smiled Travers. "George and I will have to back out ourselves as the balloons go down."

"Sorry! The fact is I was rather interested." He moved out to the narrow veranda. "See you at breakfast, then!"

"We'll be over in a couple of shakes!" Travers told him.

As soon as he'd really gone, he turned to Paradine. "Really interesting solution, that of Martin; don't you think so? It's yet another explanation of where Denis got to before the light went out!" He waited to see if there was any response to that piece of irony, but none came. "And something else: it explains that awkward way he moved through the snow. He had the telephone gadgets on him—probably under his coat! . . . What about the balloons? Got 'em all right?"

As he went forward the pencil he was carrying suddenly dropped. He peered round, then got to his knees, and it was only after he'd struck a match that he found it.

"Worst of being bat eyed, George! Balloons finished?"

Paradine had a look at his handiwork. "Think so—except these two or three by the door."

"Can't think how you remember 'em!"

"Oh, I don't know. Colours, I think. Association of ideas."

"Where'd you put that punctured one?"

"Just by the bed. That's where Martin was standing when he picked it up. This one goes by the fireplace; this here; this by the door . . . and that's the lot."

Travers began to lock away the manuscript. "Oh, by the way; how did Martin get into this gas business?"

"Well, he did bio-chemistry at Oxford and took up research work there. Then Harry—his father—had large interests in Uganda cotton and got him to join the research board of the Cotton Growers' Association, and he took over their main lab., as you know."

"Hunting the boll weevil?"

"I suppose so . . . partly. There's a fortune for the chap who can deal with that. What Martin and his people were doing was experimenting with gases known to be lethal, such as the organic isothiocyanates; then he stumbled on this Braigene. Between ourselves, I'm hoping rather well of it."

Travers nodded. Then he came to a sudden decision. Was George after all so dense as he was making himself out to be? Why not try him out by letting him see—very roughly—the lie of the land? And better still, why not give him the chance of committing himself to some definite opinion?

"By the way, George, you remember when I picked that telephone out of the snow? Martin says Fewne threw it there. But it wasn't snowing when Fewne came to the pagoda—and yet, when I picked it up, it had far more snow on it than had fallen that morning!"

"You mean, it had been thrown there before?"

"Well—er—it must have been!"

Paradine frowned. "Let me see. The telephone was going right up to the time when the party broke up. Why shouldn't Denis have taken it between then and when he turned in? We'd never have noticed him, you know!"

Travers might have retorted that that was just what they *would* have done. There was someone at that porch till the last guest had gone. Fewne, out there in the snow, must have been seen. However, he nodded in agreement.

"You're probably right!" He had a last look round. "That seems to be all. Everything's the same as we left it yesterday, except—this'll show the police how thoroughly we work!—a couple of dead matches that were under the bed last night aren't there now!"

The other said nothing; he merely laughed. Travers joined in. "Not bad eyesight that, for an old 'un, George—what?"

A few other things of unequal importance happened before breakfast. William reported a quiet night, and Challis couldn't remember the exact number of balloons that went with that costume of Fewne's. And, as he pointed out, it wouldn't be any use to inquire, since two of the balloons had to his own knowledge been destroyed during the night. Tommy Wildernesse had stuck a pin in one for devilry, and Mirabel had exploded the other with her hands. Possibly others had gone West too.

"What were they filled with?" Travers asked him. "I mean, what made them float in the air?"

"Haven't you been to Margate, old boy? Special gas, supplied by the balloon people. Perfectly harmless stuff. I brought it down with me. Pollock's got the empty gadget somewhere."

"Who filled 'em?"

"I supervised—and Charles tied 'em up."

The last thing was perfectly ridiculous. As Travers came from the dining-room safe, where he'd checked its contents, he paused before the Chippendale mirror. Then he smiled to himself as he turned back the corner of his eyelid. As he moved away he smiled again. Had he really bamboozled George Paradine, or had the green in his own eye been rather too visible?

For his announcement, Travers chose a moment at the end of the meal, when everybody happened to be present. He produced a pile of envelopes and a couple of foolscap sheets.

"I'd rather like everybody to do a small job of work this morning. It's awfully interesting and won't take more than a few minutes."

Challis eyed the envelopes critically. "What's the idea, old boy? Soup tickets?"

Travers simulated a laugh. "Not yet—thank God! No, it's something really brainy—sort of thing you'll revel in, Challis. The idea's this: I've read that manuscript of poor Denis's, and apparently he proposed to add somewhere about three more chapters. I'm not suggesting for a moment that I've the faintest chance of being appointed his literary executor—I mean, I don't want anything out of the idea. What I'm suggesting is that we state our ideas as to how he proposed to finish it. As he left it, there's a most intriguing situation. You probably won't agree with me when I say it'll be something to pass away a few minutes over. Not only that—the book will certainly be finished by somebody or other, and it'll be interesting to see whose ideas coincide most with those of the particular author who ultimately undertakes to finish it for publication." He looked round persuasively. "Now, what do you say?"

"Sounds interesting," said Braishe.

"What sort of a book is it?" asked Wildernesse. "Adventure, detective, or what?"

Paradine chuckled. "You're giving yourself away pretty badly, young man! What is it, exactly, Ludo? Got the plot?"

"I have. And I've made two copies. I wonder if you'd take one for Celia and Brenda? The other I'll leave here."

He gave his glasses a polish, blinked round, and began.

"This is the plot, as I've written it down. I need hardly say it gives no idea of the really enthralling way the characters are developed, or of the delicacy of the actual writing. This is just a bare outline. Proposed title is *Distressful Virtue*. All ready? Here goes, then!"

"DISTRESSFUL VIRTUE

"Isabel Lake, the eldest of three sisters, is a girl with strongly developed maternal instincts. The story opens with her interest in a man who somehow slips away again out of her life—not the first experience of the sort that has happened to her. And that is a pity. She is a charming girl, a delightful companion, and one with enormous potentialities for making a man happy. Then her two sisters, whom one might call modern, slap-dash women of the world, both marry; almost, it seems, in spite of themselves and rather as a matter of course. Thereupon Isabel deliberately throws herself at the head of Robert Carey, a rising young artist possessed of private means. She marries him. He apparently adores her, and they seem to be amazingly happy.

"We arrive at the second part of the book, for which the first was merely preparation. Two years later, Isabel begins to go through a period of self-recrimination and doubt.

"I should say that this outline here becomes scandalously inadequate!

"She tells herself she won her husband by a trick. Ought she to expiate that act? Does her husband really love her? She feels, in fact, that if only she could lose her husband and then win him again by legitimate means, her conscience would cease to reproach, and her life would be anchored to a definite point.

"Now, a year previously, her own cousin, a most attractive girl in the twenties, just back from completing a musical education in Paris, joins the household. Isabel deliberately throws the two together. Finally, to hasten the experiment, when the three of them are at Carey's cottage in Cornwall, she fabricates an excuse to be called away urgently, leaving the two of them alone.

"The last chapter deals with her feelings in London. She is still assailed by doubts. How is she to know if they have really profited, as it were, by her absence? Must she return and judge by their reactions to each other—by their looks and faces? But she knows she can't go down there again, with all the old doubts and wonderings. It would drive her mad. She must *know*. Life with further indecision wouldn't be worth living.

"Now we come to the very last words of the last chapter:

"Her eyes fell listlessly upon the copy of *The Times* which had fallen from her lap and lay by her feet on the floor. With an action almost mechanical, she picked it up and, her mind still remote from the set formality of print, let her eyes run idly over the pages. It was then that the idea came.'"

He took off his glasses again and peered round apologetically. "That's the thing I want you to do. *What* was the idea? *What* did she decide to do?"

"Hm! It's a bit stiff!" was Paradine's comment.

"Most unusual," said Braishe.

"Imagine it's a play without its fifth act," suggested Travers. "Try and put yourself in her place. There are the envelopes, by the way, with your names on 'em. Just jot down an answer briefly. Sentence or so'll do." He handed them out, with three for Paradine. "I'll collect 'em in about an hour, if I may."

As he left the room with Paradine, the others were already gathered round that synopsis for a second reading.

"Something I was going to suggest you'd do, George. Will you see Martin when you come down and find out what's been done about tracing that doped drink? If it *was* doped, it must have been for a special purpose—the burglary ... or worse. Trace it from where it was mixed to when it was handed out."

He watched him as far as the landing, then turned to find Palmer at his elbow.

"Ransome just spoke to me, sir." He coughed. "The remark was, sir, 'You needn't hang round me. I've got nothing to tell you!'"

"And of course you weren't hanging round!"

"Certainly not, sir."

"I see. Nothing to tell you! Find her at once, will you? Tell her I want to see her in the breakfast room—immediately!"

CHAPTER XII
RANSOME TAKES NO FURTHER INTEREST

RANSOME SAT bolt upright on the edge of the easy chair on one side of the fireplace, watchful as a cat and at the same time trying to convey an impression of deferential ignorance. The high collar of the blouse she was wearing, and the small black bow—a tribute, no doubt, to the departed—gave her an air of primness that was almost straitlaced. Travers reclined in his favourite attitude, legs crossed and finger tips together, his voice perfectly dispassionate and his words so economical as to be unpleasantly direct.

"Your words to Palmer were, 'She did it.' Will you explain them?"

Her gesture implied that nothing could be easier. "You see sir, after the misunderstanding that night, I thought—I mean I spoke without thinking. I was all upset. I didn't know what I was saying, sir."

"But you definitely thought at the moment that Mrs. Fewne had murdered her sister!"

"Oh, no, sir! . . . It was an unkind thing to say, sir, and I didn't ought to have said it."

"I see. And have you ever heard your mistress threatened by Mrs. Fewne?"

"Oh, no, sir!" The question appeared absurd. She even smiled faintly.

Travers nodded, then tried a bluff. "Well, we'll be a little more definite, but, first of all, may I give you a word of advice? Everything you tell me now will have to be repeated to the police. If your evidence has altered by the time they get here—and that may be at any moment—then I shall recommend that you be held in custody. You understand that?"

Her very tentative, "Yes . . . sir," showed that this was worrying her somewhat.

"Very good! For my own part, I shall respect any confidences you care to make. . . . That ring that was given you by your mistress." He saw her hand go to the pocket of her skirt. "You have it with you, I think. May I see it?"

He held it to the light and examined it carefully. "Quite a good ring! You're a fortunate person! You could get twenty pounds for it anywhere." He handed it back. "Why, exactly, was it given you?"

The answer was pat. "She was always giving things away, sir. She'd get a fit of it sometimes when she was in a good mind."

"I see. And will you explain some words used by you to the effect that people who want to get on in this world must use their eyes and ears?"

This time the answer was so very pat that the words came in a flood. "It was really like this, sir. Miss Quest was worried when we came down about some bills that had come in, and she was talking to me about them before dinner and saying there was nothing coming in till the show started, and then I remembered something, sir. I said, 'If you remember,' I said, 'Mrs. Fewne owes you some money—that forty pounds you told me about—so why not get it off her? They say that book Mrs. Fewne's written has brought in a lot of money,' was what I told her . . . and she was ever so pleased, sir, and gave me the ring!"

"She didn't think of selling her jewellery or pawning it to raise money?"

"She couldn't do that, sir! If she went anywhere it'd have been noticed."

"Hm! Mrs. Fewne give her the money?"

"I believe she did, sir."

"What was the quarrel about, then?"

"I don't know, sir. I wasn't there. I expect it was about the money. Mr. Fewne wasn't supposed to know anything about it."

"One other thing. Miss Quest told you you needn't wait up that night. Surely a most unusual thing!"

"Well, I'd had a headache, sir, so when I saw she was in a good mind I asked her if she needed me to stay up."

He thought that statement over. As far as he remembered, the message Mirabel Quest had given Pollock had been entirely for Brenda's benefit and more in the nature of a sneer. The thought prompted the question.

"Mrs. Fewne knew that she had you to thank for reminding her sister about that money?"

"She might have done, sir."

"Hm!" He sat up in the chair. "You and your mistress used to have rather violent scenes at times?"

"Well . . . I always did my best, sir—"

"No doubt you did! . . . Ellen, I understand, is a heavy sleeper."

She moistened her lips. For the first time she looked really scared.

"You see, you've been none too sure of your statements! You say you *think* this, you *believe* that, and so on. That won't do for the police. They might even think you asked your mistress to excuse you so that you might be waiting in the room . . . with that dagger!"

She shook her head vehemently. "Oh, no! I didn't do it, sir! I couldn't have done it!"

"I'm glad to hear you say so! . . . Now, something very personal. Mr. Challis and your mistress: did they quarrel—much?"

"I don't know, sir. . . . It wasn't my business, sir."

"Exactly! But you knew there *were* quarrels?"

She hesitated, then, "Everybody quarrels sometimes, sir."

"Hm!" He got to his feet. "Well, that's all—for the moment, Ransome, thank you. I have a lot of work to do here now. Not a word to a soul, mind you, about what we've—er—discussed!"

He led the way to the door and opened it for her with a grave courtesy. But as soon as the door to the servants' hall closed behind her, he sprinted up the stairs. The door of his own room he left open, and stood watching round the angle of the corridor. If what he had seen on Ransome's face was any indication of what she was thinking, and if his deductions were correct, then she'd soon be coming upstairs. That story of hers was a deliberately arranged explanation. Logically, it was as full of holes as a sieve. To give a ring of that value for the reminder of a debt! And Mirabel forgetting such a debt! The thing was, of course, the precise value of Denis Fewne in the affair. Would he really have been furious at discovering that his wife had borrowed money from—of all people—Mirabel? Travers thought not. A man as uxorious as he was seen to be could easily be got round by his wife. And since he was dead, what did it matter? Then he nodded. That explained the ingenuity of the tale! Denis Fewne *was* dead.

A moment or two later those arguments came to an end with startling suddenness. Challis was coming up the stairs—glancing nervously from side to side! On the first landing he looked towards the left, beckoned, then came straight on. Then Ransome appeared round the angle of the short corridor. Travers nipped back into his room like a stoat, closed the door, and put his ear against it. Almost at once, Challis's door was opened—it shut again—a key turned. When Travers peeped cautiously out, stairs and landing were deserted.

He closed his door again with infinite care, then tiptoed with preposterous precaution over to the chair by the window. As he put the cold pipe into his mouth, he shook his head and frowned. Everything was different from his calculations. It was Brenda Fewne the maid should have seen by rights! What she was doing in a locked room with Challis was altogether beyond him—unless that ridiculous bluff he'd tried had turned out to be no bluff but a direct accusation! Challis and Ransome must have some sort of understanding. Had she really done the murder—by arrangement? After all, Challis had more influence over Mirabel than anyone else. Had *he* manipulated the strings for the change over to that remarkably convenient room? Had the whole thing been worked out before they left London? That woman must be deeply in his confidence; thrown in as she was with the flat and the rest of the *quid pro quo*.

Then another idea. Could Challis have done the killing himself? Surely not. As soon as the lights went out he was in that corridor outside. But, had the murder really been done just after the lights failed? If not, why was the cord cut at all, seeing it might be repaired in a second or two once the nature of the failure was discovered? Or had Ransome worked the light while Challis did the killing? If so, that housemaid, Ellen, must have been the heavy sleeper he'd pretended she was. But then again, if Celia had really seen a harlequin? . . .

Two minutes more of that and he made up his mind. George Paradine would have to be confided in. And it'd have to be a desperately tactful job. Any approach to Brenda, and Celia's ears would prick up—and George would spill the beans. Still, there seemed nothing else for it, and, as it happened, George was in the breakfast room.

"Been looking for you, Ludo. Do you know, I can't make head nor tail out of that drink business!" He waved his sheet of notes. "Here's the recipe for that special punch. Pollock made it himself—put it in the bowl, saw to glasses and ladle; did everything, in fact. We saw Charles bring it in and Martin hand it out!"

"You imply that Charles did the tampering!"

"Well, it looks like it. Pollock guarantees the—er—ingredients."

Travers thought back for a moment to the actual scene. Charles had deposited the tray on the side table, and Braishe had gone over to him. And the lights were still out, as Mirabel had suggested! Then Charles had gone, and Braishe had handed out the drinks himself. He'd asked everybody separately. "Just a spot for you, Aunt Celia?" and taken it over. "What about you, Mirabel?" then poured out hers, and so on round the circle. Travers looked up to catch Paradine's eye.

"As you say, George—Charles seems to be the right spot. As soon as the phone's working, Martin ought to look him up."

He fussed round for a moment or two, then got it off his mind. "There's something I'm tremendously worried about, George. It's ticklish—rather. Perhaps you'd better hear it as *I* did."

The account he gave stopped short of the visit of Ransome to Challis's bedroom. Paradine attempted no interruptions, but his face was an open book. Travers could read his utter rejection of the idea that Brenda Fewne could even have come near contemplating murder. He could read, too, the desperate attempts that were being made to find some adequate explanation, and he saw the appreciation of the inconsistencies in Ransome's story. But the mention of the money interested him most.

"Do you know, that was very curious!" he said. "Part of her story is correct. Keep this to yourself, but yesterday morning, just before lunch, Celia asked me to let her have ten pounds—in cash. She said a check wouldn't do. Between ourselves, I hardly like to ask her direct, but do you think she wanted it for Brenda?"

"Possible, of course. But why yesterday morning? Mirabel hadn't any use for money then?"

That stumped Paradine completely. Travers watched him shrewdly, then came to a decision.

"We'll let that settle for a bit, George, and think it over. What about that competition I asked you to do? Got it on you?"

Paradine confessed he'd forgotten all about it.

"Well, have a shot at it, there's a good chap! Time's up long ago. The synopsis? Isn't it in the dining room?"

When Paradine came back, in a matter of five minutes, he seemed rather more enthusiastic. For one thing he had six envelopes with him.

"Splendid!" Travers looked really pleased. "Watch me seal them up, George!" and he ran his tongue across the flap of the first envelope.

"But aren't you going through them now!"

"Good Lord, no! We've got to have a meeting about it—and I rather thought of offering a couple of prizes."

Paradine went over to the writing desk and set to work. Travers finished the sealing up, then glanced at the clock. Almost eleven. For five minutes, as he sprawled in front of the fire, the room was quiet except for the scratching of George's pen. Then his voice was heard excitedly.

"I say—the end of this problem where the woman looks at *The Times* and has an idea! Don't you think that's a strange coincidence? I mean that scrawl of Denis's—on the desk?"

Travers nodded at the fire. "That's it, George! That's why I started the competition!"

Paradine turned round in his seat. "This very competition you've given us to do is the one that was worrying him. *He* didn't know how to finish the story! That's what drove him into a breakdown! That's what was on his mind and made him write all that rubbish just before he died!"

Travers had a look at him. "That sounds all right, George, only . . . there's a flaw in it. Unless he had in his mind what he intended Isabel Lake to do, he'd never have mentioned it!"

The other wasn't to be beaten. "I can explain that. As a matter of fact, I'm glad you mentioned it! He did know—when he wrote it down. *But*, the first symptoms of breakdown—and I should say, the results persist after partial recovery—are loss of memory. The subject can't remember names, for instance. He wrote down those last words, knowing—as you say—what he intended this Isabel Lake to do. Then he forgot the idea. It worried him. The whole book depended on it. The more he tried to remember it, the more it eluded him. That's what drove him mad!"

"Splendid!" He gave a nod of satisfaction. "You're a damn sight cleverer than I gave you credit for, George, and that's saying something!" He took the envelope, sealed it up, and put the collection into his breast pocket. Then he fumbled at his glasses.

"I want to put something to you, and I'm not going to act unless you're with me. I'm suggesting this to you. Brenda didn't know till after lunch yesterday that her husband was dead. Mayn't this woman Ransome have had the idea that Denis would have been furious if he'd known Brenda had borrowed money from Mirabel, and isn't it probable therefore that she put the screw on Brenda and collected the money for herself—possibly with the added threat to tell the police some tale or other as well?"

"Blackmail!"

"If you like. The proposal's this: Is Brenda to be asked point-blank before the police get here, so as to clear the matter up finally? We don't want them raking up non-essentials like that for everybody to hear at the inquest. Are we to see her and ask for her account? Or shall we search that woman's box? Or shall we confront her here and get the truth out of her?"

"Not that, I think! She might make trouble."

"What do you suggest, then?"

"Hm!" Paradine was worried. He started to speak a couple of times before he made a definite suggestion. "I don't like disturbing Brenda. I'd rather do the other. But—er—what powers have we got?"

Travers's announcement that he'd accept full responsibility, and his request that Paradine should bring along all the keys he'd got, were enough to give a start to an affair in which one member was a decidedly nervous helper. Mrs. Cairns, too, was rather in a flutter when halted just past the door of the room where those bodies were lying. But she was quite prepared to be a witness: Ransome seemed to be no favourite of hers. At the top of the narrow staircase Travers stopped.

"Let me have those keys, George. You stay here, and if Ransome comes, go and meet her and say we want her in the breakfast room. Then take her there."

It was a typical servants' bedroom with its white enamelled furniture. By the side of one of the low iron bedsteads was a fibre cabin trunk, locked and strapped.

He motioned the housekeeper over, then set to work. One of his own keys fitted, sufficiently if uncomfortably. The trunk was practically full of miscellaneous garments, but on the top lay a leather handbag. But there was no money in it. Then he felt carefully among the layers of clothes. At the very bottom was a small package wrapped in brown paper and tied round with an old silk stocking. He gave the housekeeper a look as he checked the contents. The bundle of notes, as he flicked them off, numbered twenty-four and amounted to twenty pounds!

In another couple of minutes they were out on the landing again, the trunk apparently undisturbed. Paradine, too, had neither seen nor heard a soul. Travers suggested a minute's conference in his room, and as soon as they got inside Mrs. Cairns had to let off steam.

"What'd she want that money for, sir? There's nothing to spend it on here. And they were going straight back to town! That was that other poor thing's money, sir, that's what that was!"

"You may be right," said Travers. "However, not a word! Don't let her see you suspect anything, or you may do a terrible lot of harm, besides getting the three of us into trouble."

"That's all right, sir. I know my way about!"

"I'm sure you do," smiled Travers. He turned to George. "What now? Have her in and hear what she's got to say?"

"But we can't tell her her trunk's been searched!"

"I know we can't. But we can make her talk. The more lies she tells, the better. Would you mind sending her to the breakfast room at once, Mrs. Cairns?"

Downstairs they had a five-minute conference as to the best method of approach. After that was settled came five minutes' fidgeting. Finally Mrs. Cairns came in.

"I'm sorry sir, but we can't find Ransome anywhere. We've looked everywhere, sir."

"What about Mrs. Paradine's room?" asked George.

"She's not there, sir. They haven't seen her since just after breakfast."

"Have another look, Mrs. Cairns, will you?" said Travers. "I suppose she couldn't be in one of our rooms, talking to a housemaid?"

"The bedrooms were finished long ago, sir."

"Well, have a good look!" When she'd gone he turned to Paradine. "Do you realize, George, that we've actually got on to something at last? Wait till we suggest to Ransome that she shows us her trunk!" He shook his head complacently. "There'll be some funny happenings before lunch, you mark my word!"

The other nodded—but with much less enthusiasm.

"Wait till the police get here!" went on Travers. "They'll turn that scheming little brain of hers inside out—and show it to her!"

He got to his feet and began a restless promenade of the room. A couple of minutes of that and he clicked his tongue.

"Curious she can't be found just when she's most wanted! . . . I think I'll have a look upstairs."

Paradine got up too. "I'll go with you. She might be in Celia's room by now."

Travers left him at the top of the stairs, then set to work to look into the rooms for himself. As he returned to the first landing Paradine joined him.

"I didn't suggest anything to them, but she wasn't there!"

Travers shook his head. "I don't like it, George. Hallo! Somebody coming!"

The somebody was Mrs. Cairns. Travers produced a smile.

"Any luck?"

"No, sir. We can't find her anywhere!"

"Well, never mind. She'll roll up sooner or later. Just send her along when she does turn up."

He stood there for a good minute, like a man trying to make up his mind. He clicked his tongue, then he frowned. Then as he looked round, his eye caught something—the sill of the window above the servants' stairs.

"Look at that window, George! Who's been spilling water on it?"

The other peered at it, then began to mount the stairs. Travers followed him.

"The window's been opened! That's not spilt water—it's melted snow!"

All at once he felt an overwhelming fear. His heart began to race, and he bit his lip nervously. Paradine watched him as he stood there indecisively. Then he leaned across and opened the window. The snow blew in as he leaned out and peered below. Down there was the blurred outline of a body, already covered by a white film!

Paradine clutched his arm.

"What is it? Aren't you feeling well?"

"I'm all right. Better get downstairs, George. I rather think that's her body in the snow."

The other started to stammer something, but Travers had already moved off. Inside the breakfast room he locked the door, then squinted through the far window.

"That's a body all right, George. We'll open the window and get her in this way."

It *was* Ransome's body. As they placed it on the floor beneath the window Travers saw the bruises on the throat, the distended lips, and the staring eyes. Paradine's examination took several minutes, and his voice was oddly nervous as he spoke from time to time.

"Strangled . . . from behind, by the look of it. . . . Larynx probably dislocated. . . . Must have been unconscious a second or two after the hands gripped her. . . . Dead under an hour."

Travers waited till he'd finished.

"She'll have to be smuggled up there, George . . . with the others. We'll wrap her up in this rug. You watch at the foot of the stairs and say when the coast's clear."

They were lucky. In a couple of minutes Ransome s body was placed on the rug before the window of the temporary morgue.

"We'll leave her here till the police get here," said Paradine quietly. "And what about sealing up the room and having Palmer on guard?"

"Right! I'll see to it."

Then, as they stepped out on the landing and Travers closed the door, Pollock appeared at the head of the stairs with a suddenness that was almost terrifying.

"Excuse me, sir, but I've been looking everywhere for you, sir. Mr. Franklin's on the phone, sir, and would like to speak to you!"

Travers took a deep breath. "Thank you, Pollock. We'll be there in a second."

He watched him turn down the stairs, then shook his head. "That wasn't a godsend, George, it was a miracle! You stay here till Palmer comes. Then tell Mrs. Cairns that Ransome's been found and won't be down for some time. And, for God's sake, pull yourself together and don't let a soul see anything's happened. Not a word to a soul! If Ransome's mentioned, don't know anything!"

After which jumble of instructions he sprinted down the stairs for the dining room.

CHAPTER XIII
CRASHAW LENDS A HAND

IT WAS WELL OVER half an hour later when Travers went out of the front door, past the loggia, and along the hedge path almost as far as the pagoda, with the snow flickering down spasmodically and the whole prospect as miserable as he felt himself. Then he turned and had a good look at the house. High up in the roof were two gable windows, each with a sheer drop to the ground and not an inch of foothold for a cat-burglar. He nodded to himself, then returned to the house. William, in the hall, was dispatched for Pollock.

"Just a minute, Pollock, please!" He led the way upstairs to the side staircase, past where Palmer sat on duty.

"There's a gable window at each side of the house. Does that mean an unoccupied room, by any chance?"

Pollock ruminated. "Gable window, sir? Yes, sir; that'll be the attic."

"Right! Let me have a look at it."

"Very good, sir!" He led the way up the stairs, round to the right, away from the servants' rooms, to where a short flight of steps led almost vertically to a species of loft. Pollock pointed to a door.

"You wish to see inside, sir?"

Travers nodded. Inside was a room like an inverted V; ten good feet in the middle. In a corner were some discarded trunks and boxes. Travers went over to the window, looked at the snow and the pagoda, then tried it. The window didn't open. Pollock explained.

"That's a sort of dummy, sir. There's a ventilator up there, sir—in the gable."

"I see. Now, Pollock; sometime this afternoon the police are going to be here. You can keep a still tongue in your head?"

"Most certainly, sir!"

"Then, not a word to a soul—including Mr. Braishe! Have a small packet of sandwiches made up at once, and a thermos of coffee, and bring a rug along. Put them in the corner by those boxes. And is there a key to this room?"

"In the door behind you, sir."

"So there is!" He pocketed it. "How long'll it take you to do all that?"

"About . . . ten minutes, sir."

"Good! Use the back stairs—and not a word to a soul! And send William to the breakfast room at once."

A two-minute talk with William, and he strolled along to the dining room—in time to see Braishe replacing the phone with Paradine standing by. Braishe appeared to be rather annoyed.

"No go about Charles. I can't get through to town."

"How'd you first get him? Through an agency?"

"Yes—County Employment Association. They backed his references." He scowled at the phone. "If we're not careful, he'll bolt."

"Not he! He couldn't get through half a mile of that snow. It'd kill him!"

Braishe grunted as he closed the doors of the miniature cupboard; then, "Know who's coming with Franklin?"

"Afraid I don't. He wasn't too sure himself—except that the Yard had been called in."

Braishe nodded. "Well, they can't come too quickly for me—that's how I feel about it."

Travers glanced at Paradine, then looked away again. "Everything else settled? Lawyer, undertaker, and so on?"

"My God! It's hellish!" Braishe broke out. "Think of it, Travers. Two days ago—all you people coming here—"

"*Don't* think of it!" said Travers quickly. "Walk about! *Do* something!" He took him by the arm and steered him out of the room. "Suppose you don't know where Crashaw is?"

"I don't. I think I heard Challis tell him he'd have to do something or go balmy. I think that's how he put it." Braishe's tone was very irritable. "They're probably in the billiard room."

"They might do worse!" said Travers cheerfully. "There's no disrespect for the dead in keeping sane."

He left them standing there and hurried off to the basement staircase where the click of the balls told him Braishe's supposition was correct. This time the pair of players looked much less self-conscious at being discovered. Challis finished his shot before he spoke.

"Good news, old boy—what?"

"You mean about the police." He nodded. "By the way, why exactly did you choose that Chinese costume for the dance?"

Challis's eyes nearly popped out of his head. Crashaw looked startled. "Why! what's the idea, old boy?"

"Just curiosity! You see I know the reason for everybody else's." Then he smiled.

"Oh, I see!" Challis smiled too—rather warily. "It was like this, old boy. Just another stunt we were doing in the show. You know those comic jugglers you see on the halls—all bounce and bunkum? Well, I'm doing an impersonation of one. Damn funny—though I say so!"

"I expect it will be! What I really came for was Crashaw. He's been bewailing the fact that he hasn't anything to do, so I've got him a job."

"I say—really?"

"Come along with me!" Travers took his arm. "Challis won't mind being left for a bit. Hallo! here's the gong! Better hurry up, or we shan't be finished by lunch."

Travers prattled away as they mounted the stairs. At the top of the servants' landing he caught sight of William.

"What about bringing William along to lend us a hand?"

"What's the idea precisely?"

But by the time the footman had joined them they were mounting the steps to the attic room. William opened the door for them to enter. Travers waved Crashaw in first. Then the setting changed dramatically. Travers closed the door and stood with his back to it. William backed alongside him. Crashaw, in the middle of a sentence, stopped with his mouth open. Then he looked suspicious.

"I say—what's the idea?" His voice still had its plaintive quality.

"I'm afraid you know it!" said Travers. "Here you are, and here you stay till the police come. You'll find something to eat in that corner. The window's a fixture, so you—"

"Here—I say!" broke in Crashaw.

"Shut up! Don't keep up that ridiculous pose! You'd be far more sensible to own up and ease the strain on yourself." There was no cheap irony in his voice as he went on. "You had a bit of bad luck, you know, Crashaw. You claimed to be at a school ten miles from Wroughton Park, where my young nephew is. You mentioned Westover, and we talked about its O.T.C. They haven't got one, and haven't had since—" He stopped suddenly. "Who's the chairman of your governors?"

"I'm afraid I can't say. You see, you didn't give me the chance to tell you I'd only been there a couple of terms!"

Travers shook his head reprovingly. "Been at Westover two terms and not know Lord Dillingwater! Really, Crashaw!"

"Of course, I know the name—"

"Of course you do! However, here you are, as I said. William's going to sit outside that locked door—with a loaded revolver. If you break down the door or try to escape, he'll let you have one in the nearest place. Isn't that so, William?"

"That is so, sir!"

Crashaw wasn't going to take all that lying down. "You're making a mistake, Travers—and you'll be sorry for it. I want to see Mr. Braishe. I insist on seeing him!"

Travers shook his head.

"I tell you, you've *got* to send him up here. If you don't, I'll kick the place down!"

"If you try that, you'll be tied up." Without any more argument he nodded to the footman to leave the room. The chair was brought to the very foot of the steps, and William took his seat.

"You've had lunch?"

"Yes, sir."

"Good! Here's the key. If Mr. Braishe does come up later on, let him have it. Let me know if that chap tries any monkey tricks."

In the dining room the men were standing round waiting.

"Sorry!" said Travers. "Don't wait for Crashaw, by the way. He won't be down for a bit."

The meal went on its way even more cheerfully than he'd anticipated. Moreover, being something to do, it was extraordinarily spun out. In the air was quite a new feeling. Another hour or two, and there'd be yet more people in the house, and a set of wholly new conditions to break the monotony and finally end it. George Paradine was almost his old genial self, more, as Travers suspected, to hide than to express what he was feeling. When the servants had gone someone asked again what had happened to Crashaw.

"As a matter of fact, he's locked up in the attic. William's on guard at the door."

"Good God!" exclaimed Braishe amid the general consternation. "What on earth for?"

"Because he's our burglar!"

He waited till the questions were all fired.

"One reason I know is because he knew nothing about old Dillingwater—the pacifist peer. And, by the way, Martin, Crashaw insists on seeing *you*."

Braishe looked exceedingly annoyed. "Really! I say, Travers! I think I might have been consulted about all this!"

Wildernesse looked very sheepish. Paradine looked watchful and startled. It was Challis who relieved the situation.

"About this Lord What's-his-name, old boy. Hadn't you better lock *me* up? 'Cause I'm damned if *I* know much about him!"

"Sorry!" said Travers most apologetically. "It's a most annoying habit of mine—being cryptic. Dillingwater is the big noise at the particular school Crashaw's claiming to come from—"

"What about his footprints?" interrupted Braishe. "Franklin said there was only one set. Even Crashaw can't work miracles, you know!"

"That's true enough—but he could create an illusion! Franklin knew all about that. Before he left he gave me a note—as you know—telling me to keep an eye on Crashaw. May I tell you what Franklin knew had happened? Crashaw slipped into the house last night—possibly as the harlequin Celia saw; possibly not. At any rate, he slipped in *after* the guests had gone, since his prints are over those made by them and the car wheels. He was kept hanging about because he was disturbed two or three times in the night—by Charles and Franklin and myself. I should say in any case he hung on till the very edge of dawn, when perhaps he heard the household on the move. Then he slipped out of the front door—"

"But Charles found the door locked!"

"I know! I'm coming to that later. Crashaw slipped out to the porch, and he saw the snow. He knew what a job he'd had getting here, and he didn't like the idea of tackling it when it was infinitely worse. Also, he was cold—and most damnably hungry. Very well, then: he decided on a bluff about a car. He therefore walked backwards, choosing the ruts as much as possible, as far as the end of the kitchen garden wall, where he was partly sheltered. Then he came back, treading in his own steps, knocked at the door, and was let in. Franklin found out all that from the footprints. What's more, he took the pains to go to the end of Crashaw's steps and found they ended—in the air!"

That, of course, cleared the atmosphere.

"My God! Would you believe it!"

"Sorry, Travers!" said Braishe. "But you've only got yourself to thank for the misunderstanding."

"I know that. But if you people had suspected Crashaw it might have been far more difficult. He might have bolted by hook or crook."

"Why didn't he bolt after breakfast?" asked Wildernesse.

Travers hesitated for a moment, not because he wasn't sure of *that* point. What he was thinking of was the ridiculously thin excuse he'd given—and had had accepted—for Crashaw hanging on in the house at all, once he'd collected the spoil.

"Why didn't he bolt after breakfast? Well, why should he? He was welcomed here by a set of charming people—so decent and so intelligent that they couldn't conceivably have any real low-down sense. Also the morning blizzard arrived and he *had* to stop. May I recall something to you there? Remember how he advised Franklin to go by the hedge and the wood? Why? Not only was it the way he realized he ought to have gone himself; but he didn't want Franklin to see those footprints of his that ended nowhere!"

"Good for you, old boy!" Challis looked round as if to lead the applause. But Braishe was still somewhat reserved.

"Then you've not only got the burglar upstairs—you've got the murderer! And you think he's that type?"

"That's for the police to decide," said Travers mildly. "We've got our man, ready to hand over—with a full statement."

"What about the boodle, old boy?"

"That's probably secreted somewhere at the end of the footprints. We can get that at any time."

"Then I vote we have a look now," and Challis got to his feet.

Travers smiled. "Then you'd better get a diving suit. It's under a couple of foot of snow!"

Paradine's voice came in quietly. "*What about that door?*"

"Oh, yes!" Travers fumbled at his glasses. "If Martin will be good enough to let me have a free hand I'll try to prove it. Even if I don't, I shall still hold—with Franklin—that the case is proved against Crashaw. Would you mind if I pushed the bell for Charles?"

The footman had obviously no idea of what was in store for him, in spite of the fact that five pairs of eyes were regarding him curiously.

"Oh, Charles! I'm authorized by Mr. Braishe to ask you a very direct question!"

The footman's face coloured. His expression altered at once.

"Mr. Braishe guarantees that if you answer this question perfectly frankly he'll pass the whole thing over and make no further reference to it. Also, the police won't be informed. . . . You locked the front door on the night of the dance?"

"Yes, sir."

"It's a spring lock?"

"Yes, sir."

"And you bolted it top and bottom?"

"Yes, sir."

"And in the morning, when you got up, everything was as you left it?"

The hesitation might have been due to the five pairs of eyes, all fastened on him. Travers cut in again before the answer came.

"You imagined that Mr. Franklin and I were suspicious of you, when we found you wandering about. Also you had on a pair of shoes—done up; probably because you hadn't been to bed. Is that why, although you found the door unbolted, you decided to say nothing about it?"

Charles looked round for a lead.

"Speak out!" snapped Braishe. "You hear what Mr. Travers is asking!"

"Well, sir . . . the door *was* unbolted."

"That's all right," said Travers. "You can go now!"

He turned to the others. "I may be doing him an injustice—and her too—but I think if you find out, as I did, which one of the maids arranged after all to have a room to herself, you'll know why Charles was careful how he brought himself into prominence after being discovered wandering about!"

"I'll certainly have *that* seen into!" said Braishe angrily.

"That's your own private affair," Travers told him quietly. "I may be wrong. I hope I am."

"You say Crashaw—if that's the fellow's name—wanted to see me. What about it? You think I ought?"

"That's just as you like. I don't think perhaps I'd let him know—well, just all that *we* know. We're running no risk in holding him." He got to his feet. "Now, if you fellows will excuse me, I think I'll turn in for a bit. I have an idea I shan't get a frightful lot of sleep to-night."

As he went out of the door he heard the babble of conversation begin. On the landing he halted for a word with Palmer.

"All right, Palmer? Had lunch?"

"Yes, sir—thank you."

Travers nodded kindly. "Mr. Franklin and the police'll be here in an hour or so—at least, we hope so."

"What was the matter with the telephone—if I may ask the question, sir?"

"Elm bough broke the wires—on the bye road."

Palmer shook his head. "It may not be my place to say it, sir, but I shan't be sorry when . . . something does happen, sir. This place is getting on my nerves, sir."

"Well, you've got to stick it for a bit. Anybody been along?"

"Only Mrs. Fewne, sir. I told her the door was sealed up."

"Good!" He nodded again, then moved up the stairs to the main landing. There he stopped. Should he have a confidential word with Brenda before the police got there? He made a step forward—stopped again—then entered his own room and locked the door. Things were too deep for him to handle. That last terrible business had made him feel so mentally tired that his mind refused, with something more than horror, to think it out from the mass of devilish complications that held it in.

He prowled about the room restlessly; hopelessly at a loss. The only solid ground had gone from under his feet when Ransome's body had been seen down there in the snow. The murder couldn't have concerned Fewne at all! That money business must be an unimportant side issue. If it were not—where was the connection? Ransome in Challis's room—the dagger that hadn't been in the rack—that awful position of Fewne's body—that uncanny scrawl on the sheet of paper—the packet of treasury notes—the dead matches beneath the bed—the phone that should have been free from snow—Ransome's body out there where it might have been hidden for days: a dozen things like that came crowding into his mind as he prowled round the room.

Something would have to be done to keep his mind off it; something to concentrate it on a single point. His eye caught that file of newspapers on the table. He got into his dressing gown, had a cold wash down, then, with a rug over his knees and his pipe going, set to work again to search those papers for a clue. From time to time, as things occurred to him, he jotted them down—literary notes, a mention of Cornwall, a discussion of the law of copyright. That lasted till just on three, when it came to a sudden end.

From somewhere above him he heard the scamper of feet. A shot! Another! A shouting that became frantic! Then the noise shifted ground. It died away as quickly as it had begun.

Travers, with more than a vague wonder, stepped out to the corridor. Where had those shots come from? William had no revolver! That statement to Crashaw was merely a ridiculous bluff!

CHAPTER XIV
CRASHAW LIVENS THINGS UP

FOR A MINUTE or two things happened so suddenly that Travers seemed to be turning his head in several directions at once. Braishe and William came rushing up the stairs, and a yard or so behind, Wildernesse, well ahead of Challis. Behind, on the landing, came Celia's voice and the yap of Ho-Ping. The advancing forces met with Travers in the middle.

"Where is he? Have you seen him?" This from Braishe.

"Martin! What *is* all this noise about?" boomed Celia.

Braishe put his hand on her arm as if to lead her away. She shook him off angrily.

"Martin! How dare you treat me like a child! What was that noise?"

He gave Travers a look, then explained. "It's the burglar, Aunt Celia. We had him in the attic, and he's got out. Now, go back to your room, please! You're holding everything up."

"Seen anything?" he asked again.

"Nothing," began Travers. But the hunt had moved on. Celia was just disappearing inside her room, and with the murmur of her voice as she consoled the Pekinese came the sound of scurrying over the bare boards towards the attic. Then came Braishe's voice, issuing instructions; steps receding, then more steps, this time down the side staircase as Palmer came into view. All *he* knew was that he'd heard a noise; then William had come bounding down to the hall like a lunatic. Thereupon, still scared stiff after those revolver shots, he'd gone along himself to investigate.

Travers, with a sudden feeling of alarm, glanced quickly at the door knob, then drew a breath of relief. The seals were undisturbed! At the top of the servants' landing, William was standing as if on sentry.

"What's up, William?"

The footman shook his head sheepishly. "He did me, sir—clean in the eye!"

"How do you mean?"

"Well, sir, after Mr. Braishe had gone I heard him fumbling—or tinkering, you might say—with the lock. I didn't pay any attention to that, sir, because I thought he was doing it to annoy me. Then, a minute or two later, sir, I heard his voice at the keyhole, sir. 'Good-bye, William; I'll see you later!' That's what he said, sir. I didn't say a word, sir; thought he was pulling my leg. Then I heard the glass smash, sir. 'The window!' sir: that's what I thought. 'He's gone out of the window!' So I got hold of the knob and put my shoulder to the door, and what do you think happened, sir? The door was unlocked! and in I fell, and when I looked at the window, it was smashed and there wasn't a sign of him. So I went over to have a look, sir, thinking he'd let down a rope or something, when what do you think happened, sir?"

"Don't know."

"He nipped out of the door, sir! He'd been behind it all the time! And when I got there he was just going down the steps, so I loosed off a couple of shots at him—"

"Shots! Where'd you get the revolver from?"

"The master gave it to me, sir. He said he was the murderer, sir, and I was to let him have it point-blank if he tried any tricks."

"Hm! . . . And what happened then?"

"Well, I chased him as far as our staircase, sir, then I went down to the hall and saw Mr. Braishe."

Travers suddenly wondered—then clicked his tongue involuntarily.

"Then Crashaw must have thought that revolver business was all bluff, William?"

"He didn't give a damn, sir; that's all I know. He just nipped out and ran."

Travers rattled the loose silver in his trousers pocket. "Mr. Braishe with him . . . long?"

"About ten minutes, I should say, sir."

"Hm! You didn't hear anything, by any chance? He wasn't threatening or anything like that?"

"I didn't hear a word, sir. Oh, and after he'd been in a minute, Mr. Braishe looked out, sir, and told me to wait at the bottom of the stairs till he came out."

"I see. And what did you think of that?"

"Well, I knew, if he cut up rough, Mr. Braishe'd eat two like him, sir . . . and I was there if he bolted. But nothing did happen, sir, and when the master came out he locked the door, and then he fetched me the revolver and asked if I could use it, sir."

"Had you said anything to him about a revolver?"

"Well, sir, I told him when he first come up, what you'd said to Mr. Crashaw inside the room, sir, about a revolver."

"And are you a good shot?"

"Not so dusty, sir!"

"And Mr. Braishe knew that?"

"He did when I told him, sir!"

"Exactly!" Travers smiled. A couple of coins changed hands. "Keep what we've been talking about to yourself, William! Don't even mention that you've been talking to me at all. Not a word to anybody, mind!"

As he hurriedly dressed in his room, he felt no particular gratification. The fact that Crashaw had, by bolting, acknowledged the truth of the accusations was merely an unnecessary confirmation of the obvious. It was the other factors—the disturbing ones—that kept coming into his mind. Why had Crashaw insisted on seeing Braishe? True, he was the owner of the house, yet somehow Travers felt there was more to it than that. Then *after* Braishe's visit, he'd escaped. Then there'd been that revolver. Crashaw, in his opinion, had had no hand in the killing of Mirabel Quest—and almost as certainly not in the killing of Ransome; but, wherever he'd gone, there might be delay in laying hands on him, and that might mean holding up a good many things else. In his movements about the house that night, for instance, he might have heard or seen some very strange things.

Down in the hall the search party reassembled, chattering and excited. If their reports were to be believed, Crashaw had disappeared into thin air, with devil a footprint anywhere.

"Can't think how he did it!" Braishe exclaimed angrily. "If he *picked* the lock, where'd he get the wire from?"

"If he's a first-class man," smiled Travers, "he probably had some on him. Still, he's gone; the thing is, what to do about it. You see, all he's waiting for is a chance to slip into the drive as soon as the plough arrives. He can't possibly get away till then. He must be lying handy somewhere." Then an idea: "Why not call up Levington and tell them to have a man or two waiting for him at the drive gates?"

"Good!" Braishe slipped off at once.

"Don't think I'm being funny," said Travers, "but have you checked the route Franklin took yesterday morning?"

"Martin looked out of the window," said Paradine. "So did I—and we couldn't see anything."

"What about the door—and the hedge path? You couldn't see as far as that." On a sudden impulse he moved off, the others trailing at his heels. But the breakfast-room door, when they tried it, was locked!

"That's the way he's gone—and he's taken the key!" was Travers's opinion. "Slip upstairs, Tommy, and have a look out of a window."

The others looked away across the wild garden and the wood, behind which nothing could be seen. The branches of the larches made a screen that shut everything off, but within the small field of view nothing was seen stirring, not even a black-bird. Then Wildernesse came rushing in.

"You can see the footprints outside the door—but there isn't a sign of him!"

"He's gone, old boy! Taken the line Franklin took."

Travers shook his head. "Franklin said it took him two hours to get to the side road—and there's been a couple of foot of snow since then."

"I've got it!" exclaimed Wildernesse. "I'll bet you he's in one of those evergreen trees—what d'you call 'em?—pines of some sort! That's the only spot of cover there is—and it's handy for the drive!"

"I think you're right," said Paradine, looking round. "And it'll be a tree close up to the hedge. Let's follow up the footprints."

"Just a minute!" said Travers. "Tommy and I'll be enough. We've got the longest legs. You fellows watch."

"What about your clothes?"

"Oh, damn the clothes!"

The window was opened, and the pair of them set off in Crashaw's footprints along the hedge, floundered along in the wild garden, sogged across the shallow ditch and into the wood. Twenty yards, and the holes made by Crashaw's progress turned sharp left to a clump of Douglas firs. There they stopped short. Travers's eye ran up a trunk, with its disturbed snow and the scrape marks where feet had slipped. Halfway up a pair of legs were visible.

"Coming down, Crashaw—or are we going to fetch you?"

Nothing happened for a moment; then there was a movement. Crashaw came down hand under hand, then dropped to the snow. He was a forlorn figure: trousers sticking to his legs, and collar wet with snow and perspiration; for all that, he was looking perfectly resigned. Then he actually laughed.

"Well, I've given you a good run for your money!" There was nothing plaintive about his voice now.

The procession of three, Crashaw in the lead, battled back to the house. Crashaw produced the key from his pocket, but he kept his eyes averted when they joined the main body. Everyone seemed tongue-tied and remarkably self-conscious. Challis bobbed up first.

"Ask him where he put the boodle!" he whispered to Travers.

Travers nodded. "If you people don't mind, *I'll* stay here with him. Get me a pair of trousers, somebody; and a pair for him. We don't want him to get pneumonia."

"Sit down, Crashaw!" He indicated the chair opposite his own. "What made you do such a baby trick as scrambling up that tree?"

Crashaw raised his eyebrows. "Baby trick! My dear fellow, if you'd given me a few minutes more till the snow had covered my steps—or crevasses, rather—that'd have been the last you'd have seen of me!"

"I see! . . . And how did you get into this game?"

Crashaw smiled. "You're not asking me to start snivelling, are you?"

"Oh, dear, no! I merely wondered. I suppose, by the way, you went to Westover?"

"I did . . . as a matter of fact. Pretty bad break, that of mine, wasn't it?"

"It was . . . rather. And you made a good many more. Where'd you put the—er—boodle, as Challis calls it?"

"In a handkerchief—in the soil by that rambler rose up against the front porch."

"I see! Well, here's our changes of raiment!" He sent Challis off with the news about the boodle and set about his own toilet.

"Of course, you're not bound to answer me—as you know. I might perhaps do you a good turn with the police. Already, I believe, Franklin's arranging for you to be held on his charge only. The others'll be withdrawn. . . . You didn't commit the murder?"

Crashaw sneered. "Should I be such a fool as to say yes?"

"Everybody assumes you did it. The police'll assume it. You're in a bad way, Crashaw!"

"Don't you believe it! May I smoke?"

"Do, please!" He even passed over his own case. "See anything suspicious that night?"

"Perhaps! . . . I saw you and Franklin, and if it's any use to you, I can corroborate that little love affair of your friend Charles!"

"I say! That's interesting!" His tone changed. "But about that petty pilfering of yours—that's what it amounts to really, plus a certain amount of nerve—I'd be glad if you'd tell me something. When did you go into Miss Quest's room?"

"Well, I waited till Braishe went upstairs, then I started—"

"Where were you, by the way?"

"Clothes cupboard—servants' corridor. I waited till I heard the first snore—Wildernesse, that was—then waded in. Everybody slept like a log. I was actually just inside Miss Quest's room when you and Franklin disturbed me. As soon as you'd gone 1 slipped up the side stairs."

"But you came back to the room?"

"I didn't. Honestly I didn't. I looked in—that's all I did—and thought the room was unoccupied. Then I went down to the dining room and made myself comfortable for an hour or two."

"Have a drink?"

"Teetotaler—as you know." He smiled. "It's no use asking me to prove the last tot was doped!"

"Quite! And to get back to the point. You didn't know Miss Quest was murdered?"

"Good God, no! Do you think I'm a fool? I'd have been out of the house if it'd killed me! I'd have been a thousand miles away by now!"

"Did you wear a harlequin costume, by any chance?"

"Good Lord, no! Came in just as I am—except these trousers!"

"And why exactly were you so anxious to see Braishe?"

Crashaw hesitated. "Oh—er—merely thought I could tell him the tale. I rather hoped he'd override you!"

"And you found him a tougher proposition than you'd anticipated?"

Crashaw's voice was at variance with the subtle sort of smile that crept over his face. "Oh, yes! Frightfully so!"

"Are you prepared to give evidence against Charles?"

"Depends on what sort. If you mean . . . his little rendezvous—well, no!"

"What other evidence is there?"

Crashaw raised his eyebrows. "None—that I'm aware of!"

"Did you cut the light cord?"

"Good Lord, no! Light or dark, it's all the same to me!"

"What about the phone?"

Crashaw smiled. "Rather funny, that! I went to do it, but somebody'd done it already!"

"When was that?"

"Oh—er—just before I left."

Braishe and Challis came in just then; the former with Travers's missing notecase.

"Here's your share of the proceedings, Travers. It comes to a bit less than you thought. Do you mind if . . . he's asked whether he pocketed any notes?"

Crashaw answered for himself. "Never do it—not when I'm coming back to breakfast!"

Braishe's face flushed. "We've only your word for that!"

"*My* word means a good deal!" Crashaw looked at him with what Travers thought unnecessary directness. After all, Crashaw's word wasn't the Bank of England.

"Damn funny!" cut in Challis. "Your share's forty-five, old boy. We've settled with everybody else."

"Pardon me!" Crashaw got to his feet. "Mr. Travers should have forty-nine ten. I don't know if you've helped yourself to the ten you claimed to have lost. If you have, you're a profiteer. There was a fiver, all told, in your pockets!"

"You're a liar!"

"And you're a dirty little swine!"

"That'll do!" snapped Braishe. "We'll settle that with you afterwards, Travers." He lowered his voice. "The tractor's getting pretty loud. They should be here in a few minutes."

"Splendid!" He felt for his glasses, then restoked his pipe instead.

"I wonder if you'd care to be there when they turn up? I'll carry on here."

"No, really!" Travers smiled gratefully. "Awfully good of you, but I'll stay on with Crashaw. You'd better be there. You're the real person in authority!"

Braishe paused, then. "Right-ho! Sure there's nothing you want?"

"Quite . . . thanks." He waited till they'd gone—Challis, for once, rather subdued—then leaned forward to Crashaw, who was watching him superciliously. Crashaw spoke first.

"Taking no risks?"

"No . . . not again! I've taken too many in this case already, Crashaw. A woman got strangled because I took risks!"

"I thought she was stabbed!"

Travers ignored that. "You spoke about snivelling, just now. Ever been caught before?"

Crashaw lighted another cigarette, very deliberately.

"Yes . . . once or twice. It's all in the game, you know!"

"Like it much?"

"Like it! Good God, did I like it!"

"You'd do a lot to avoid—shall we say—another term?"

"I would! I'd even commit murder—and you may tell the police so!"

"Why should I?" Travers shook his head like a father. "I might even commit murder myself. But would you do something else? Would you break your word?"

Crashaw looked at him queerly. "Why all this . . . hypothetical stuff?"

Travers shrugged his shoulders. "Just curiosity. . . . Your name isn't Crashaw, of course!"

"It certainly isn't!"

Travers got up and went over to the light switch. When he came back he was looking amused.

"Do you know, I'm awfully grateful to you for that information . . . Crashaw? You don't mind my continuing to call you that? It tells me quite a lot!"

The other laughed. "Then you're damned easily satisfied!"

"I am! Er—would you mind pushing the bell?"

William, as it happened, came in. The request that he should sit there with an eye on his former prisoner seemed to give him considerable satisfaction.

"Don't let him get away this time!" said Travers.

"Don't you worry about that, sir!" and he took up a position unpleasantly close.

Out in the hall George Paradine, Wildernesse, and Challis were waiting, with the front door open. The roar of the tractor sounded pretty close.

"Soon be here now!" said Paradine. "Get anything out of that chap?"

"Not much. . . . Martin about?"

"He just went into the dining room with Charles."

Travers looked startled; then turned on his heel. Outside the dining-room door, he ran into the couple just emerging. In the half light it was impossible to see Braishe's face as he spoke.

"Oh—er—Travers! Just a moment!"

He drew him into the room. Travers, with a sudden feeling of irritation, switched on the light.

"I've been trying to get through to town again . . . about Charles." He broke off to see if the corridor was clear. "I couldn't get through at all—but I had an idea. I asked him to come in here; then I tried him out. I offered him fifty quid and a permanent job if he would open that safe!"

Travers's eyes opened. "And did he?"

"He couldn't—or he said he couldn't! He didn't know the first thing about it—even when I showed him the safe!"

"But didn't Fewne take the siphon?"

"I know he did. But this chap might have been after a formula. And he might have been surprised down here by Mirabel." He lowered his voice to the merest whisper. "Why should she necessarily have been murdered in the room where she was found?"

As Travers opened the door he was shaking his head perplexedly. Then he looked up. "Keep an eye on him till the police get here—and after, if it's necessary." He watched Braishe nod and move away, then returned to the breakfast room. Outside the door he stopped. Voices were heard in the hall!

Inside the room Crashaw sat smoking with a perfect indifference to the presence of the footman.

"See if Mr. Franklin's arrived yet, William, and tell him where I am."

The footman hurried off. In the door he collided with Franklin himself, whose eyes went straight to Crashaw. Behind him came a figure that warmed Travers's heart: Wharton, fatherly and suburban as ever, wiping the moisture off his huge moustache with a silk handkerchief.

"Well, Mr. Travers? And how are you, sir?"

"Splendid! And damn glad to see you! All right, Franklin?"

"Rather! Here's Norris!"

Wharton got up from the fire where, as if unaware of Crashaw's presence in the room, he'd been warming his hands. Before Norris could speak he got into action.

"Now, Mr. Travers. Any men you want specially placed?"

"Yes. The upstairs room, pagoda, dining room . . . and the attic. Pollock or William can show you."

"See to that, Norris, will you? Franklin might show you where. Take this chap along"—he nodded back at Crashaw—"and charge him. Then have him handy!" He stooped to the fire again. "Where's the best place to start, Mr. Travers?"

Travers shook his head, then raised his hands hopelessly.

"God knows! I don't. . . . Anywhere. . . . Everywhere!"

Wharton looked at him.

"Pretty bad, is it? Well, come along to the entrance hall. We'll have a consultation out there."

CHAPTER XV
WHARTON MAKES A START

IT WAS TRAVERS'S frantic message to Franklin that led to the appearance of Superintendent Wharton. Of the two available members of the Big Five, Wharton had the advantage of knowing Travers's little ways—and he'd known Franklin for years. Moreover, Wharton was ideal for that case and its particular setting. He was so quietly paternal in appearance, so disarmingly jovial, so obviously understanding and sympathetic, that he might have been a popular medical practitioner. As to his colossal patience, his tenacious memory, and his occasional outbursts of perfectly terrifying and snarling indignation, these were sides that the unwary never expected. And he was a good mixer. He could be deferential, suave, retiring; even a damn fool, if circumstances demanded it.

That consultation he had mentioned to Travers took the better part of half an hour; then, in the dining room, which he had chosen as headquarters, began the grilling of Crashaw. Wharton saw Travers's point. As the keystone of the whole case, Crashaw must be made to talk. If he refused to volunteer information, then he must be made to betray it.

"I don't think you'll scare him," Travers had said. "He just doesn't give a damn—and I think he's got something at the back of his mind that's cheering him up. I don't quite know what it is, but it's there!"

Wharton's handling was masterly, as Travers had to admit. He hinted delicately at the withdrawal of the charge; then more than balanced that by hinting at facilities for murder. He got a detailed statement of movements; tried to find a flaw in it by a series of superbly disguised suggestions; sympathized with him; laughed at him; threatened him; then threw his hand in—apparently.

"All right!" he told the local sergeant. "Take him off to Levington! I shan't want him to-night—unless I phone." Then, at the very door, "Oh, Crashaw! How, exactly, did you get out of that room? Pick the lock?"

"That's right!" Crashaw nodded jauntily.

"Where'd you get the wire?"

"Oh—er—had it on me!"

Wharton turned to the sergeant. "Show me the list of what was found on him!" He produced a pair of old-fashioned glasses from a disreputable case, adjusted them with extreme deliberation, then peered over the top of them like a burlier Chester Conklin.

"Hm! What did you do with the wire?"

"The wire!" He smiled. "Fact of the matter is, I threw it away. Homicidal weapon, you know!"

Wharton shot a look at him but said nothing. Then he handed back the sheet. "All right! Take him away!"

He watched the departure, then turned to Travers. "You were quite right! We'll have the lock in. Fetch it, one of you!"

The plain-clothes man brought it in, already dismantled. Wharton got his glass to it, then nodded to Franklin to come over. That lock hadn't a single scratch mark; moreover, as Travers pointed out, since Crashaw must have thought he'd actually succeeded in escaping from the house, there was no need for him to throw away either wire or skeleton keys. He'd have retained them for future use, as he did the key of the outside door of the breakfast room.

"Ask Mr. Braishe to come here for a minute!" Wharton ordered.

Travers felt a sudden apprehension, but he needn't have worried. As it happened, Braishe showed up rather well. There was a sort of board of directors' air about him. He looked alert, supremely collected; ready to be judicial and prepared to be helpful. Moreover, the visit was not a business one—on Wharton's side.

"Sit down a moment, Mr. Braishe, will you? We want you to help us. You see, it's this burglary affair," he explained. "We want to get it out of the way. Now, when you went to see Crashaw, I take it he wanted to tell you he was unjustly accused."

"Precisely what he did do—or try to do."

Wharton smiled. "I imagine he got no change out of you!" Then he frowned. "What we can't make out is that he claims to have picked the lock. That, of course, is ridiculous!" and he waved a contemptuous hand at the pieces of metal. "Now, I wonder! It's a thing I've done myself, for instance. Could you have thought you turned the key one way but had actually turned it the other?"

Braishe pursed his lips. "Possible, of course. Mind you, I'd swear I hadn't."

"Naturally. I was merely wondering if you could think back to what you actually did." He shook his head. "That's a very difficult thing. However, we're very much obliged. Everybody perfectly normal? They don't think we're going to be a nuisance in any way?"

Braishe smiled. "I'm sure nobody thinks that! Naturally, they'd all like to get away as soon as they can. Some of them—of *us*, I might say—have all sorts of important things to attend to."

"Quite so! Quite! At the earliest moment, Mr. Braishe!"

Once more he watched the exit from the room, then leaned over to Travers. "Just wanted to put him at ease! Now, then! What's *your* opinion of the Crashaw affair—briefly?"

"This!" said Travers. "And it's an opinion and nothing else. Crashaw had a hold of some sort over Braishe and sent for him to show it. Braishe hadn't any idea of that when he went into the attic—but he soon did! That's why he ordered the footman to go to the foot of the steps. The hold was so great that Braishe *had* to let Crashaw go. He pretended to lock the door but didn't. He advised him which way to take out of the house, and when the place was searched, took that sector himself to report on. *But* the secret was so deadly that Braishe gave William the revolver, hoping to God Crashaw got shot. Just before you arrived, when I was questioning Crashaw in the breakfast room, Braishe tried to get me out of the room so that he might stay with him. If I'd gone, Crashaw might have got away again—or he might have been shot while attacking Braishe. The only other thing that seems fairly certain is that Crashaw gave Braishe his word that he'd never give him away provided Braishe facilitated the escape—and Crashaw means to keep that word ... unless ..."

"Unless what?"

Travers smiled. "I was hoping *you'd* suggest that! Unless Braishe lets him down—I mean, doesn't keep his part of the bargain."

"Braishe, of course, is screening somebody!" put in Franklin.

"Well—er—he may be."

"You mean he isn't likely to have had a hand in it himself?" asked Wharton.

"I very much doubt it."

Wharton nodded. "That ought to simplify things. However, ask Dr. Paradine if he can spare us a minute, Franklin, will you?"

"Do you know, Mr. Travers," he said, "I feel like a man who's arrived exceedingly late at the theatre. Something's going on the stage, but I haven't the least idea what. I haven't got anywhere near this case yet. I'm a stranger; an interloper. House, people, things that happened; everything's hearsay from you and Franklin. . . . Ah, here's the doctor!"

He beamed affectionately on Paradine. "Just the merest second! About that affair out there." He waved his hand in the wrong direction for the pagoda. "What, between ourselves, are you and Menzies agreeing on? Suicide?"

"I think so. The gas, of course, as the direct agent."

"Quite! That's all I wanted, thanks. The idea is to eliminate everything *outside* the house, then we can concentrate on what took place in it. Make your own arrangements, by the way, about P. M.'s and removing the bodies. Menzies'll show you the ropes."

He pottered for a minute or two round the table where lay Travers's collection of exhibits.

"And you say finger prints are pretty hopeless?"

"I think they are," said Franklin. "The door knob'd have been the great thing, if it hadn't been smudged. And nobody would have been such a fool as to leave any on the dagger."

"Hm!" He thought for a moment. "Well, we've got to earn a living some way. We'll *try* the dagger. Send those print people in, one of you!"

Wharton stood by the table as they got to work. Something was evidently happening at the first puff of the insufflator, for he craned his neck round and got out his glass.

"Take a whole series!" he told Matthews, and the dagger was forthwith fixed and three close-ups taken. Then he beckoned the others over.

"Take a look at those! Beautiful! Beautiful!" He rubbed his hands. "We'll get the prints of everybody straightaway!"

"I think I've got most of them here!" said Travers, lugging out his collection of envelopes. "I got them for quite another reason, which I'll tell you about later."

Wharton took a look at them, then at Travers. "What's inside?"

"Merely some papers. If you don't mind, I'll write the names on them, too, as we open the envelopes."

There was a tense silence as the insufflator was puffed and Wharton checked against the dagger. The women's passed without comment, as did Paradine's; then Crashaw gave the first surprise. His half sheet had no prints at all!

"Probably smelt a rat!" said Travers.

Tommy Wildernesse's showed two prints—his own and Paradine's. Next came Braishe's—and there the test ended. Wharton stared, snatched the paper, and held it alongside the dagger. Then he looked round dramatically. Franklin picked up the glass and had a look.

"Incredible! Fancy a man being such a fool as that!"

"Just a moment!" said Wharton. "Are we sure they *are* his prints! Could he have asked somebody to write this for him?"

"I doubt it," said Travers. "Also he wasn't such a fool as all that. He left the prints on the dagger because he hadn't gloves on and he was disturbed—"

"By Crashaw?"

"Possibly. But he knew he *had* left the prints. That's why he tried to get Charles to open the safe!"

Wharton clicked his tongue. Another one of the things Travers hadn't had time to tell him!

"I'll tell you what we'll do," he said. "Push that bell for some tea. While we're eating, you can go over all the things you've left out."

Twenty minutes later Wharton wiped his mouth, pushed the tray on one side, then got to his feet.

"Better see Mrs. Fewne first. Her account of the quarrel might give some ideas."

"If you'll excuse me," said Travers, "I don't think there's any reliance to be placed on that. If Ransome had been alive we could have had *two* interviews and noted the discrepancies. Now there's nobody to check Mrs. Fewne's story. I don't suggest for a moment that hers would be wrong! All I mean is, that if hers differs from what Ransome told *me*, she can maintain—and probably prove—that Ransome was wrong."

"What's your suggestion, then?"

"A peculiar one." Wharton sat down again. "I don't agree that because Fewne died over there he was cut off from other events in the house. I believe the three deaths are connected. I believe they're tangled up as tightly together as the knot in a ball of string. I believe the solution to all three lies in that pagoda!"

"Hm!" went Wharton. "You ought to know—at least you ought to be well enough steeped in the atmosphere of the place by now. All the same, how do you reconcile your latest statement with your first one—that *Crashaw* was the key to the case?"

"So he is—in a different way." He polished his glasses nervously. "If you'll bear with me, I'll try to differentiate. Imagine you've a clock, the age of which you don't know. Then a man turns up and tells you that eighty years ago he helped to make that clock. His is direct evidence. He's Crashaw—*if you could get him to speak*. But you might do something else. You might call in an expert who'd deduce the age of your clock by its style, its wood, its works and so on. That's indirect evidence that's always there—waiting to be read. That's Fewne—if we can read what he tells us."

Wharton's comment hit the nail on the head with considerable abruptness.

"You have no doubt that Fewne was murdered?"

Travers smiled. "You don't expect me to tell you that—in the face of medical evidence?"

Wharton snorted. "Tell me! Every word you say tells me!"

"Well, that may be so—but it's not official or repeatable. When I can add motive to event and explanation to suspicion, then I'll write it down—and sign my name to it!"

Wharton thought that over. "What are you proposing to do now? Start over there?"

"Yes—and no. I'd like you, when we do go over there, to be a witness of something that'll take place. Then I'd like you to take advantage of the evidence of Braishe and the doctors and press for a suicide verdict at the inquest. In other words, I'd like you to let it be known that you're finished with the pagoda. You're satisfied. Then let me make use of special points of contact for a day or two, to see if I can find anything out. I'll keep you informed of all that happens. In the meanwhile it'd be an impertinence for me to say that you'll naturally carry on where and how you think necessary. Suppose, for instance, you decide to start at the two murders in the house; then, if you come across anything that concerns Fewne—and the pagoda—you'll pass it over to me. One thing, for instance, you *may* be told."

"And what's that?"

"That Mrs. Fewne was terrified her husband should know she'd borrowed money."

"Hm! Hardly a murder motive, that!"

"Exactly! But the whole of the *obvious* problem lies here— the doped drink, the cut cord, the murders, the suspects; the evidence—what there is of it—is all here." He looked at Wharton with a disarming smile. "Well, what do you say?"

"This," said Wharton, less bluntly than it seemed. "You're extraordinarily anxious to be let alone with that pagoda! You wouldn't be sorry if I never set foot in it—except that you might want me to do some cross-examination for you! However," and he gave Franklin a wink that Travers didn't see, "we'll try it out! I shall be up to my eyes for a day or so, merely getting hold of facts. Then there'll be the inquests on Monday, and that'll mean the chief characters away. Then there'll be the funerals."

Franklin cut in there. "Knowing Ludo better than you do, George, I think all he wants is that whoever was responsible for the death of Fewne should think he's got away with it. That'll leave you free for all manner of—"

"All right! All right!" Wharton waved his hand. "Haven't I said I agree? . . . Hallo, here's the medical evidence!"

Menzies and Paradine seemed perfectly satisfied with what they'd done, and that was a feather in George Paradine's cap, since the police surgeon wasn't the easiest person in the world to get on with.

"Had them both back where they were found?" asked Wharton.

"Aye! Everything's as Dr. Paradine found it—except the dagger—and you have that here."

"You leave that alone for a bit!" Wharton shot his hand out just in time. "There's some pretty pictures to come off it yet."

"Is that so!" Menzies raised his eyebrows—and had his look all the same.

"Finished?" asked Wharton. "Right! Then we'll go upstairs for the photos there. We shan't want you for a bit, Dr. Paradine, thanks."

Some time later Wharton and Franklin were standing in the pagoda. As Menzies had reported, the body had been taken there; not that Challis's drawings were useless, but rather that they necessarily created no atmosphere. Now the body had gone again; this time to the ambulance, and the two were talking things over by the light of the acetylene lamp.

"How's it working out, George?"

"Seems all right! It *may* be suicide." He shook his head. "Don't think I ever saw a more horrible sight!"

Franklin nodded. It *had* been pretty ghastly.

"Paradine's sure enough—and Menzies doesn't disagree. The curious thing is that what they find normal, Travers finds unusual." He waved his hand at the writing desk. "Take that extraordinary scrawl, for instance, and compare Paradine's and Travers's theories. Take the manuscript. Travers says he'd never have committed suicide and left it as it is. He'd have burnt it first. Paradine says he was so mad that he forgot all about it."

"And. who are you backing?" Wharton asked quietly.

"I?" He shrugged his shoulders; the reply was enigmatical. "Travers isn't Braishe's uncle—even by marriage!"

"Come, come! Paradine's an honourable man!"

"Implicitly so. But honour and prejudice are different things."

"I know they are. But why *Braishe?* I see the contacts, of course: the gas, the fact that it's his house, and so on. Also, there's this dagger business—though Travers spoke before he knew that. But why did *you* mention Braishe?"

"Because I know Travers," said Franklin cryptically. "Sh! Here he is!"

Travers came in with Tommy Wildernesse.

"Frightfully cold out there. Freezing like sin! This is Tommy Wildernesse—Superintendent Wharton. Tommy's a thundering good chap!"

Wildernesse blushed as he shook hands. Travers explained.

"I got him to have a look at something for me, just after we discovered the body—knowing he could keep a vital secret. Now, if you don't mind, I want him to have another look. Put the lamp on the floor; just down here." He pulled up the valance. "Now, Tommy, imagine you're going to drain the sump of your car. Get on your back, wriggle under the bed and have a look where you did before."

Wildernesse did as directed and elbowed himself along. Travers chattered away as if to keep up the spirits of his new assistant.

"Mind your head against that mattress! . . . Now, then! What about the joint between wall and floor?"

"Can't see it. I'm on my back!"

"Damn it, of course you are! Roll over, then! . . . Now what do you see?"

"Damn all!"

"Good enough! . . . Come out again the way you went in!"

"Is that all?" asked Wildernesse rather sheepishly when he'd dusted his knees.

"That's the lot, Tommy!" Travers told him. He turned to Wharton. "You can absolutely depend on him not to say a word about all this."

"Good!" said Wharton, who was feeling as if the conversation had been in Chinese. "I'm sure Mr. Wildernesse realizes the importance of it!"—and he might have added, "Which is a damn sight more than *I* do!" However, Travers saw his assistant off, had a word or two with him outside, then came back for the balloon to go up. It went up!

"What's the idea of this joint business, Mr. Travers?"

"There isn't any. I don't give a damn what happens to the joint!"

"I see. No sewerage or lighting connections with the main lighting or drainage?"

Travers smiled, very apologetically. "Sorry! but if you're thinking a pipe was tapped to let that gas in—you're wrong! If you grub up this place by the foundations, you'll find nothing. There isn't a crack where gas could have been let in—Wildernesse'll swear to that!" Travers was getting quite excited. "What's more, I hope Braishe says he loathes the sight of the place as much as I do. I hope he suggests wiping it off the face of the earth; grubbing up the foundations and sowing salt. And I hope you'll agree with him—and clear out of the way so as not to watch it being done! I'd like to come here in a couple of days' time and see turf laid here, where we're standing now!"

Wharton shrugged his shoulders. "You're talking riddles!"

"I'm not! My God I'm not! Wharton, will you do that? If he suggests what I say, will you let him?"

"Why not? But what's the point?"

Travers suddenly looked very hopeless—even miserable. "I can't tell you. It's not a point—it's not even an intuition. When you've done something—something I can't do—then I'll tell you . . . and you'll probably laugh like blazes. Find *this* out for me— find it out in the house. Why did Fewne tip that last drink into his pocket? Why did he run like a lunatic through the snow instead of round by the hedge? Why did he write that scrawl? And why did he dance with three people only—one of them a woman he must have loathed?"

Wharton shook his head and said nothing. Franklin tried a short cut.

"If Fewne *was* murdered, the balloons did it!"

Travers smiled ironically. "That's what I thought—at first. Suppose one of his balloons was filled with that lethal ingenuity that Braishe invented. The gas was heavier than air! That particular balloon would have flopped about—not floated!"

"Yes, but the temperature of the room would have expanded the gas and made the balloon float."

"Oh, dear, no! The temperature of the balloon and the temperature of the room would have remained relative! And there's something else: we know that at least two of those balloons Fewne carried were burst during the evening—and nothing happened. Not only that: Braishe couldn't have known that Fewne was going to run amok and slash those balloons about!"

"That's right enough!" said Wharton decisively. "The balloons didn't do it." He clicked his tongue. "All the same, I can't see why he took all that trouble to do himself in—unless Braishe had dinned into him that the gas was so damnably deadly that when Fewne went mad he had it on his brain as an obsession."

"Then," said Franklin, "why didn't he take a sniff and get it over?"

"Exactly! That's where I'm beaten. Now, if Mr. Travers could say to me, 'I had a good look round that grate and fireplace and there wasn't a siphon there!' *then* there'd be something to go on!" and he looked at Travers hopefully.

"I'm afraid I can't do that. I looked in the fireplace but not round the inside. Why should I? And it was as dark as blazes." He suddenly fumbled in his waistcoat pocket. "He didn't burn anything that I could see, except—well, what do you make of these?" He produced the metal tabs. "Pair of tabs from bootlaces by the look of 'em."

"Not a pair!" corrected Wharton. "A single lace has two tabs. But why should he burn a bootlace?—unless—"

"It wasn't that!" interrupted Travers. "At least, I couldn't find a new lace in any of his shoes."

He pocketed the tabs again. "Got any ideas about that scrawl?"

"Not a one. Paradine was telling us his theory."

"Quite! It's a good theory. However . . ." and he smiled insinuatingly. "Perhaps during dinner—assuming you get any—you'll be so good as to read that synopsis I was telling you about. Then you can fill in the official form."

Wharton grunted. "The only official form I feel like filling in at the moment is my own! What about getting back? Any other key to this place? It's too cold to keep a man on duty."

Norris met them in the hall with a piece of news. Mrs. Cairns, whom he'd got to look through the clothing of the two women before the bodies went into the ambulance, had made a discovery. Inside the blouse Ransome had been wearing were three one-pound treasury notes tied round with a wisp of a handkerchief. Wharton didn't grasp the point—he couldn't be expected to. He was still trying to digest the mass of heterogeneous information he'd received from Franklin and Travers. However, he nodded to Norris: "Put 'em with the other exhibits!" and left it at that.

It was Travers who suddenly saw a gleam of daylight.

CHAPTER XVI
WHARTON DOES HIS TRICKS

TRAVERS AND FRANKLIN both went in to dinner that night. Wharton, however, definitely but courteously refused Braishe's invitation, in spite of the opportunity it might have given him for a first-hand survey, under reasonably normal conditions, of the men with whom he was soon to come in contact. The General—to give him his nickname—contented himself with a pot of tea and a plate of cold meat, then got Pollock to take him round the house; photographers and what Menzies always called "the circus" following on behind. "Quite a nice, pleasant-spoken gentleman!" the butler afterwards told Mrs. Cairns. By the time Wharton had got some idea of a first objective and had told Norris what he wanted him to get from his interviews with the servants, Travers and Franklin were available again.

That meal, in the breakfast room with a solitary footman on duty, was a most lugubrious affair. For one thing, the room was a change that kept on reminding people why they were in it at all. Then George Paradine was absent, on post-mortem work, which was a gruesome enough reminder. Worst of all, the third murder had leaked out, and there the very incompleteness of the information seemed to cause an uneasiness that set everybody to strange, distracted moments of thought, set nerves on edge, and gave the meal an atmosphere of unreality and disquietude. Nobody seemed to be hungry. Wildernesse and Challis more than once snapped at each other. Braishe was quiet in a nervy, restless sort of way, and altogether it was a pretty deadly business.

As Wharton sat waiting for Challis to come to the dining room he was thinking of the very invidious position that Travers had been forced to occupy during those two days. Yet in one matter he was doing him scant justice. When Travers, in his report, had insisted that what had struck him most was the comparative readiness of the men to be questioned about the murder of Mirabel Quest, and had deduced from it the fact that none of them was therefore guilty or else was sure of getting away with it, Wharton had an interpretation that was private and different; that Travers was such a good sort generally and so obviously not a detective that the whole lot of them—murderer included—suffered precious little disquiet on his account. In other words, Wharton, as he watched Challis enter the room, saw no reason why he should not reach safely where Travers had merely travelled hopefully.

"We want your help, Mr. Challis, please. Take a seat, will you!" and all the rest of the preliminaries.

Challis looked round like a partially deflated balloon, but he soon brightened up.

"Let me see, Mr. Challis. You're the manager-producer of the Hilarities?"

"That's right!" He checked the "old boy" in time. Travers nearly laughed.

"You're a sort of coöptimistic theatrical party, aren't you? Like the Follies when they first took a London theatre?"

"Yes, that's it!"

"I saw your last show. Remarkably good, if I might say so. What's your new one going to be like?"

"Oh, very good! Splendid, in fact!"

"Miss Quest going to be a great loss to you?"

That pulled Challis up with a jerk. "Oh, yes—I mean, of course! She'll be very difficult to replace."

"Exactly. Now to hard facts. You needn't answer my questions unless you like. There's no record being taken—as you see." He leaned forward till he caught Challis's eyes, and held them. "We're not here to discuss morals or pay the least attention to them—but may we take it that your personal and intimate relations with the deceased were . . . what they were rumoured to be?"

"I don't see what you're getting at!"

"You will!" said Wharton confidently. "Just yes or no, Mr. Challis!"

"Well—er—I'm damned if I know what you mean—but I'll say yes."

Wharton nodded. "She was rather trying at times?"

"She had the hell of a temper, if that's what you mean!"

"Quite! You'd even thought seriously of a change?"

Challis's face coloured violently. "What do you mean by a change?"

"I'll tell you," said Wharton. "Never mind who they are, but witnesses are prepared to swear that Miss Quest had a violent scene with you over—well, let's call her A. M.—who was in your spring show. She more or less gave you your choice. She'd go if the other didn't. Now, unknown to Miss Quest, you've engaged A. M. for your new show. The last time, A. M. went! This time you're prepared to stand the racket!"

"I was prepared to be master in my own show!"

"Exactly. But, tell me. Suppose the alternative had been given you again—as it certainly would have been if Miss Quest had remained alive—what would you have done?"

Challis looked down, snapped his eyes—and said nothing.

"Let me put it another way," went on Wharton. "Suppose you had been the strong man and had let Miss Quest leave the show, would she have been still agreeable to continuing in—er—any other capacity?"

Challis shuffled again as he caught the drift of the argument. His face flushed. "If you think I ... got rid of her, you're on a wrong tack. Ask Travers. He'll tell you where I was. I couldn't have done it!"

Wharton smiled benevolently. "Mr. Travers *has* told me! It would have been a remarkably ingenious feat if you *had* done it!"

"Then what are you hinting at it for?"

"I'm not. I'm handing out caps, and you're fitting them on! However, let's get to something else. Ransome—what was your opinion of her?"

"A hellcat—that's what *she* was!"

"Exactly!" He caught Challis's eyes again. "Now a question which you've *got* to answer—either here or on oath in the coroner's court. Why was Ransome alone in your bedroom with you this morning?"

It took a long time and a good deal of patience to extract that story. According to Challis—and Wharton believed him—he'd asked Ransome to keep her ears open if anything was mentioned about himself, in view of the particular relationship in which he stood with the dead woman. He'd met Ransome by appointment, and she'd told him the questions Travers had asked her. She'd gone on to say she could tell Travers quite a lot of things if she were so minded: quarrels with the dead woman and unsavoury titbits generally. Challis had anticipated that. He'd borrowed some money from Braishe, who'd some spare cash in the safe, and had coughed up three quid, to use his own words. Five minutes after, he'd seen the coast clear and gone off, leaving her to follow; the idea being that if she were seen in the room it'd cause no particular comment. On his way down to the hall he'd seen nobody.

"Where'd you go then?" asked Wharton.

"I saw Pollock and asked if he'd send in some beer. Then I went to the billiard room and knocked the balls about a bit. Then I went and found that swine Crashaw and got him to have a game."

"Know where the others were?"

"I don't . . . only Crashaw. He was in the dining room—when I found him."

"And what did Ransome do with the notes?"

"She stuck 'em down her dress."

"Tie 'em up at all?"

He hesitated for a moment. "Yes—she tied a handkerchief round 'em. Just like her—clutching hand and all that!"

Wharton got to his feet. "Well, I think that's all. You've helped us a good deal, Mr. Challis," and so on, to all the rest of the apologetics and smoothings-over that Challis rose to with really pathetic faith. When he left the room he was almost himself again.

"We've got him scared!" said Wharton. "What's your opinion? Did he kill her to save blackmail?"

"I don't think he did," said Travers, and smiled at a certain recollection. "I know Challis'd do a lot to save money, but I don't think he did that. Also, if he killed her, you can bet your life *he'd have had his three pounds back!*"

"The very point!" Wharton nodded confidently. "And that gives us a lead. She'd already put twenty pounds in her trunk. I should say that as soon as she left Challis's room she'd go straight to the trunk to put the new proceeds with the old. She was killed on the way there! If you try to work out when it was she left Challis's room, that'd give us the time when she was killed—and therefore who was absent from downstairs and might have done it."

"Did Mrs. Paradine hear anything in her room?" asked Franklin.

"She might have done if there'd been anything to hear," said Wharton. "Menzies says she was seized from behind by someone she knew and didn't suspect. She was dead and out of that window almost as quick as we're talking about it. There wasn't a print anywhere, by the way."

He put on his glasses and wrote some notes. Occasionally he put out a feeler.

"A fairly clever chap—Challis?"

"At his job—first class."

"Wildernesse was keen on her, you said?"

"'Was' is right," said Travers. "If she came to life to-night he'd bolt if she looked at him."

"And Fewne loathed her?"

"Well—" Travers hesitated—"Fewne couldn't loathe anybody; I mean he couldn't show it. He'd the most perfectly charming courtesy for everybody."

"Suffered fools gladly?"

"Yes—and the other sort, too; and they're even more trying . . . at times!"

He finished his notes, then got up and rubbed his hands at the fire. "We'll have Braishe in now; not an inquiry—just a free-and-easy! You two get up and lounge! Get your pipes alight and start chattering. Laugh like hell if there's anything to laugh at!"

Braishe must have been pleasantly surprised when he came in. Wharton was positively effusive. He congratulated, apologized, prophesied, and hypothesized. He even became mildly pathetic.

"I'm in an awkward position, Mr. Braishe. Much as I'd like to talk things over with you, I daren't! I'd be bound to drop a brick somewhere. You see, everybody in the house is a friend of yours!"

Braishe smiled as he sipped his whisky and splash.

"I don't think I'd go so far as that. In any case, one's got no friends at a time like this."

"Challis a friend of yours?"

"Yes—and no! He's a useful sort of chap . . . and his new show's a very attractive proposition. And he can be damn good company at a house party, if he likes."

"Exactly!" Wharton thought heavily. "Do you know, one thing has been troubling me a bit. Stop me if I'm on delicate ground! You and I are men of the world. We're all men of the world—except Travers."

Franklin laughed, as directed. Braishe smiled.

"Still, to be serious. Tell me. Knowing the relationships between—er—Challis and the unfortunate lady who's dead, why did you risk having her here—say, with Mrs. Paradine?"

Braishe smiled. "Aunt Celia's still in the early nineties!" Then his tone altered. "Mind you, I don't agree that things are as . . . notorious as that. People will exaggerate a lot. And you must remember she was Mrs. Fewne's sister."

"What did Fewne think of it?"

"Nothing. Why should he? Also the house party was as much for him and Mrs. Fewne as myself."

"Quite! And ideas change. People don't pay any attention to that sort of thing nowadays. And why should they?" He glared round belligerently.

"That reminds me!" said Franklin, and told the extremely risqué story of the ultra-modern house party and the bishop who had a strange experience. Travers shuddered; still, the air was cleared considerably. Then Wharton pottered round the exhibit table like a suburban gardener round his salvias. His voice suddenly lowered.

"Would you care to see the weapon ... she was killed with? It's rather an unpleasant sight."

Braishe went round at once. His eyes narrowed slightly as he looked at it, lying in the cardboard box, with the darkish stain that stopped just short of the handle. The triteness of his remark showed what he thought about it.

"Ghastly—isn't it!"

Wharton nodded. "I've seen worse. You've never seen it before—of course?"

The other looked startled, then grunted. "You mean—did it come off that display board in the entrance hall?"

"Well, we wondered. Travers tells me nobody seems to recognize it, yet it's the same pattern as some that are still there."

"Really!" Braishe didn't seem to be interested.

"We're hoping to identify some finger prints on it," went on Wharton casually.

"Finger prints! That sounds bad for somebody!"

"Hm! Yes."

"What about taking everybody's prints? Take mine as an example! I mean, nobody can grumble if you're in a position to say I've had mine done."

Wharton laughed at the idea, then allowed himself to be persuaded. And he made considerable display of labelling the sheet of paper and setting it aside as a nucleus. That concluded the visit, except that Wharton had one last question.

"How's Mrs. Fewne keeping?"

"Oh—er—bearing up very well. She doesn't know anything about . . . that other business yet."

"Good! Don't let her know ... or Mrs. Paradine, either. I must have a word with them both in the morning, if it can be managed. Say down here, at ten o'clock. Oh, and we might like to try out again that harlequin idea Travers has told me about. Might as well explode it officially. Let me have your own and Mr. Wildernesse's costumes; do you mind?"

There was a certain amount of desultory conversation till he returned with them, and a certain amount more while they made their examination. There was nothing else really to say. Each was of a stockinet material; hose that fastened round the waist by a belt of the material itself, and a tight-fitting upper garment with an opening for the head, closed by pression studs and concealed by the ruff worn high up the neck. Each had a design in lozenge pattern, the colours alone being different.

Wharton made no further reference to them when Braishe had gone, but he did ask about Braishe—his scientific standing and so on.

"I don't know that there's any enormous merit in his discovery of this gas," said Travers. "I admit he wasn't forced to work for a living, and therefore deserves credit for a certain number of laborious days. Still, he's a queer type, really. Sheds his professional outlook like a garment, I'm told. Quite a man about town—in his leisure."

"Hm! He's a fine, robust specimen, mind you. Pretty good breeding, I should say."

"What's that got to do with it?" asked Franklin curtly.

"Nothing at all!" Wharton replied mildly. "But if we had to go by his reactions at the sight of that dagger just now, I'd swear he'd never seen it before in his life. He wasn't acting. He was natural!"

"You never know!" said Franklin oracularly.

"No, but you can judge," said Wharton. He drew up the chair and lighted his pipe. "You probably noticed I was working at one idea with Braishe. What's your idea? Could Fewne have killed his sister-in-law?"

"You mean he knew just how she stood with Challis? That he was sort of cleaning the family escutcheon?"

"I think that idea's being stressed too much," broke in Travers. "Fewne couldn't have been such a fool as that. Mirabel had the opportunity of taking a short cut to where she wanted to be—on the stage; where she knew she could make good—as she did. If she took that short cut, why harp on it? She was a free agent."

Travers's defence was more vehement than Wharton anticipated. He smiled.

"Not only that!" Travers went on. "If you look round, you can find perfectly adequate reasons why everybody in this house should have killed Mirabel Quest—the women included."

Franklin laughed. "George is merely putting up Aunt Sallys to show his skill in knocking 'em over."

"That reminds me!" said Travers. He hopped up so quickly that he spoiled Wharton's retort.

"Here's that synopsis I told you about, and here are all the other people's ideas. Just add your own. It won't take you five minutes!"

A few more explanations, a lot more persuasion, and he got them down to it. The time was then about ten-thirty. Outside, it was freezing hard, and when he left them to it and went in search of Tommy Wildernesse, he found the house as good as deserted. Pollock alone was hovering about round the corridors, and there came the sound of voices from the breakfast room which Norris had commandeered as a headquarters. Every other room was in darkness.

CHAPTER XVII
THE WEAKER SEX

TRAVERS, TAKING a few minutes extra in bed the following morning, was having another look at those solutions he'd induced people to do for him. More than once he had to smile. Talk about the triumphs of the palmist! Palmistry wasn't in it with the revelations of character that had been made by that collection of persons who'd tried to put themselves into the place of Isabel Lake!

CELIA PARADINE: *Go and see a mental specialist and make her husband her hobby.*

That was Celia every time, to the vicious snap of the writing, and the confusion of ideas.

CHALLIS: *Go down and catch them in the act.*

Crude, perhaps, but very much to the point. Challis spoke as one having authority.

BRENDA FEWNE: *Go into a convent.*

Like Brenda—that; reacting to her own emotions!

GEORGE PARADINE: *See her husband and ask him plainly.*

George, that, to the last detail! But suppose the positions reversed. George tackling Celia, for instance!

TOMMY WILDERNESSE: *Write to her husband, offering to divorce him. If she thinks he is merely being generous, let him have the girl.*

That was the only one that gave Travers any difficulty. Was Tommy weaving in some sad thoughts of his own, or was it an echo of the movies?

CRASHAW: *I think she should go back and watch faces, as suggested.*

A little irony there, on Crashaw's part, surely!

BRAISHE: *Let her go and live with one of her own sisters. If her husband really wanted her, he'd guess where she was and find her.*

Travers thought he saw through that, and yet, in some peculiar manner, it disturbed him. Braishe had evidently put to the problem a scientific mind; he'd thought things out. That was the disturbing point; though precisely why, Travers couldn't say; unless, perhaps, that it showed Braishe's mind as one that couldn't relax; that it was *ready* to think things out.

WHARTON: *Have a good cry, get it over, then go home again.*

Travers chuckled. Wharton had probably meant to put, "Have a good cup of tea," and so on. And he remembered that he'd never met *Mrs.* Wharton.

FRANKLIN: *Engage a private detective and read his report.*

Travers didn't smile at that, for an excellent reason, he was actually shaking his head over it when Franklin's voice came from the other end of the room.

"Wonder what the General's been doing all night. Bet he had the whole circus there with him!"

"He'd want a couple to keep the samovar going!" said Travers. "Did you hear them outside, shortly after we turned in? I should say they were doing that harlequin business."

Franklin hopped out and had a look at the weather. "Snow's stopped. Thought of anything new yourself?"

"Not really. Unless I've discovered why you gave me a certain answer to that conundrum of mine. Quite a coincidence there, by the way!"

"Really!"

"Yes. I wrote practically the same answer myself! Notice anything about the whole of those answers?"

"You mean the revelation of character?"

"That's it. So were yours and mine; perfect warning to people like Wharton and yourself who profess to be above prejudice!

You're the head of a detective bureau. I'm an interested party—more or less. Very well, then! We both thought in terms of bread and butter—and Durangos Limited. We forgot Fewne!"

"But your advice was to imagine we were that woman—what's her name?"

"Isabel Lake—the heroine. I know that, but she *was* Fewne. She merely moved as he directed. If you say she didn't, that she obeyed her own impulses, then I say Fewne created those impulses."

"I wish to God you wouldn't do that devil's advocate business!" snapped Franklin. "How the devil do *you* know what I'd say? In any case, you're too highbrow for me. If I'd put the truth on that paper, I'd have said I'd wring the other woman's neck!"

"If you'd said that, I should have—Damn it, there I go again!" He laughed. "What about getting down to breakfast and hearing the latest?"

Practically everybody seemed to have gone when they got down. Franklin stopped for a word with Norris, and Travers pushed on to the breakfast room, where William was clearing away the ruins of a meal. He didn't know where the gentleman was. In the pagoda, he thought. Travers was halfway through his meal before Franklin came in, and clean through it when Wharton looked round the door.

"Had a good night?" Travers asked him.

"Off and on. Cleared the air a bit."

Travers drew back his chair. "Come and have a warm up! That pagoda's frightfully cold—in the morning!"

Franklin laughed. "Not bad that, George, for one who's not a man of the world!"

"Mr. Travers has his moments," said Wharton, perfectly unperturbed. "To be perfectly candid, I *have* been over there. I hoped to find some memoranda in his writing desk, but either he didn't keep notes or else he burnt 'em. All the information I got was his check book. He drew a check on self for seventy-five pounds, seven weeks ago, and you found about four pounds on him, all told."

"What's the inference?" asked Franklin.

"You'll hear that later. Think of anything else relative to Mrs. Fewne?"

"I don't think I have," said Travers. "The main point, of course, is how Ransome got that twenty pounds—and why."

"Exactly! Now, then. Mrs. Fewne's coming down to the drawing room at ten. I want you to be there, just to make small talk and be decorative. She'll want something of the sort."

"Right-ho!" said Travers. "Give me a holler when you're ready!"

That was not before another half hour. When Travers went in, Wharton was nodding heavily; probably breathing out some heartfelt sympathy or other. Brenda looked very much her old self; paler, perhaps, and a bit heavy eyed. The slight droop of the mouth took away all that aggressive aloofness, but the face itself was as perfect as ever. Travers, the old, small antagonisms disappearing in a flash, felt a certain sort of pathos as the eyes looked tragically into his.

"Awfully glad to see you, Brenda. You must stay down here now . . . and forget things."

She smiled faintly but said nothing. Travers was reproaching himself for ever having thought her cold . . . and virginally inhuman. Then Wharton's voice cut in.

"I was telling Mrs. Fewne that we're all here to help her. And we want her to help us—just for a minute or two."

"That's it. Anything we can do, we will." He drew his chair up between them. "I suppose Wharton hasn't advised you to have what he calls 'a good cup of tea'?"

She looked rather puzzled. Travers explained Wharton's weakness and managed to make her smile again. Wharton thought things promising enough for an opening.

"You've been away a long time, Mrs. Fewne, I believe?"

"Away!" The grey eyes opened innocently. "Oh, yes. Some people asked me to go to Switzerland with them—as a guest, of course. I only got back on the Sunday."

"You were away for about six weeks?"

"Yes—about that."

"Then you stayed in town with your sister?"

"Yes. ... She was coming down here."

Travers watched her anxiously at the first mention of the tragedy, but he needn't have been anxious. The face seemed rather more wistful, but there wasn't a sign of tears. If anything, the old level-eyed look seemed to come back.

Wharton nodded, and looked very appreciative of nothing in particular. Then he took on his most consolatory tone.

"Your husband's sad . . . most tragic death, must have been a terrible shock to you. You had no suspicions that—er—things were worrying him to such an extent that he might take his own life?"

She stammered a faint, "No-o!"

"His letters to you were cheerful?"

"Oh, yes, quite cheerful. He was hoping a lot from the new book." She hesitated slightly. "I thought he was just a bit dispirited at times."

"Have you a—er—letter that illustrates that? Not too intimate a one, of course!"

"Oh, I couldn't dream of . . ."

Wharton smiled. "Not to keep. Just to see!"

She shook her head and bit her lip nervously. Wharton let that point pass.

"You won't think me impertinent, Mrs. Fewne, when I suggest that monetary matters may have worried him—perhaps, a little?"

"Yes . . . perhaps they did. You see, we were really . . . very poor, considering . . ."

"Considering the people with whom you'd been used to associate!"

"Yes." She smiled gratefully. "But things were much better. The book sold quite well."

"I'm very glad to hear it." He nodded with satisfaction. "Mr. Fewne didn't have a lot of extravagances?"

"Oh, no! He thought most about his work."

"Exactly! Strictly between ourselves: it was expensive for him, your holiday?"

"Oh, no! Not really. I had to have some money, of course—for clothes."

"Quite! Now, Mrs. Fewne; we've had to go into all these matters. Your husband drew a check for seventy-five pounds on the eve of your holiday."

She looked startled for a moment, then nodded quickly. "Yes, I had to have some clothes. I told you that." She gave a deprecating smile. "Only fifty pounds!"

"Then you must have gone rather carefully!" broke in Travers.

"I did. I had to!"

"And your birthday was about three weeks ago?"

That really surprised her. "How did you know that?"

"I didn't. Only there was just one other counterfoil after that check. It showed ten pounds—and was made out to B. I guessed that was you!"

Somehow Travers didn't think she liked Wharton's methods, in spite of the half smile that accompanied her comment.

"Yes . . . he wanted me to get something for myself; something I might like."

Wharton nodded. "Now, just one last matter. It's got to be mentioned, so we might just as well get it over and done with! Precisely why did your sister want to change rooms with you?"

"I don't know—quite. She said she liked the room I had."

"And why did you give in to her?"

She shook her head wearily. "I knew . . . well, we were with other people. Anything was better than unpleasantness."

"Quite! And when your sister reminded you of the money you owed her, did you think that was a sort of blackmail?"

"Blackmail!" She gave him a look that made him lower his eyes. "Is that a reflection on my sister—or myself?"

"On neither, Mrs. Fewne. I ask you to believe that. All I mean is that your husband might not have been very pleased to be told you were in your sister's debt."

"Does that matter so much . . . now?"

"I don't know that it does." Wharton was looking decidedly uncomfortable. "But just one last question. Did your sister take the money?"

"She did . . . only she didn't! I mean, it wasn't her money really. It was Ransome's!"

"Ransome's! You mean you borrowed from Ransome?"

"Surely you don't think that of me! Mirabel offered to lend me money—but she could never keep money. When I had to go to her, she had to go to Ransome. I didn't know it—till that night when she told me. That's why I gave it to Ransome the next morning. I felt I . . . wanted to get rid of the money . . . to forget all the awful things . . . all but the good ones." Her eyes filled with tears. As she turned her head away Travers saw her lip quiver. He made a motion to Wharton, then got to his feet. Wharton rose too.

"That's all, Brenda. Sorry it's been so . . . rotten for you! Let me take you upstairs."

Wharton hobbled forward to open the door. As she passed, he took her hand.

"Cheer up, Mrs. Fewne! And thank you for helping us. Er—ask Mrs. Paradine if she can spare a moment, Mr. Travers, will you?"

He closed the door behind them, then made his way back to the fire again, shaking his head as if at a loss to know just where his questions had led him. In three minutes Travers came back.

"She's feeling better now. Mrs. Paradine'll be down in a minute."

Wharton nodded. "She's a plucky woman—or a coldblooded one!"

"Women like Brenda don't shriek," said Travers rather curtly. "She's had two days to cry in . . . alone."

"So she has," said Wharton gravely. "And she's what I'd call a really beautiful woman; sort of unapproachable."

"Oh, no, she's not, George! She's got a heart underneath—don't you delude yourself!"

"I know. Fewne thought so. Paradine told me he gave her everything and kept nothing."

"Well, wouldn't *you* do as much?"

"I don't know." Wharton spoke more to himself than to Travers. "Perhaps I would . . . but my wife wouldn't take it!"

Travers suddenly saw a glimmer of sense in Wharton's questions. "Is that an aspersion on Mrs. Fewne?"

"Not at all. But she was pretty poor when he married her—the daughter of a country vicar." He changed the subject. "By the way, those women know what happened to Ransome. Paradine let it out last night!"

"I say, that's bad. Do you know, I rather guessed as much, just now, upstairs." Then a sudden question. "When'd you get all this from Paradine?"

"Rang him up at Levington—before breakfast, to hear how things were going."

Celia Paradine came in under full sail and was far more gracious to Wharton than Travers had anticipated. She had clearly decided that the occasion was one when a certain amount of nicely graded unbending would not be amiss. Travers smiled to himself more than once, but more often felt a glow of affection. If the heavens had fallen, Celia would have contemplated the ruins. It took more than a murder or two to scare her—particularly with Brenda and Ho-Ping to be mothered.

Wharton regarded the Pekinese with some interest and put out his hand as if to rub its ears, but at the curled lip and incipient snarl shot his hand back in a hurry.

"Poor darling! He's so distressed this morning! He misses his master!" explained Celia.

"Dr. Paradine'll be here for tea, at the latest," said Wharton. "It's been a responsible time for him, Mrs. Paradine!"

"And you've been simply splendid, Celia!" added Travers.

"I! Rubbish! I've been scared to death. Daren't put my nose outside my own room!"

"Mrs. Fewne seems to be bearing up well," remarked Wharton.

"Very well!" Her tone was one of approval. "Terrible shock at first, but, there, she's young. She'll get over it!"

"They were a happy couple?"

"Most affectionate! He adored her, and she simply worshipped him. And admired him. We all did."

"Rather well connected, his people, weren't they?"

"Oh, very! Lady Barbara—his mother—was an Alveston! No money, but frightfully old—as you know."

Wharton nodded comprehendingly, then, "Well, Mrs. Paradine, we mustn't keep you long. Just one or two things you might help us with—things we couldn't very well ask Mrs. Fewne for fear of distressing her. For instance, has she told you what she did when the light failed?"

"Oh, yes! She suddenly remembered she'd left her bag down there, where we were."

"And didn't she see her husband down there?"

"She did! Most peculiar, if you ask me! Unless he was mad, as George said."

"How do you mean 'peculiar'?" asked Wharton earnestly.

She shrugged her shoulders. "The man didn't speak to her! And he must have seen her, because he came close up—and there was a candle there!"

"Hm! . . . And the quarrel with her sister. Do you know anything about that?"

"Quarrel!" She snorted. "It takes two to make a quarrel, Mr. Wharton! Brenda's of *my* opinion. There's nothing so undignified as brawling."

"Exactly! My own views entirely. And, of course, sisters can't be alike. You slept pretty well yourself, that night?"

"Too well!"

"You're convinced that last—er—health you drank, was drugged?"

"I'm certain of it! Everybody's certain of it!"

"Quite! We shall have to inquire into that later. I hope we didn't disturb you last night with our experiments on the landing. Tell me—" he leaned forward confidentially—"you'd swear you saw a man in harlequin costume that night—as you told Mr. Travers?"

"Swear it! Of course I'd swear it! Haven't I the evidence of my own senses?"

Wharton turned to Travers. "Just what I told you! I knew Mrs. Paradine couldn't be deceived!" Then he rose. "We're very grateful to you, Mrs. Paradine, very grateful! And in more ways than one." Wharton was fond of little obscurities like that. "And we shan't bother to trouble you with inquests: not that you wouldn't be prepared to do all in your power—because I know you would!"

Travers, with an ironical smile, watched him shepherd her out; then pulled out his pipe and got his back to the fire. Wharton found the same smile on his face when he returned.

"Well?" asked Travers.

"Well what?"

"What did you mean by shamelessly playing me off against Celia Paradine?"

Wharton waved his hand with a gesture of superb dismissal. "Pure diplomacy, my boy." His tone changed. "You heard what she said about that harlequin? There wasn't a sign of blood or cleaning on either of those costumes!"

Travers nodded.

"They've gone away now—for detailed inspection. Tell me. Why should that harlequin have gone across to Wildernesse's room? Was it, as you hinted, to throw suspicion on him?"

"I've changed that view," said Travers. "Why should Braishe want to throw suspicion on Wildernesse? *He* didn't want Mirabel. He didn't want Wildernesse out of the way. . . . But aren't you forgetting the other side of the problem? Suppose it was Brenda Fewne that should have been killed!"

"If that's so, then you or Franklin or Fewne did the murder, because the others knew of the change of rooms! No. We'll exhaust one possibility first. Unless—" and he gave the other a wily look—"you can tell me why anybody should want to kill Mrs. Fewne . . . compared with the several who'd have been glad to see her sister out of the way?"

"I know no reason. If I had one, I'd put it up to you."

"I'm sure you would!" Wharton told him, and almost looked as if he believed himself. "But of course you believe Braishe doped that drink!"

"Yes. Perhaps I do. One thing I didn't tell you was that he made considerable show about being sleepy and the nasty taste in his mouth next morning."

"More show than others?"

"To be fair—no! Still, he did complain very patently."

"Fewne tipped his into his pocket, you said?"

"Either that or an earlier one. But why not have the coat analyzed—to see if the drink was doped or not?"

Wharton looked very apologetic. "As a matter of fact, I've sent it away already." He got up again. "What are you doing now?"

Travers smiled. "I take it you mean, in the immediate future! At this very moment, however, I'm wondering why, with the prints on that dagger, you don't arrest Braishe?"

"Hm! Finger prints don't lie. Isn't that so?"

Travers nodded. "So I'm told!"

"Well, *that's precisely why I'm not arresting him!*"

Travers was puzzled. "What's your riddle?"

"Riddle! There isn't one. If there is, it isn't harder than the one you set me, in the pagoda. . . . However, what *are* you going to do?"

"I'm going to get out of this house for a bit. If the road's clear, I'm going as far as the village. Why don't you come? Do you the world of good!"

Wharton shook his head. "Sorry! I'd love to. But I must see Norris."

CHAPTER XVIII
CRUMBS FROM THE TABLE

WHATEVER TRAVERS had been thinking out during his hour's exercise, the fact remains that immediately after lunch he hunted up Wharton again.

"I want you to do something for me," he said. "I'll tell you why afterwards. Is it possible for me to be excused those inquests?"

Wharton thought it over; hemmed and hawed, then reckoned it *might* be managed. After all, there'd be merely formal proceedings for the purpose principally of burial orders—except in the case of Fewne, which ostensibly would be finished with. But what were Travers's reasons?

Travers blinked away as he polished his glasses. "There are things I feel I *must* inquire into about Fewne. I'd like to know just what he did with his time while he was doing no writing. I've gathered he went out two or three times, and I want to know where and why. I'd like to see his publisher—and I'd like you to see his solicitor."

"He'll be down to-morrow morning."

"Splendid! And his bank manager. And I want to find out how he spent the balance of that big check. There wasn't anything here to spend it on—and he never went out till last week."

Wharton nodded. "All very useful information, of course. And after all, every bit of string has two ends. You prefer Fewne's; I prefer Ransome's. That doesn't deny that Fewne leads to Ransome."

"As I see it," said Travers, "Fewne, Ransome, and Brenda Fewne are sides of a triangle—with two sides gone. What's left for you to get hold of?"

"Plenty!" said Wharton grimly. "It's Mrs. Fewne I'm relying on. I've got a whole lot of awkward questions to ask her yet."

"Such as?"

"Well, how she spent her money!"

"Good Lord! Why, a woman like that could spend a hundred quid in necessaries without wasting a sou!"

"She wasn't forced to go on that holiday. Holidays are never force-work—except by doctor's orders. And why did her sister use those particular names?"

Travers shrugged his shoulders. "Merely the unbridled vocabulary of a vulgarian."

"Why did she borrow at all, from her sister?"

"That's got me. But why *do* women run into debt?"

"And why did Fewne have three dances all that evening, as you pointed out yourself; two with one girl—"

"Cecily Harrise, you mean. That was just for fun. I saw the whole thing."

"Very well. And the other with his sister-in-law!"

"You're forcing my hand," said Travers. "I think I know why he danced with *her*. It was to be in a position to flick that note to Tommy Wildernesse. I think he wrote the note and threw it; and I think he made some remark about Wildernesse so that she appeared to be smiling at him at the time."

Wharton looked serious. "Why did he do that? If it was he who lured Wildernesse to the loggia, then it must have been to commit the murder. Even then it doesn't mean Wildernesse wasn't in the way!"

"Don't ask me why!" said Travers. "I might say lots of preposterous things—that Fewne killed her and his wife; that he and his wife did it between them." He shook his head. "I know one thing—and only one. Something keeps telling me to find out all about Fewne. No matter which way I turn, I can't get away from it. That's why I asked to be excused inquests—and that's why I'd like to question all of the people in the house—if I have your permission."

Wharton waved his hand. "Get on with it—and good luck to you!" He suddenly shot out a finger. "I'll make a small bet—that we meet at the crossroads!"

"I won't bet," said Travers. "But I hope we do. If I go up from Fewne, and you come down from Fewne, won't the meeting-place be Brenda Fewne?"

Wharton nodded. "If you only knew it, that's the wisest thing you've said to-day!"

Wharton as he heard the case as Travers put it, showed every disposition to help. Travers was convincing about those preliminaries. He painted in colours—almost pure gold leaf, in fact—the admitted fact it would be important to know how Fewne intended to use that book. A clamorous public was waiting for facts—they wanted Fewne; not Fewne and a collaborator. Fewne might have mentioned his intentions to someone in town; that was why it was so important to know just where he'd been and what he'd done.

"What I can tell you," said Braishe, "is this: I'd planned on the Friday night that I was going to go to a short conference on the Monday. I wanted to call in at town on my way up—Colonial Office, for one thing—and I wanted to see some people about preliminaries on the Sunday. What happened was that just as I was leaving on the Saturday morning, Denis came over in his dressing gown and asked if I could hang on for a bit, as he'd like to go to town too. Of course, I said I'd wait—and I did."

"Did he mention why—on the journey down, for instance?"

"He didn't. Now you come to mention it, I wondered why he didn't, at the time. He was a taciturn sort of chap, you know, always mooning about."

"I know. 'In worlds unrealized.' Where'd you drop him?"

"At my club—the Isis. That reminds me. One curious thing did happen there: I told him where I was going and said I might be back there for lunch at twelve-thirty, so he'd better look in then. It so happened that I couldn't call at the club till half-past one, and they told me he'd been there twice, asking for me urgently, but well after the time we'd arranged. On the Tuesday night, when I got back, I asked him about it: why he wanted me so urgently and so on. What do you think he said?"

"Lord knows!"

"He said, 'Did I?'—just like that. Then he sort of pulled himself together and said, 'Oh, yes! I wanted to ask you if you'd mind if I went out in the car with Bruce.' What do you think of that!"

"Who's Bruce?"

"The chauffeur. I left him behind with the small car and drove the Daimler to town myself."

"I see. You mean he needn't have asked that!"

"Precisely! What was mine was his—and he knew it. He mumbled something about getting out more; wanted some local colour or something. Scenery, I gathered."

It appeared to be all that Braishe knew. Travers judicially noted it all down while he had it on his mind, then went in search of Bruce. The chauffeur was a youngish man—about twenty-five—and swallowed up every preliminary that Travers gave him.

"Well, sir, I met him at Levington station by the eight-thirty on the Saturday night. No, sir, he didn't have parcels or anything with him. Just come back and went, sir. How'd I know about him going, sir? The master told me when I brought the car round on Saturday morning."

"And what did Mr. Fewne talk about on the way to the station?"

"Nothing in particular, sir. Then he said, 'Bruce, I need you to take me in the car to Folkestone on Monday after an early lunch,' and that's all he said, sir, so on Monday morning, sir, I sent word by William to see if he'd changed his mind, but it was all right, sir, so after lunch we went to Folkestone."

Travers suddenly felt extraordinarily curious. Surely late to start off on a journey like that! And with the nights drawing in at about half-past three!

"What did he talk about on the way there?"

"Not much, sir. He sat alongside me in the coupé, and he hardly opened his mouth. He seemed a bit preoccupied about something, sir, but he didn't tell me what. But he did say, sir, that was he was going to have to go to a house in Kensington. I remember that, sir, the last job was there. Then he said he was going to have a look round the antique shops to see if he could find anything suitable in the way of furniture, sir."

"Good! What happened when you got there?"

"Well, sir, I put up at the Royal, and he said I was to be ready at tea-time. Well, tea-time come, sir, and he didn't turn up; and six o'clock, sir, and seven, and I was getting the wind up pretty bad when he rolls up at half-past. He told me to start right away, sir, and all the way home he sat there and didn't say a word; just grunted if I spoke to him, sir; so I got fed up and kept my mouth shut. When we got in he gave me a quid, sir; and he said he had a splitting headache, and he was sorry he'd been—well, not chatty, sir."

"I see. And how'd you like him—personally?"

"Mr. Fewne, sir? A toff he was, sir; one of the best!"

Travers nodded. "Anything else happen?"

"Yes, sir. Next morning he come to me and asked me if I could tell him where he could hire a car. I told him he needn't do that, sir: I could go anywhere he wanted. Then he said, sir, he wanted to go somewhere alone, so I told him Downers', in Levington Church Street, and he gave me ten bob, sir, and said I wasn't to say anything about it—and I haven't sir, not till you just asked me!"

Travers nodded again. "Between ourselves, where *did* he go?"

"A chum of mine who's at Downers', sir, told me he had to drive him to Folkestone, sir. They went about eleven and got back just after three."

"And what happened there?"

"Don't know, sir—only they didn't put up at the Royal but the Bristol, and Joe—that's my chum, sir—didn't clap eyes on him from the time he got out till the time he came back."

Travers thought for a moment. "And when did Mr. Braishe get back that week?"

"Tuesday, sir—just before dinner."

"Hm! Anything else happen between you and Mr. Fewne?"

"No, sir . . . that is, not between me and him, sir, only on the Wednesday—day you come down, sir—while I was at the station, they told me in the kitchen they'd seen Mr. Fewne coming from the garage."

"The garage! What was he doing there?"

"Well, sir, I thought he was looking for me to tell me something, but as he gave me that ten bob to keep quiet, sir, I kept my mouth shut about it."

That was all for Bruce. Travers took best part of an hour to get it all down, then joined the others at tea, then hunted up Pollock. There he found himself to a certain extent forestalled. Wharton had reaped that field—but he hadn't raked or gleaned.

"As I told Mr. Wharton, sir," said Pollock, "I knew Mr. Fewne had something on his mind. I saw him sit in that chair of his, sir, and look at the fire as if he was mesmerized. He was more like a corpse, sir, or one of those mummies."

Travers nodded sympathetically. "And the Saturday morning when the letters came. Was there one for him?"

"No, sir. Nothing, sir!"

"You sure of that?"

"Positive, sir! I distribute the letters, sir. I should have seen it dispatched to the pagoda personally, sir."

"When did a letter come?"

"There was a letter on the Monday, sir . . . and a parcel on the Wednesday night."

"Good! Now, don't be offended, Pollock. I'm not going to suggest spying or anything ridiculous like that, but do you remember the writing on the envelope?"

"I do, sir—and I know who it was from, sir! It was from Mrs. Fewne, because he told me so, sir—in so many words. He tapped his pocket, sir—all smiles—and he said, sir, 'Mrs. Fewne'll be down on Wednesday, Pollock!' and I said, 'Very good, sir. Pleased to hear it, sir!'"

"And Mr. Fewne wasn't in to lunch on the Tuesday. You were surprised at that?"

"Well, I was in a way, sir. It was just a bit unusual, sir, if I may say so. He'd been here for five weeks and never left the house—and then he goes out three times in a matter of days, sir."

"Between ourselves, Pollock, what was your opinion of him—as a man?"

"As a man, sir?" Pollock screwed up his mouth and rubbed his chin. "Well, sir, he was a gentleman, sir! And when I say that, I mean a real gentleman—like yourself, sir!"

Travers blushed, mumbled his thanks—and disappeared up the stairs. Franklin was in the room, frowning over some notes.

"Hallo! Where've you been all this time?"

"Folkestone, principally!"

"Really! . . . Oh, I see. Why the devil can't you be direct occasionally?" Travers thought for a moment he was really annoyed. Then he told him all about it. Franklin was hopelessly at sea.

"Damned if I can make head or tail of it! The first time, he seems to have gone to look over antique shops—as Bruce said."

"But I don't see even that!" said Travers. "Why didn't he go *before* lunch? He must have been very much of an ignoramus. Even I—and I say it with all humility—wouldn't trust my judgment of antique furniture in artificial light."

Franklin grunted, then changed the subject.

"Wharton's sent Norris to town."

"Really! What for?"

"Don't know. He's got to be back for the inquests to-morrow. Wharton's got one of his enigmatical fits on, but I rather gathered he's trying to see what happened in Switzerland."

"Good God! What on earth for?"

Franklin shrugged his shoulders. "Don't know—unless he wants to see how much money she spent. Oh, and something else he said to me: I happened to say Fewne rushed through the snow because he'd already lost control. 'Not necessarily!' says George. 'He might have been laying a deliberate trail—making footmarks that nobody could miss!'"

"What was behind it?"

"Lord knows! He's just got a fit on—as I told you.... What about getting down? Bit cold up here."

"You push on!" Travers told him. "I'll be down in a minute."

It was several minutes that he spent, lying back deep in the chair with his eyes shut. What actually lay behind all that information of the afternoon he had no idea whatever. In a way, that was a very pleasing thought. If he'd had to set off on Fewne's trail with a straight road to follow, there'd have been no thrill. As it was, what he'd listened to had been one continual mystery. At every step, Fewne had done unusual things without a suggestion of motive. There was not *one* mystery to trace but half a dozen! In Folkestone itself there seemed to be at least five distinct problems—the time of the first visit, the lateness of the return, the taciturnity on the way home, the bribing of Bruce, and the next day's visit. And all in the absence of Braishe. And Braishe knew nothing about it! Travers nodded with satisfaction. Folkestone it should be—and first thing in the morning! Then he went to find Wharton and make his report.

Palmer brought the Isotta round to the front porch the following morning, and as Travers came across the hall, Wharton joined him for a final word.

"I'll ring up the station at Folkestone," he said. "After all, there's no knowing when you might want the help of the police."

"Thanks very much!" Travers got in. "Suppose you can't do anything to make Crashaw talk? Make somebody commit himself in writing, for instance?"

"That'll be all right!" nodded Wharton. Then he mumbled something. Then cleared his throat. "So you really expect to get something definite—about Fewne! Er—ever read the Bible nowadays?"

Travers laughed. "You mean ... as prose? ... or what?"

"As anything you like. Remember the story of the ewe lamb?"

"The ewe lamb?" Travers thought furiously. "There was something about a lost lamb—no! that wasn't it. And the lamb caught in a thicket—no! that was a ram!"

"Sorry, but I'm afraid I don't."

"Hm!" said Wharton and made a wry face. "That's a pity. You might have found it useful!"

He drew back. Travers looked at him curiously—then pushed out the clutch.

PART II
THE SOLUTION

CHAPTER XIX
STRANGE CONDUCT OF AN AUTHOR

As TRAVERS DROVE the Isotta to Folkestone that morning, he was feeling quite a different person from the buoyant individual of the previous night, who had rejoiced at mysteries and counted on safety in numbers. The dangerous surface of the road was causing him far less anxiety than the realization that every action Fewne had taken at Folkestone could reasonably be accounted for. Fewne was taciturn, absent-minded, and subject to nervous headaches: that accounted for a lot in itself. Then he might have been displeased with either Bruce's driving or his attitude and have hired a car for his second trip; and he'd tipped the chauffeur to keep quiet in case Braishe heard about the change and felt justifiably offended.

As for Wharton's hint that Fewne had left a *deliberate* track in the snow, that, in Travers's opinion, was manifestly absurd. Whatever Fewne had done before he left the house for the pagoda, he'd had no hand in the murder of Mirabel Quest. That theory of cleaning the family escutcheon was gorgeously romantic but incredibly remote from possibility. A much stronger urge would have been needed to make Fewne commit murder, and Travers very much doubted if anything on earth could have done it. And Fewne *wasn't* the harlequin. And he'd been murdered himself, under circumstances as fantastic as a nightmare. That part Travers *was* sure of. He knew who had done it—and how, or he thought he did; moreover, once a motive was established he'd put his cards on the table. As for Wharton's cryptic remarks about ewe lambs, Travers wasn't so sure. The General never leaped before he'd looked; every reason therefore to take a safe line by being enigmatical.

He garaged the car at the Bristol, ordered his lunch, then found the police station. Of the two photos of Fewne which he'd managed to get hold of, he kept one and produced the other. The superintendent, after Wharton's phone message, was keen enough. He suggested rushing through a couple of dozen reproductions and handing them out to such of his men who might have run across the original. Travers thought the idea a capital one, said he'd look in again after lunch, then started off with a complete list of the antique shops in the town.

The first shop was soon found, and the proprietor was in. Travers pulled out his photo and delivered the official speech he'd rehearsed for the occasion.

"Sorry to be a nuisance to you, but I'm making certain inquiries on behalf of the police authorities. Superintendent Dollis will give you my credentials, if you ring him up. All we want to know is whether this gentleman called in here last Monday or Tuesday."

The proprietor had a quick look at the hander-over of the photo, then decided to dispense with phoning. The photo itself appeared to interest him.

"Yes, sir; the gentleman came in—on the Monday afternoon. I attended to him myself."

After that came a quarter of an hour of exhaustive inquiries, and all that could be gathered was this: Fewne had entered the shop so diffidently that the owner had at once placed him as an inexperienced amateur. He was, nevertheless, a "perfect gentleman"; had said he was shortly furnishing a smallish flat in town and wanted one or two nice pieces—an oak dresser and a bureau, for instance. The latter wasn't available in the quality required, but a Georgian dresser with shelved top was actually set aside for the "Denis Fewne" of the card, who agreed to send in a day or two the address where the dresser was to be sent, if his wife, whom he was bringing along, decided to have it. That was all. The conduct of the gentleman was normal throughout. He did not complain of a headache.

Here something important is to be noted. It was the Royal from which Fewne started out on the Monday. Proceed from there a hundred yards due south, and you arrive at the police station. Turn sharp left, and you are in the High Street. Cross the road, and fifty yards on, with windows so prominent that the most uninformed of amateurs could tell it, was the antique shop Travers had just quitted. Proceeding in the same direction, a hundred yards on, came the next. Travers entered, produced his photo, said his little piece, then got his first surprise.

"Yes, sir; the gentleman came in on the Monday. He particularly wanted a bureau."

"Did you sell him one?"

"No, sir; not actually sell it. Here is the actual bureau," and he pointed to a Chippendale effort which the dealers euphemistically call "late." "He liked the look of this one and asked if I'd give him an option for a couple of days, when his wife would be coming along to see it."

"And you haven't heard from him since?"

"Oh, yes! He came in again on the Tuesday morning and said he'd like another look. I showed him this secret drawer . . . and this one—"

"That's all right," said Travers. "No need to show 'em. Did he give you an answer?"

"No, sir; he said he'd wait till his wife had seen it. Mind you, sir, it's a very nice piece!"

Travers smiled. "Oh, quite! Anything happen?"

"Yes. On the Tuesday he took a poker to show his wife!"

"A what!"

"A poker, sir. You see, on the Tuesday he had another look at something he'd taken a fancy to on the Monday." He led the way to the back of the shop. "This pierced fender and set of irons to match. He said he liked them and he'd probably have them. Then on the Tuesday I said to him, 'And what about the fender, sir?' He said he couldn't bring his wife over for a day or two, but might he have a look over the oddments—this lot, sir—to see if there was a poker, as his wife had laughed at him when he said there were such things as antique pokers." He smiled. Travers smiled in keeping. "So he found one up, sir, and I let him have it for five bob, and he took it with him. Oh, and something else: I had to give him a receipt which distinctly said, for his wife's benefit, that the poker was a genuine antique."

"What was it like, exactly?"

"Ah! there you've got me." He fussed round the collection of odd candlesticks, trivets, bellows, and fire gadgets till he found what he wanted. "Something like this it was. Of course, I wouldn't swear to it."

"Exactly!" Travers had a look at it and saw—nothing but a poker. "Tell me," he went on; "did you pick out the poker or did he?"

"He picked it out."

"And any difference in his attitude on the Tuesday? Was he nervous or strange in any way?"

The other frowned. "Can't say he was. Mind you, the gentleman was a bit nervy, but I put that down to the fact that he didn't know very much."

Travers set off again. A hundred yards or so on his left was the post office, and well beyond this the third of the shops he had to visit. This time he drew blank. The proprietor called in his wife and an assistant, but neither had seen the gentleman in question. Then, finally, well off the main road, he found the last shop—a small affair with a mixture of modern and pseudo-antique. Here again he drew absolutely blank.

During lunch he tried to think it all out. Apparently Fewne *had* set off for Folkestone with a very definite object in view. He had mentioned at the first shop two pieces of furniture he must have planned to fit into his new flat. At the first he'd found one; at the second the possibility of the other. What would he do then? It was getting well on to the time he'd given Bruce as that of the return, otherwise he'd have sought out the other shops for a second string to his bureau. But he *hadn't* gone to the other shops; therefore he'd remembered Bruce was expecting him. And he *hadn't* gone back to the Royal; he'd disappeared for another three hours. Where—and why?

Finding no answer, he tested the Tuesday. Fewne hadn't gone to see his dresser again: he'd gone to see the bureau. He'd therefore made up his mind about the dresser but not about the bureau. But wouldn't it have been more natural to have a look at the remaining shops in the town to see if they had a bureau more likely to suit him?

Then there'd been that poker—purchased on the plea that he and his wife had had an argument! Travers checked his smile—

then frowned. After all, why not? The argument might have taken place months before. *But*, if Fewne had taken that poker with him, then what had he done with it? Not sent it by post. That would have been absurd, with his wife coming down the next day. Then where was it? Not in the pagoda—he'd swear to that.

All the same, he decided to test that one point. At the police station he got through to Levington Town Hall. Mrs. Fewne was still there, so Wharton told him. And that was all that happened. She knew nothing whatever about a poker—and, as far as she remembered, had never had an argument with a soul about one. Wharton's tone, as he reported it, showed that he knew still less.

Travers was puzzled. Within half an hour he was to be more so. While he'd been phoning, the superintendent had seemed to be waiting expectantly, and as soon as the receiver was hooked up he produced his news.

"We've got something about your man, sir. He was seen going towards Dover—about four-thirty. My man's here if you'd like to question him. And as he isn't so sure, would you mind giving extra details about dress and so on?"

The constable's story was this: At about four-fifteen on the Monday he'd been on duty at the end of Albert Road and had noticed a man, whom he now definitely recognized. The man appeared to be under the influence of drink, since his gait was none too steady and he was muttering to himself. He watched the man till he got out of sight, along the cliff road towards Dover. Later on that evening he'd met a colleague who'd been on duty still farther along that road, and he'd seen the gentleman still proceeding in the same direction.

That was all the news at the moment. Travers sauntered back to the smoke room of the hotel and sat and thought things over. Immediately after leaving that second shop Fewne had seen or heard something that had sent him, half distracted, away from the definitely appointed place of meeting towards the open country. What had been the deciding impulse that had set him going? Had there been no external cause? Was the whole thing a sudden breakdown, temporary in character, foreshadowing the far more serious one that was to come a few days later? Travers wondered. Everything was so hypothetical and problematic that conjecture seemed a waste of time.

Then he found himself looking at that rough map they'd drawn for him at the police station earlier in the day. His eye ran along that main thoroughfare—first shop, second shop . . . post office! Had that anything to do with it? Was it a letter Fewne had received? If so, it must have been *poste restante.*

He hopped up, grabbed his hat and coat, and fairly scurried along the High Street. At the post office he saw the postmaster and said his little piece. This time his credentials were checked before inquiries were made.

"No, sir. Nobody of that name."

"On neither Monday nor Tuesday?"

"No, sir. Neither day."

Travers thanked him and was turning away. Then he realized the mistake he'd made.

"Oh, it's possible he didn't give his name as 'Fewne.' Would you mind checking it again for the Monday only? He was a very quiet-spoken man; charming manner and voice; and he had on a felt hat and grey overcoat."

The photo was taken again, and this time there was a bit of luck. According to the assistant, the gentleman had given the name of Alveston—D. Alveston—and had taken over a foolscap envelope bearing that name. Travers was delighted. Fewne had given two thirds of his name—D. Alveston Fewne—and had taken over what was presumably a business letter. And he hadn't returned to the hotel to read it. Then where had he read it? Probably in a tea shop. Then would he go forward or back? Undoubtedly forward—or else he'd have gone the whole way back to the hotel.

Again he was lucky. Fifty yards beyond the post office was the sort of place Fewne would choose; through the window one could see spotless coloured tea cloths, flowers, and basket chairs. The proprietress told a story that confirmed his new hypothesis. The gentleman had come in—it was dusk at the time—and had ordered teacake and a pot of China tea. She had taken the order personally, and just as she re-entered the room, some five minutes after, she was in time to see him rush from the room without his hat; his expression one that positively scared her. She'd set down the tray and hurried to the door but was far too late. What she did therefore was to give a boy a penny and tell him to hurry after the gentleman with the hat. When she returned to the shop she thought she'd done a foolish thing. The gentleman might have gone out, leaving his hat, because he'd seen a friend pass. However, he hadn't returned; and that, in fact, was the last she'd seen of him.

It was a trifle early, but Travers ordered some tea and cake and sat there for some time, trying to recreate the atmosphere. But that was hopeless. However well the trail of Fewne had been followed, the fact remained that the end was a cul de sac. Fewne's brainstorm had been due to that letter—that was a reasonable assumption—but to discover either who had sent it or what had been its contents was quite a different matter. There had been no trace of it in the pagoda—either in the desk or in his pockets.

But what else might be reasonably deduced? He jotted down every idea that seemed anyhow relevant and arrived at the following: The letter had come from somewhere which was a day and a half's post—or half a day's post. Fewne had expected it to be at the post office in the afternoon and *not* in the morning. That was why he had left for Folkestone *after* lunch on a winter's day.

Very well, then. Fewne had known he was going to be in Folkestone that Monday, and he'd had the letter sent there. But why all the secrecy? Why send it to Folkestone—and under an assumed name? And it was presumably a business letter. Now surely that meant that the sender couldn't be aware of Fewne's real name—and had been given his instructions orally? Such instructions couldn't have been given in writing, under his real name and from the Little Levington address. And when had Fewne had an opportunity of giving anybody such oral instructions? Surely only in London the previous Saturday! The thing to do, then, was to trace his movements from the time he'd left the Isis Club. He might even have spoken of his intentions to the secretary or someone he knew. And if the letter had been posted from London very late on the Sunday night, it couldn't have reached Folkestone before Fewne expected it. Travers gave a nod of satisfaction. The logic seemed sound; in any case, the matter was worth a trial. London, therefore, seemed to be the order—and at once!

He called again at the police station before he left. A further idea had occurred to him. That theory of Braishe's might as well be inquired into. If Fewne had cut the telephone—and Travers was pretty sure he *hadn't*—then he must have had the necessary pliers. True, he might have got them from the garage, on that occasion when he'd been seen coming from there in the absence of Bruce; but then again he might not.

"Keep the photos for a bit," he told the superintendent. "And could one of your men make inquiries as to whether he bought a pair of pliers or wire cutters? On the Tuesday, that'd be."

It was about half-past four when he left in the Isotta, driving at what was, for him, a snail's pace. The roads were treacherous, and he wanted to think rather than concentrate. Once more he reviewed the day's doings, step by step; then tried to correlate them with problems that were still unsolved. Why, for instance, had Fewne, at the very end of his novel, wasted a day on going to London, another on his return, and so on, all without a word being written? Then suddenly Travers clicked his tongue in annoyance. One big mistake had been made. Suppose it *had* been something in *The Times* that Fewne had seen—the thing, perhaps, that he'd made Isabel Lake see—then it hadn't been in the Saturday's issue that he'd seen it, but the Friday's; since those final words must have been written on the Friday. On the Saturday Fewne had had no time to see *The Times* before he'd left for town. In that case Pollock ought to have been asked for the issues beginning with the Friday. However, that could soon be put right by a check through *The Times* files at the club.

Travers instinctively trod on the accelerator. Then came another idea, so startling that he let the car slow to a standstill. Preposterous, of course! Fewne would never do a thing like that! And yet . . . but *The Times* would solve that problem, too.

Travers set her going again, and this time the car really travelled. As soon as he drew up before the club steps he found himself darting up the stairs like a man possessed.

CHAPTER XX
THE DEAD SPEAK

TRAVERS WAS UP too early the following morning, after one
of those nights when, afraid of over-sleeping, one wakes at all
hours. In the smoke room after breakfast he still found himself with an hour to spend before he could test these overnight
discoveries. Not that they promised too well; they were far too
nebulous for that.

First had come that wonder whether after all Franklin's
suggestion—and his own—had been right. Would a man like
Fewne—sensitive, one to whom the least crudeness or vulgarity would be abhorrent—have contemplated for his heroine
so drastic a solution as the employment of a private detective
agency? Isabel Lake might, perhaps, have done such a thing
through ignorance—or through a sudden whim caused by a
glimpse of an advertisement. And the fact remained, recorded
in Fewne's own words, that whatever it was that Isabel Lake
had intended to do, it had been a sudden glance at *The Times*
that had prompted the resolve.

The Times of the Friday week had, moreover, two such advertisements.

THRING & MABBERLEY 33a, Gt. Took St., undertake
confidential inquiry work of all kinds. Tact and discretion
guaranteed. First-class references. Phone. Cav. 4336.

BEWLAY'S DETECTIVE AGENCY, 173 Courthope Sq.,
W.C. 2, undertake confidential inquiries and detective
work of all kinds. Blackmail a specialty. Consultations
free. Phone Oxford 1145.

Of these the former seemed much the more likely. There was about it an air of respectability and solidity that might have appealed to Fewne and his heroine. In any case, there'd be no harm in making a few discreet inquiries.

The second discovery was a link with the first and arose out of the same issue of *The Times*. He had hunted it through for anything which by its literary bearing might have attracted Fewne's attention, and once more found nothing which might have prompted a dying man to make a last desperate and even frenzied attempt to write a letter. Travers was deciding, indeed, that *The Times* was not the source of Fewne's impulse, when the juxtaposition of ideas sent him off in another direction. Fewne wanted to write a letter. Then what of the correspondence in the paper?

There one thing struck him as decidedly unusual—though its interest for Fewne was none too apparent. A senior officer of the C. I. D. had written a letter which, to a novelist, must have been rather intriguing in its references to fidelity and craftsmanship. And Braishe had been under the impression that Fewne had been worrying about local colour. After that, of course, the sequence was plain. What local colour was Fewne not exactly sure of? Surely—and Travers had to smile at the idea—the office of a private inquiry agent was the last thing in the world with which he was likely to be acquainted. And if so, why shouldn't Fewne, after reading that letter, have been determined to be sure of his local colour by paying a visit to—say—Thring & Mabberley?

The whole idea arrived so spontaneously that Travers trifled with it for some time before rejecting it. Then he toyed with it again. After all, it was a perfectly good theory—with one flaw only. It didn't explain why Fewne was so pathetically eager—even in the last moments of his breakdown—to write a letter himself to the editor of *The Times*. But then, as he consoled himself, that could be explained later, if the examination of the theory warranted it. The whole thing was so hopelessly vague. Fewne probably hadn't visited the offices of any inquiry agent, whereupon the business could be abandoned straightaway.

Next came the reading of the inquest reports, with nothing at all electrifying. As far as Travers could see, Wharton hadn't made Braishe commit himself; in other words, there was nothing in print to show Crashaw as proof that Braishe had broken his part of the contract. Then Wharton most likely had some other statement with which to confront Crashaw. One of the pair would soon be realizing that he was being driven into a corner, and whoever realized it first would be bound to incriminate the other. What the hold was that Crashaw had over Braishe, Travers had a shrewd idea. He knew—he was almost certain he knew—what Crashaw had *heard* in the night. The problem, and an infinitely more important one, was what Crashaw had *seen.* And if Braishe was shielding somebody else, there was a short cut which would be only too apparent to Wharton—to get that somebody to speak.

Travers had no difficulty in discovering the offices of Messrs. Thring & Mabberley. The clerk took in his card and was back in a minute.

"Mr. Mabberley will see you, sir."

He found himself in the presence of a dapper-looking man, obviously as shrewd as they make 'em. His clothes and the room were much of a muchness—both severely "city." The first thing Travers really spotted was that his name had been recognized, and, he rather suspected, his face too. Mabberley stood tapping the card on his fingernails as he gave the conventional welcome.

Travers gave his best smile. "Sorry to be a nuisance to you, Mr. Mabberley, but I'm here on behalf of Scotland Yard. Just a trifling matter." He produced the photo. "Did this gentleman by any chance make a professional call on you, say, last Saturday week? Everything in strictest confidence, of course."

The other took the photo. At the first look his face changed so curiously as to be almost comical. Then with an, "Excuse me!" he went over to the desk and picked up a copy of the *Daily Record*. Travers wondered why, till he remembered the inquest report and the photo of Fewne on the front page. Then, with the realization he had a sudden feeling of elation which went as soon as it came, and left behind it a vague foreboding. As he watched Mabberley comparing the two photos his heart started to race like a mad thing.

The inquiry agent gave a quick look, nodded, then consulted a card index. In half a minute he was waving Travers to a seat and brandishing a small foolscap dossier.

"Now, Mr. Travers; am I correct in saying the photo you showed me was that of Mr. Denis Fewne?"

"That's right. The one who died suddenly a day or two ago. I was down there at the time."

"Really! A friend of yours, may I ask?"

"Not precisely. We were members of the same house party. I knew him pretty well, of course."

"And why exactly do you want the information?" Travers smiled. "Scotland Yard want the information. I'm merely a special emissary who happens to be making inquiries along certain lines. You and I can talk the whole thing over here and now, or, if you prefer it, you can come round to the Yard. In any case, I expect you'll want to check my bona fides."

"Oh, no!" Mabberley nodded briskly. "Not in *your* case, Mr. Travers." He passed over the cigarettes, lighted one himself, and leaned back in the chair. "I'll take your word as man to man about the confidential nature of this affair. It was a funny thing, you know, you showing me that photo! I saw the picture in the *Record* this morning, and I kept saying to myself, 'I'm sure I've seen that chap somewhere before!'"

"It's a very bad photo," said Travers. "Probably an old one resurrected."

"And he didn't come here under the name of Fewne."

Travers smiled apologetically. "Mr. Mabberley, you're keeping a hungry man smelling a meal! Tell me all about it—all he did and everything!"

"Quite so! Well, it was on the Saturday at about eleven-thirty he came here. Usually I shouldn't have been here myself on a Saturday—just after Christmas, too—only I did happen to be here at the time. My clerk said a Mr. Alveston would like to see me, so I said, 'Bring him in!' and—er—he came in. Perfectly charming man he seemed to be; most delightful voice and manner, but very shy and—well, nervy. I don't mind telling you I put him down as an author—highbrow, probably—and I wasn't far out, though I didn't think so when I looked him up and couldn't find his name."

Travers nodded. "Excellent shot, as you say!"

"Yes. . . . Well, I spoke to him as usual; you know, 'What can I do for you,' and all that, and all the time his eyes kept going round this room. Then he caught my eye and apologized; said it was all very novel and interesting. Then he asked if we watched people, and I said of course we did; that was what we were here for. Then he sort of hemmed and hawed and hesitated. Between ourselves I thought he didn't like coming up to the scratch; you know, all very *infra dig.* and so on, so I assured him everything'd be very confidential, and we'd guarantee tact and secrecy. Also I rather hinted at divorce proceedings, because that was what I guessed he was driving at. However, he assured me it wasn't that; matter of fact, he seemed to think that idea rather funny. Then he said, 'Could you watch somebody and give me a report?'

"I said most decidedly we could, and got out my pad ready to write. I said, 'What name?' Oh!' he said, 'Alveston, D. Alveston!' So I said, 'Not *your* name! The name of the person you want to have watched.' Then he sort of dried up again, as if he was doing a bit of hard thinking. I was watching his face pretty closely at the time to see if I could gather anything; then all at once he gave a funny sort of smile as if he was tickled to death with something. Then he said, 'Oh! it's a Mr.—'" Mabberley broke off to consult the notes—"'a Mr. Braishe. Martin Braishe. He'll be at the Isis Club at twelve-thirty probably, but he's now at the Colonial Office.' I asked him to describe personal appearance and so on; then I hopped up to set a man going, as there wasn't any too much time. When I got back he was still here. He said, 'I want a report—the barest outline will do—up to to-morrow at midday, and when can I have it?' Then we arranged about getting it off on the Sunday night and where it was to go to—"

"*Poste restante y* Folkestone."

"That's right!"

"And you told him it wouldn't get there till the afternoon."

"I did."

Travers nodded. "Sorry to interrupt you, Mr. Mabberley. Carry on, please."

"Well, that's all there is to it. He paid a tenner on account and promised to look in after he got the report, and pay or receive the balance either way."

"Quite! I'd like to congratulate you, if I may. Your memory's perfectly marvellous."

The other smiled and shook his head. "We have to remember things in this office—and form rapid decisions. Merely habit."

"You're too modest," said Travers. "And this report. Have you a copy handy?" He left the rest unsaid. Not only was Mabberley paying no attention; he was turning over the typewritten pages of the report with a concentration that was of far greater moment. Then he grabbed the paper and ran his eyes staringly over that. When he finally leaned back again in his chair it was to let out a deep breath.

"This is going to be a bad business, Mr. Travers!"

"It is!" said Travers. "An extraordinarily bad business!"

Mabberley's face showed every sign of annoyance and alarm.

"Can't make out why I didn't spot it! But of course you'll understand it was merely a routine case for us; sort of thing that happens every day. I couldn't be expected, really—"

"Of course you couldn't!" said Travers consolingly "Er—may I see the report?"

The other hesitated tantalizingly. "Yes . . . I think you might see it. It looks as if it might cost this man Braishe his life. I mean, I suppose she *was* the woman?"

Travers nodded—and held out his hand. As he sat reading the three or four quarto sheets Mabberley watched him. He read stolidly through, with never a comment, but when he'd handed back the tiny file he sat for a good minute like a man who's had a sudden and extraordinary blow. It was only when Mabberley spoke, that he roused himself.

"I take it this man Braishe killed Mirabel Quest?"

Travers looked at him. "But why *should* Braishe want to kill her, even if Fewne did know—" He broke off. No reason what-

ever for Mabberley to know everything. And Fewne was dead—
and Mirable Quest as well.

He got to his feet. "Keep that report under lock and key, Mr.
Mabberley. I won't have anything to do with it myself, but Superintendent Wharton'll want it in a day or two. And may one of
your people get me through to him now. I'll jot down the number."

Mabberley gave the order, then put the report away in his
safe. "You think there's the least danger of an attempt being
made to get hold of it?"

Travers smiled. "I'll bet a thousand pounds to a dead match
that till I came in here this morning not a soul outside your people who handled it had the wildest idea there was ever such a
thing in existence. If there had been"—he waved his hand at the
paper—"two of those three people—perhaps the whole three—
would have been alive now!"

"Really!" He pushed the cigarettes over expectantly. "Curious how a quiet-looking man like Fewne had all that under his
hat! Regular cat-and-mouse business he'd been playing!"

Travers shook his head. "Not he! Er—tell me. Why do you
think he came to this office?"

"Why, to have this man Braishe watched!"

"Oh, no! He came merely to have a look round; to get atmosphere for a chapter of a novel. He'd have drawn this room—
and probably yourself. And he really did want a report of somebody—or anybody—just to see how it was written: the language
employed, and so on. And he was prepared to pay for it—though
I rather suspect he wasn't anticipating paying nearly so much.
That isn't to say your charges weren't reasonable, because I'm
sure they were!"

"Then why did he suggest watching Braishe?"

"Because it was the most ludicrous thing he could think of!
Braishe was going down to Oxford for a scientific conference.
Also he intended seeing Braishe himself at twelve-thirty and
telling him all about it. He was so anxious for Braishe to know
the joke that he went twice to the club to get news of him. Then
he thought the joke would keep till Braishe got back to Leving-

ton. He might have decided to say nothing about it—though that would have been contrary to his nature."

"You might say that Fewne drew a bow at a venture!"

"Exactly! Do you know that story of O. Henry? The one about the chap who took poison?"

"Can't say I do."

"Well, as far as I remember it, it was like this: A chap took poison by mistake, so they gave him an emetic and kept him walking up and down the room, and all the time this chap would keep drowsing off—a perfectly fatal thing to do, I believe. Then one of the men who was keeping him on the move thought of something to rouse him. He started to curse the head off him about a wholly imaginary girl in a wholly imaginary place. 'Damn dirty trick that was you played on that little girl down in Virginia!' or wherever it was. As a result, the chap who'd taken poison began to rouse himself—and actually recovered. Next morning his friend called round to see how he was getting on, and found a note."

"Thanks for your advice last night. Am just off to Virginia to marry the girl."

Mabberley didn't quite see it. "But there wasn't one!"

"Yes, there was! It was that bow you were talking about—drawn at a venture."

The bell rang. Mabberley took off the receiver, spoke, then handed it to Travers.

"That you, Wharton? . . . Splendidly, thanks! I'm coming down at once. . . . Something very urgent. Can you hold Braishe for the M. Q. Case? . . . Aren't the prints and harlequin business enough? . . . Well, you know best. But about Crashaw. You got anything to tell him yet? . . . I have! How? . . . Oh, I see! Oh! and can you make Wildernesse stay on? Most important. . . . Yes. . . . Really! Anything left? . . . Well, get the foundations grubbed up! . . . I say I know you're itching to get the foundations grubbed up! . . . Very good! . . . Good-bye!"

Travers buttoned up his coat and prepared to go. Mabberley looked at him inquiringly. "Anything special you want done, Mr. Travers?"

"Don't think so, thanks very much. There's been a bit of a fire down there, by the way."

"Really!"

"Yes. A sort of summerhouse—pagoda, they call it—got burnt down during the night."

Mabberley was still looking somewhat swindled as Travers took his leave.

CHAPTER XXI
THE LINKS ARE JOINED

TRAVERS DID NOT return to Levington—at least, direct. The reason again was one of those happenings that might be called coincidence.

As he stepped out to the pavement he made up his mind to run round to the Isis Club for confirmation of one or two points. Strolling along the Strand towards Trafalgar Square he was still very preoccupied. So many things remained unexplained: those metal tabs, for instance, found in the fireplace; the finger prints on the dagger, which nobody but a fool could have left; and then Celia's harlequin, which went across to Tommy Wildernesse's room. How Ransome got into it all seemed fairly clear, though some connecting link might have to be found. Those were some of the things he was thinking over as he turned into the Tube station; then the taking of his ticket made him forget for a moment those particular trains of thought.

The lift was practically empty, and the attendant stood waiting for it to fill up. Travers ran his eyes over the massed advertisements of gadgets, clothes, books, and theatre programmes. It was at the Paliceum programme for the week that the particular thing happened—merely the catching sight of one of the star turns.

> THE GREAT MALLARMO
> *in his protean song act introducing*
> *twenty nationalities*

It was a recollection that made him smile. A long while ago it had been, on almost his last holiday from school, and his father had taken him to the Paliceum, then recently opened. One of the turns had been a sort of protean act, and the boy had been almost as puzzled how one man could be so many people, as the unfortunate monarch had been about the apples and the dumpling. At one moment there'd been an Italian on the stage; he'd merely made his bow and had passed rapidly behind a screen, emerging almost at once as an Irishman, complete with stage hat and shillelagh and bottle-green suit! And so on through the other transformations. Travers smiled again—then his face straightened as if he'd felt a sudden spasm of pain. Instinctively he felt for his glasses—then turned to leave the lift. It was already in motion.

At the bottom he remained in. A quarter of an hour later, he was in the Isotta—Isis Club and lunch completely forgotten. This time he drove at a speed that barely missed being dangerous; schooling himself to think of the road and not of those importunate things that would come crowding into his mind. In spite of that, by the time he drew up before the police station at Folkestone he had formed certain definite theories, and all that remained was the final testing out.

The superintendent, phoned up urgently, seemed rather anxious to see him.

"We've got some news about those pliers, Mr. Travers," he said. "The gentleman in question bought some at Wallace's in the High Street, on the Tuesday. Insulating pliers they were."

"Insulating!"

"That's right, sir. Insulating. Were you expecting ordinary ones?"

"I was!" said Travers. "But I'm damn glad they weren't. . . . By the way, could you spare a few minutes to do a job of work with me? I'll tell you what it is as we go along."

With the Bristol as starting point, the pair of them moved off along the High Street. It was the superintendent who had the luck of the find, and he called Travers across to a branch of one of those first-class, outfitting, multiple concerns, where he'd evidently got the news he wanted. The manager was waiting for them.

"Good-afternoon," said Travers. "You've definitely identified the man whose costume you saw?"

"Yes, sir. I saw him myself—and the assistant says he's sure."

"Splendid!" said Travers. "In any case, there wouldn't be another man in the county likely to come for what *he* wanted. Tell me, did he order a costume for a fancy-dress ball?"

"That's right, sir. A harlequin costume. He approached the assistant—Mr. Green, over there, if you'd like to speak to him—and asked about the costume. Green hadn't met an order of the kind before, so he sent him to me."

"What was his manner like?"

"Manner? Well, pleasant. What we should call a good customer. At any rate, he asked if we'd any costumes in stock, and of course we hadn't. Fortunately we had some material left over from the hospital fête." He raised his voice. "Mr. Green, bring along that silk we had for the harlequin costume! . . . I'd rather like you to see it," he explained, and then inquiringly, "Some trouble or other about the gentleman who came in?"

"Oh, no!" said Travers. "We're just trying to trace his movements." He gave a humorous nod towards Dollis. "You know what the law is like!"

The manager smiled. "So long as it's not *me* he's after! Now, sir, here's the material. Purple, with white lozenges, as you see. Quite a good quality silk, as I told him, and he said he'd have it, provided he received it in twenty-four hours. I told him we could do that all right—and I took his measurements. You see, sir, there wasn't anything to it. A couple of people could run it together in an afternoon. At any rate, he paid three pounds down; any difference to be adjusted later."

"Any ruff for the neck?"

"No, sir. There wasn't any mention of a ruff."

"And you sent it?"

"Just a minute, sir. I'll look at the book!" and he moved away to the cashier's desk. In a minute the manager came scurrying back with a look of interest on his face.

"Excuse me, sir, but is this the Mr. Fewne all this case is about?"

Travers told him it was—to a certain extent. Then Dollis added a cautionary word about gossiping. The manager made a hasty disclaimer.

"You needn't worry about me, gentlemen. I know how to keep my mouth shut. Now, sir, about the parcel. It was sent off as arranged—late the same night, and registered. Oh, and we forgot the lace—"

Travers stared. "Lace! What lace?"

"The lace for the neck of the costume, sir. It fastened at the neck by a plain white lace; through eyelet holes."

"Something like a football jersey?" suggested Dollis.

"The very thing, sir. We forgot it, as I said, so we sent it on by special letter, with an explanation."

"And were the eyelet holes of metal or celluloid?" asked Travers.

"Composition of some sort, sir."

Travers nodded. "We're much obliged to you, Mr. Adams. Much obliged!"

After a belated lunch Travers again thought things over. Practically every detail was now complete. Thanks to the forgetfulness of somebody in that outfitting shop it was possible to follow events almost moment by moment. As he leaned back in the chair with eyes closed he could see the light snap out . . . hear the quick rush up the stairs . . . the half gasp in the room . . . the blow . . . He shook his head. That was the one link missing. How had that particular piece of devilry been done?

It took him half an hour to arrive at a possible solution, and only after he'd gone over again the movements of Fewne on the Tuesday. Every action must have had a motive, and the more bizarre the action, the easier to find the motive. And, as he realized, it wasn't necessarily the actions that were eccentric in themselves: it was the peculiar intricacy of the motives governing the whole series of actions. In any case, he'd make the first test. If it fitted, the rest must follow.

This time his visit was to the antique shop—the second of those Fewne had visited. Travers reintroduced himself to the manager.

"If you'd be so good, I'd like to have some more details about that gentleman's visit on the Tuesday; you know, the one to whom you sold the poker. May I see the set you offered him originally?"

"Certainly, sir!" He led the way once more to the back of the shop. "Here's the set, sir: fender, poker, tongs, shovel, and fire dogs."

Travers nodded, then picked up the poker and tried its strength with his hands. The manager chuckled.

"You won't bend that, sir. Good stuff they made in those days!"

Travers agreed. "And these knobs on the fire dogs—are they soldered on, or what?"

"There's a rod running through the upright, sir. The knob screws on flush." He illustrated the point. "Quite simple, sir—and ingenious."

"It is!" said Travers. "Like a good many things when you know how. And may I see the odd assortment of brass where he found the poker?"

Travers got down on his haunches before the miscellaneous collection. In less than a minute he found what he wanted.

"When the gentleman grubbed among these things as I was doing then, did you leave him to himself, or did you stay here?"

"He was all alone. He wasn't that sort, sir."

"Quite. He wasn't a sneak thief, in other words." He nodded to himself abstractedly, then looked down at the poker he was holding in his hands.

"I'll take this, if I may. What's it worth to you?"

"Five bob, sir—and cheap at the price."

"Wrap it up!" said Travers.

Along the main road the countryside was still under snow. The air was now muggy, and some rain had fallen, and a couple of days at the outside should let the fields show themselves again. Whether, somewhere under the snow away beyond the pagoda, that pair of insulating pliers was ever found or not mattered very little, except as a possible exhibit for the museum at Scotland Yard. Every step was clear, each with its cloud of witnesses, knowing or unknowing. All that remained was to bring the guilt home, and that was a matter of infinitely greater, if not insuperable, difficulty.

Along the drive the car splashed through slush. At the turning to the house he slowed the car up and let the headlights play across the lawn where the pagoda had been. Nothing was visible. Even the foundations were indistinguishable in the general mass of melted snow and shadow. The house itself was lighted up, and as he sounded the horn Pollock appeared on the porch. To Travers, at that moment, it seemed as if it were weeks he had been away, rather than a bare two days.

"Glad to see you back, sir!"

"Thank you, Pollock. Where's Mr. Wharton?"

"At tea, sir, in the dining room. I'll send yours in immediately, sir."

He found the General behind a pot of tea and met with a remarkably genial reception. Franklin had been called back to town but was hoping to see him the following day.

"Any other news?" Travers asked.

Wharton shrugged his shoulders. Elimination seemed to have gone on fairly well. Wildernesse had been retained, as Travers had suggested. Braishe, too, was still available.

Wharton lowered his voice almost to a whisper.

"You know what I was telling you about those finger prints on the dagger—how they couldn't lie—and that was why I wouldn't arrest him? Well, they were a washout!"

"How?"

"I'll show you." He picked up the poker. "Look at my thumb, down the poker shaft, the handle resting in the palm of my hand, and three fingers round the handle. Those are the prints on the dagger. It was *pushed* into the wound—not *struck*."

"Was it pushed?" Travers asked bluntly.

"Well, it wasn't. There's no point in being clever or secretive. The prints on the dagger showed the end of the thumb as left clean in the air! Impossible, of course, since the end of the thumb ought to have been pressing against the shield. That gave us the idea. The dagger was *struck* into the body, but that brass handle was screwed on afterwards. The dagger came from the hall stand—I don't think there's any doubt about that. Where the handle came from is another matter."

"I can tell you about that," said Travers, and produced his small parcel. Then he told that much of the story: how Fewne took the dagger with him to Folkestone; how he noticed the handles and knobs of most antique fire irons unscrewed, and how he found among the lumber of the antique shop one that fitted near enough. Perhaps the final fitting of the poker handle to the dagger was done just before lunch when he'd been seen coming from the garage, with its tools and turnscrews all ready to hand.

"Is Braishe handy?" Travers asked.

"Yes, he's in the drawing room with Wildernesse. They've been to the funerals to-day. We let Mrs. Fewne go back to town with the Paradines—and Challis too."

"Right. I'll have a word with Braishe. Is he pretty normal?"

"Oh, quite! I've let him know he can go where he likes."

"Verdicts all right?"

"The usual. Both adjourned for a fortnight."

When Travers came back he seemed on quite good terms with himself.

"It's all right, George!" he said. Wharton looked up at the unusual address. "Fewne did ask Braishe to stir up the fire in the pagoda; that's when the prints were made. Then he unscrewed the handle, put it carefully aside, and put the usual poker in the fireplace. We shall probably find the shaft of the antique poker under the snow where Fewne threw it. By the way, how'd the pagoda get burnt down?"

"No one knows. We were all away—hadn't got back from Levington. Braishe was here—and one of my men. They had the sense to take all Fewne's things away earlier in the day. When I got here it was burning like hell. Braishe said let the damn thing burn—and we did. The sparks went into the snow, and there wasn't any danger." Then Wharton slewed round in his chair and gave the other a shrewd look. "Rather seems as if you were right about that pagoda!"

"Just a shot in the dark. If he grubs the place up by the roots, it doesn't matter a damn. The evidence is that the pagoda *is* burned down! If it had vanished into thin air, it'd still be evidence!"

"You're too subtle for me," said Wharton.

"Oh, no, I'm not! You'll see why in a minute, when you hear the whole story."

"Just a moment before you begin that," Wharton said. He pulled out his pipe and got it going before he asked his question. "You've found out a good deal?"

"Yes. ... I have."

"And was I right about the ewe lamb?"

"The ewe lamb! I don't follow."

Wharton told him the story of Uriah the Hittite—at least, he got out the first few words when Travers remembered the reference. Wharton put his question again.

"Was I right?"

"You were—though how the devil you guessed it, I can't imagine."

"Think it out!" said Wharton. "You hinted that Braishe had killed Fewne. Very well, then, why? What was the motive? What did he want from Fewne? Not money—that was absurd. He wasn't jealous of his reputation, because he had a bigger one himself. All that Fewne had which another man might envy him was—the one ewe lamb. That's why I sent Norris to the Yard to make arrangements for an inquiry into that holiday Mrs. Fewne spent in Switzerland."

"Found anything yet?"

"Oh, no!" said Wharton unconcernedly. "But there's plenty of time. There'll be what you're now going to tell me, for instance."

"Then you'd a damn sight more faith in me than I had in myself," said Travers with a wry smile. "However, here's the story." He pushed back the table with one hand and felt for his glasses with the other; then leaned forward confidentially.

"The story begins with a certain Chief Inspector of Scotland Yard who had a sensitive soul. Were I a writer of fiction, I should call it—'A Bow at a Venture.'"

Wharton, knowing something of Travers's methods, nodded resignedly.

CHAPTER XXII
FEWNE TRIES TO PAY

TRAVERS WAS well on the way with his story.

"Every time it comes back to me it makes me wince as if someone had struck me a blow. There's Fewne, strolling into that office of Thring & Mabberley, looking round like a boy at a circus. Then he realized he'd have to give some definite excuse for his visit, and when Mabberley rushed him into it, he gave the name of the most nonsensical person one could possibly imagine—Martin Braishe! reliable old Martin; the chap who was like a brother; the steady-going, scientific-minded Martin; just off to the Colonial Office and then to a greybeards' powwow at Oxford. Lord, how funny! Fancy a sleuth following *him* up! Taking down meticulously every movement—and wondering what the devil it was all about!

"I want you to imagine the rest, because it shows what happened. Fewne left that office, probably chuckling to himself inside. He couldn't find Braishe, to tell him the joke, but it would keep. All the week-end he'd be looking forward to getting that report and carrying on with the book. Then there'd be that trip to Folkestone, looking out a piece or two of furniture he and Brenda had thought of for the new flat. And there'd be the thought of Brenda's coming down after six weeks and more away.

"Then he went to the post office and got the report. He was so keen that he couldn't wait till he got back to the hotel; he went into a little tea shop and read it while his tea was coming. I expect you've guessed what was in it?"

"I have ... I think. But go on."

"I'll tell you as much as I can remember. It ran something like this:

"I picked up the suspect outside the Colonial Office and followed him to the Ravoli Restaurant in Minor Street, just off the Haymarket, where he lunched alone. He consulted his watch frequently. From there he went to the Isis Club, and from there to Victoria Station by taxi, and as he took no ticket I presumed he was meeting somebody, and therefore took the precaution of having a taxi ready myself. He inquired of a porter how the Continental train was running, and was told a quarter of an hour late. When it came in he proceeded straight from the barrier to a taxi, where he was joined by a lady, whose luggage, I heard her say, had been placed in the cloakroom. She carried a small bag only.

"My taxi followed them to Golder's Green and along the North Road as far as Finchley, where it drew in at a small detached villa standing back from the road: 'Ivydale' by name. There I dismissed my own taxi."

Travers paused for a moment. "This chap—Reid his name was—then appears to have hung about till it was dark without being able to do anything except make sure that nobody left the house. Then a light went on in a downstairs room, and he tried listening at the window. What he heard was—*inter alia*—something like this:

"'You're sure Denis isn't likely to run across the Fowlers? It might be pretty awkward if they happened to let out that you'd come back a day earlier.'

"'You silly boy! He wouldn't think anything if he *did* know! Besides, what's it matter?' Then there was the sound of kissing, a 'darling' or two, and various endearments.

"Next thing was when a light went on in the bedroom, and Reid was lucky enough to find a ladder. I needn't repeat all the intimacies he heard; the exact words don't matter. But Brenda Fewne was talking stars and romance and love, and Braishe was still a bit nervous. They discussed Fewne's suspicions again; Mirabel Quest and her relations with Challis, and Ransome's sharp eyes and tongue. They gloated over Braishe's foresight in getting hold of that handy little place at Finchley and planned what they'd do when the Fewnes came to town. Then Braishe cut up nasty; said he wouldn't have her coming to him straight from her husband's arms. She said she'd make excuses—get medical advice, and so on. In any case, she'd never live with him again—unless things got too difficult, when they could talk it over together at some delicious moment like the present.

"The rest of the report doesn't matter. Braishe saw her back to town and was actually fool enough to see to getting the luggage out again. Mirabel didn't meet her at the station—that's all surmise, of course, though it must be near the truth—but I should say she sent Ransome along to help with luggage, and so on. Ransome must have seen the whole of the camouflaged arrival. The report ends with the departure of Braishe: to de-garage his car, I imagine, though it doesn't say so."

"My God! Perfectly hellish!"

"Wasn't it! Put yourself in Fewne's place. Now we know why he rushed out of the tea shop, along the road to Dover; and why he came back like a man who's been stunned. The woman, mind you, he'd given up everything for—worried and sacrificed so that she could have a good time! And Braishe!"

"You'd never have thought it!" said Wharton plaintively. "I guessed Braishe was coveting *her*, but I'd have sworn she was as chaste as an icicle!"

"I know. That's the terrible part of it. Fewne must have gone half mad over there in the pagoda that Monday night. Then he began to scheme things out. He made up his mind to kill her and make it appear as if Braishe had done it. By the following morning he had it all worked out. He took the dagger with him, bought the poker, arranged for the costume, and got the pliers. But, throughout the whole affair, he showed a curious naïveté. He was still, in some ways, the natural Fewne—remote from actualities. It would have taken a super-first-class crook to carry out what he planned.

"Then we come to the actual night. Under his clothes he had on that harlequin costume. He took care to dance very little; as far as possible he sat apart watching, over on the settee by the door. I rather think he was afraid of the costume showing beneath his clothes. Also he kept his feet firmly on the floor—didn't sit with his legs crossed—so that his pulled-up trousers mightn't show the tights.

"He flicked that note to Tommy Wildernesse; then went back to his seat by the door, where he was sitting, as I told you when we all sat round the fire with the lights out. I should say he left the room just before we did. He could judge that. The balloons he left with their string wedged between the settee and the wall. He went straight to the electric light recess, and when he heard his wife's voice above him on the stairs, and he'd guessed we'd gone up, he cut the cord. Then he slipped up the stairs like a streak and *into that recess by Tommy Wildernesse's room.*

"Now you see the importance of that note. What Fewne hoped was that he'd remain out in the loggia long enough for his room to be empty. He needed that landing, just as a protean artist needs a screen. He whipped off his outer clothes and nipped across the landing into *what he imagined was his wife's room.* He saw the figure in white—and struck with the dagger. Then he laid down the body, locked the door, screwed on the handle of the dagger, taking care not to disturb the prints, and pushed the body under the bed. As he came out of the room again he may have heard voices, and that may have been why he paused for a moment to brush back his hair as if he were Braishe. Then he nipped across the landing again, got his clothes on, and went downstairs, where he escaped being seen. Then he got his balloons.

"We can discuss his probable state of mind with the medical people, but I would suggest that after he got those balloons he was in a highly nervous condition—to put it mildly. It was when he was coming back from the dance room that he saw his wife! He may have run into her in the semidarkness or have seen her closely by the light of a candle. *That was the final shock.* He rushed out of the front door and made for the pagoda like a madman. When he got there, his brain was on fire. He prowled up and down like a lunatic. Then he sobered down a bit; took off his clothes and burnt that harlequin costume, poking it about till nothing was left but the metal tabs of the lace. Then he got into his pajamas and tried to think again. All that would keep coming to his mind was the damnable irony of everything. He'd killed the wrong woman. All his scheming had been for nothing. His wife and Braishe could still carry on their intrigue, and he'd have to shut his eyes to it or else give her her freedom and so play into her hands. And all because a man had written a letter to *The Times!* I repeat—the hellish, damnable irony! That's what struck his poor befuddled brain. He was a creative artist, and his mind kept urging him—in spite of his body—to write down what he felt; a letter, we'll say, to the editor of *The Times*, something like this:

"To the Editor of *The Times*.

"Dear Sir:

"You printed in your issue of Friday last, a letter which had consequences so tragically ironical that . . .

"and so on. Naturally, he never intended the letter to be sent. He was putting down his thoughts on paper; giving an outlet to a devastating emotion. But his hand shook so much that he couldn't write. He tried over and over again—and his hand failed him. Then that, or something else, infuriated him. He snatched up the pen and cut and slashed those balloons—with their ghastly associations—and ripped them about the room. After that I should say he threw himself on the bed in a frenzy, clutching his hair, his face puckered up with an incomprehensible sort of agony. . . . Then he died."

Travers shook his head, then slowly rubbed his glasses. Wharton grunted, nodded once or twice, then jerked out:

"How?"

"I'll come to that later," said Travers. "Shall we go on to the following morning—and Ransome in particular?"

"The blackmail business?"

"That's it. We can fit that in now like a glove. Overnight Ransome had decided to throw in her lot with her mistress, instead of doing a little quiet blackmail on the sly from Brenda Fewne.

Mirabel was extraordinarily amused! To think that the virtuous Brenda had been having an affair! Brenda—the paragon of chastity, the ever present Lucrece, the perpetual proclaimer of virtue—oh, my God! it was too funny! No wonder she laughed! And no wonder she turned round and spat! And she let the other see how it felt, by a little threatening of exposure."

Travers shook his head again. "Now I come to look back, George, I can think of a dozen innuendoes Mirabel let out that night—perfectly venomous remarks and hints I couldn't understand at the time. However, Ransome got her reward straightaway, by the ring; then, next morning, after the murder, she put the thumbscrews on Brenda Fewne. Brenda borrowed from Celia Paradine and stopped her mouth with twenty pounds as a beginning. But Palmer had been talking to Ransome before that bit of blackmail was done—when Ransome had really decided to tell some yarn to explain away that ring. After the blackmail the two women had to put their heads together—and they invented that story about the debt. If Ransome hadn't been killed, you'd have had the whole yarn out of them in five minutes."

Wharton shook his head. "I shouldn't have been here!"

"Hm! Perhaps you wouldn't. . . . However, something else arose out of that interview I had with Ransome. Like the usual inexperienced amateur in anything, I tried to do too much. I didn't keep to bare essentials. I hinted at Challis—who happened to have the wind up pretty badly himself. Thereupon Ransome saw another source of income and proceeded to put the screw on Challis. Unfortunately for her, Braishe had seen Brenda Fewne. He spent best part of half an hour with her while Celia was having tea downstairs—and by a really delicious irony, I was the one who sent him upstairs! Braishe'd be in the devil of a hole when that disaster loomed up. All he probably did then was to reassure her. After all, she wouldn't see the seriousness of it, as he did. *She* thought her husband died from—well, what George Paradine had told her. Then Braishe made up his mind to handle Ransome himself."

Wharton looked up suddenly. "Know what happened?"

"I don't. If it came to guesswork, I'd say he watched her leave the room after I'd finished with her. Perhaps she'd arranged with Brenda to make a report to her about what happened with me—that's what I expected at the time. If Brenda told Braishe that—then he'd have been waiting somewhere upstairs for her. He got her with his hands as she was going up the side stairs—say, after they'd passed one another. Still, that's all too vague."

"Who else *could* have killed her?"

"Exactly! He was the man with a motive." He said nothing for a moment or two, then went off at a tangent. "That footman Charles? Was he perfectly genuine?"

"Absolutely. Clean sheet where he came from—and Pollock speaks well of him."

"Then he had nothing to do with that doped drink?"

Wharton snorted. "You never imagined he had—did you?"

"Well ... I did flirt with the idea."

"Hm! It was he or Braishe—I grant you that. Braishe wouldn't have dared to bribe Charles to do it. And didn't it strike you as unusual that Braishe should have handed out that drink himself? Shouldn't the footman have done that?"

"Not necessarily!" said Travers. "You see it was a special drink—and all very informal. Got that coat analysis yet?"

"Not yet. When we do get it, it won't be conclusive. Braishe mightn't have troubled to dope Fewne. Over in the pagoda he'd have been quite safe."

Travers's eyes opened. "Safe! How?"

"Well—out of the way!"

"I don't follow," said Travers. "What's *your* idea of the reason why Braishe doped that drink?"

Wharton smiled. "Different from yours—which is that he wanted a quiet house while he faked the burglary—gas from the safe, and so on. You and Franklin and Charles interfered with that; then next morning the genuine burglary turned up like a fifth ace. Wasn't that your idea? ... I thought so! Mine is that he intended as well to spend some part of that night with Brenda Fewne."

Travers hopped up. "George, you've told me the very thing I wanted to know." He smiled. "Hell of a thing to suffer from purity of mind, as I do. No wonder Crashaw smiled when I hinted that it was Mirabel who'd spoken to Braishe!"

Wharton slewed round in his chair.

"I say, what *is* all this?"

Travers squinted round. "Have a look outside to see the coast's clear; then I'll tell you."

Ten minutes later, Wharton was nodding his head as if satisfied; against his better judgment, perhaps, but still satisfied.

"What do you suggest?"

"This, I think," said Travers. "Get hold of Tommy Wildernesse at once and make sure he doesn't see Braishe again except in your presence. He'll go with us to Levington station and be packed off to town—to a perfectly quiet hotel like the Melton. Fix an appointment there for to-morrow evening—we two, he and George Paradine. Get that evidence absolutely officially."

"But no jury'd convict!"

Travers glared at him. "Jury! Who's worrying about juries? Get the evidence while the going's good! You can do your window dressing later."

Wharton looked at him—and said nothing.

"Tell Braishe you've finished here altogether. Be discreetly effusive. Thank him for his help, and so on. Tell him to go his way in peace. Then you and I and Palmer leave at once—but only for Levington, where we see Wildernesse off, then have a heart-to-heart talk with Crashaw. You got his record?"

Wharton tapped his pocket.

"Good! All that suit you?"

"It'll do," said Wharton laconically.

Travers pushed the bell, then remembered something else.

"What was that you were mentioning on the phone —about the evidence we'd got, to show Crashaw, to make him talk?"

Wharton nodded complacently.

"Do you know, I was so interested in hearing you discuss the intelligence of juries that I forgot to ask *you* that!" He heaved himself out of the chair as William entered the room. "I'll tell you that on the way down."

CHAPTER XXIII
CRASHAW TALKS

WHARTON HUNG up the receiver.

"It's all right! The chief constable's quite agreeable. Is he in the charge room yet?"

"Just gone in," said Travers.

Wharton rubbed his hands. "Right! We'll see what he's got to say."

Crashaw didn't look any the better for his three days' incarceration. There was some attempt on his part at jauntiness, but its only effect was one of pathetic tawdriness. He was none too robust at any time; now he looked distinctly fragile—a wisp of a man who was biting the bullet but feeling most damnably uncomfortable inside. The room, too, was none too cheery; with its scarcely discernible fire, the cold linoleum on the floor, the rigid chairs, and the admonitory uniform hanging from a peg.

Wharton dismissed the sergeant and waved Crashaw to a chair. The General's face was intended to be inscrutable—with a dash of the offhand thrown in. And he resorted to one of his own tricks—wrapping up his meaning in such a spate of words that it would have worried a wiser head than Crashaw's to see precisely what he was driving at.

"I won't insult a man of your intelligence by attempting any sort of bluff," he began. "I'm here to talk about the murder of Mary Kathleen Ransome, on the morning of January the 3rd last. A good deal depends on certain answers you give to certain questions. Also I'm prepared to give you the official warning about those answers—that they may be used in evidence—but the whole thing's a matter for your judgment. If I decide to make a charge, that'll be a different matter altogether."

Crashaw watched and said nothing.

"Your name is Henry Mortimer Crewe. Your aliases—some of them—Charles Mortimer and the Hon. Charles Carewe."

Crashaw nodded. At the first name Travers had seen him flush.

"You have three previous convictions—details don't matter. You're now on remand. If you go before the Quarter Sessions you may get three years—or more."

"It'll come to an end," said Crashaw with exaggerated indifference.

"It will!" said Wharton curtly. "Only I don't happen to be interested in the flight of time. The interesting thing is that you'll be what's known as a hold on. If, for instance, you'd committed murder, there'd be you—nicely put away inside while the evidence was being collected. I don't mind telling you we've quite a lot of evidence now. But why be precipitate? You'll be safe—and our principal witness is no longer afraid of you!"

Crashaw sneered. "I thought you weren't going to bluff!"

"You can't annoy me," said Wharton. "Mr. Travers will give you some news that will show you whether I'm bluffing or not. Mr. Braishe—we're being very frank, you see!—has done some foolish things, but not criminal ones. For his own sake, he refused to incriminate you Now he's changed his mind, because we know—well everything! There's no longer any need for him to be afraid of you." Then Wharton made his first gesture. He leaned forward, chin thrust out. "Suppose a witness would swear that Ransome saw you on the night of the murder. Where'd you stand then?"

Travers was horrified. Wharton had said nothing about that prodigious bluff when they'd discussed procedure. Crashaw, however, was unsettled.

"But you haven't any witness! You can't have!"

Wharton waved his hand. "That's to be seen. But, let me tell you, it's this witness or you; his word against yours. However .. . Mr. Travers has something to say to you about that."

"Nothing very pleasant, I'm afraid," smiled Travers. "Don't you think, between ourselves, you've been made rather a fool of, Crashaw? I'm not going to flatter you. There's no point in doing that silly sort of thing. You're what we call a sportsman. You took a risk and you take your medicine. You're a good sort in many ways, but you're a fool to yourself. You've got a lot of kicks out of this—er—burglary business. It's given you a thrill. You've occasionally thought of yourself as an up-to-date Raffles. But you're not nearly so clever as that. You didn't fool Franklin, and—in all modesty—you didn't fool me; and you've been made a tool of by Braishe! Isn't that right?"

"It's a matter of indifference to me either way."

"Ah! now you're sulking. Let me tell you the exact position as between you and Braishe. Your real name isn't Crashaw. But when we were talking about nicknames the other day at lunch—a subject which was deliberately introduced by yourself—you gave a most ingenious account of your own nickname as derived from 'Crashaw.' Therefore that nickname was non-existent! Therefore the conversation was for the purpose of determining the nicknames of the rest of us! And as soon as you knew that Braishe's nickname was 'Broody,' you stopped—and therefore you had your information. We know, then, that during the night you heard Braishe addressed as 'Broody,' and you wanted to know who 'Broody' was. Thanks to Braishe himself—and I give you my word that that statement is correct—we know whose voice you heard! Shall I tell you, or will you tell us?"

"You carry on!"

"Very well. During the night you entered Mrs. Fewne's room. To put it picturesquely, she stirred sleepily on the bed and said—or whispered—'Is that you, Broody darling?' You possibly grunted and backed out of the room. Later you saw a figure, whom you couldn't identify, enter her room. Mrs. Fewne told Braishe about the visitor. He was scared and came out again sooner than he intended. You—with the eye of a genius for the possible chance—saw the likelihood of blackmail. That explains why you did such a mad thing as to return to the house in the rôle of the Unfortunate Traveller. You decided that a bird in the bush might be worth several in the hand. And that's why Braishe came to let you out of the attic. Isn't that so?"

"Carry on!"

"Braishe was badly scared, or he'd never have let himself be held up like that. You told him if he let you go, you'd keep your mouth shut about that affair with Fewne's wife. Braishe agreed—*but he let you down!* When I told you William had a revolver, that was all bluff. But after Braishe left the attic, *he* fetched a revolver for William, told him you were the murderer of Mirabel Quest, and instructed him to shoot you point-blank if you tried any tricks. Braishe meant to do you in!"

Crashaw looked at him queerly.

"You remember when I was questioning you in the room, after your escape? How Braishe suggested he could look after you for a bit? If I'd gone out, as he suggested, he'd almost certainly have shot you then—in self-defence. Isn't that true? Can't you see it?"

Crashaw still said nothing.

"Take when the police came," Travers went on. "You don't know how galled Braishe was to think he'd given way to you. He's a person of some standing and importance; you're a negative quantity—socially. He felt the vulgarity of his position in letting himself be blackmailed by you. The offense wasn't deadly, and he was ready to come more than halfway to meet the police over a confession—if he thought they knew anything. I give you my word that they do know something. They know everything. They know that Ransome was more of a menace to him than to you. That's the problem. It's your life or his. Which'll a jury believe?"

Crashaw bit his lip and fidgeted with his fingers.

"Of course, I realize the position. You gave Braishe your word—and you've kept it. You haven't said a thing. *We've* done all the talking! But this position is a wholly new thing which you hadn't anticipated. The Ransome Case—"

"All right!" broke in Crashaw. "There's no need to go on. Give me your word of honour that what you told me about the revolver is true."

"I certainly do. Also I think Superintendent Wharton will let you hear William tell his own story—if you insist. And I tell you, here and now, that it'll be a case of you or Braishe, and—between ourselves—I'm on your side!"

"Mr. Travers is right!" said Wharton. "But before we go any further, we want two things from you. Your definite undertaking to put yourself in Mr. Travers's hands, and your implicit promise to treat what we tell you with the most absolute confidence."

"Right-ho!" Crashaw nodded. "You don't want to know any more about that bedroom business. That's near enough right, and so is the way I got out of the bedroom. Braishe planned the route I took, but you've probably guessed that. All I held over him was the intrigue with that dead chap's wife. I didn't know who she was at the time, but it looked promising. If he hadn't given in, I'd have told him more. I did rather hint at it, as a matter of fact. All I wanted at the moment was to get well clear before the police came, then I intended to blackmail him for a pretty good sum on the strength of what I *hadn't* told him. That let me out of the promise I'd given."

"Do you know, I'm rather surprised at you, Crashaw!" said Travers. "A blackmailer's a loathsome swine."

Crashaw nodded. "I know that. But I shouldn't have done the dirty on him. One decent sum, and I'd have gone abroad—Kenya, probably—and stayed there." He smiled with a touch of his old chirpiness. "Prodigal's reform, and all that!"

Out of the corner of his eye Travers could see Wharton getting restless. Evidence—that was what Wharton wanted, not flippancies. Travers cut Crashaw short.

"And what was it you really knew?"

"This. My original entry was to the drawing room, which opens on the loggia. You had it as a sitting-out room, and a window was opened for air. I took a look in and saw it was empty and then got well behind that big settee in the corner—and waited. I got to know about the show being cut short, and people going, and naturally I heard all the noise outside. Then, still later, when everybody'd gone, Braishe came into the drawing room carrying a raincoat on his arm and something under it; what, I couldn't see. He slipped over to the window, then locked the door. Then he put what he was carrying on a chair; put on the coat; put out the light, then slipped out of the loggia door, which he'd unlocked. I nipped up and squinted out of the window.

It was snowing like hell, and all I saw was him going towards the pagoda. In five minutes he was back. He locked the outer door, listened at the other door, then went out of the room. Next morning, when that poor devil Fewne was found done in, I thought quite a lot. I pumped Challis pretty hard, and I soon knew the strong hand I held, since I knew of the intrigue with Fewne's wife. As you said, I found out Braishe by his nickname."

"Do you know what he was carrying, concealed under that raincoat?"

"I don't—but it was something he treated with considerable care. Next morning, when there was all that talk about the telephone, I thought it was that—only it didn't seem the sort of thing one would handle carefully."

"It *was* the telephone—for one thing," said Wharton. "He made out that Fewne had thrown it out there in the snow. Mr. Travers happened to find it—as you know—and that's when he guessed things weren't all they seemed. If Fewne had thrown it there, there'd only have been the morning's snow on it. Braishe forgot that—or rather, he didn't know it was going to stop snowing. Hear anything else in the night?"

"Only what you know. When people started to wander about downstairs I thought I'd better beat it. Then that other business occurred—so I decided to rely on the blackmail possibilities and give the other rooms a rest."

"What about the Ransome business? Did you see anything of Braishe at the time?"

Crashaw smiled. "Surely you're not trying to catch me out! I knew Ransome was dead—killed, if you like—and that's all I do know."

"I don't think there was a catch in it!" Travers smiled over at Wharton. "But tell me something. When you told me you hid in a closet in the servants' corridor, I take it you said that because you wanted to shield Braishe."

"That's right. I didn't know what you might tell him—and I didn't want him to know all *I* knew. . . . Anything else you want?"

Travers caught Wharton's eye. "Just this. The worst you'll get is to be let out on bail. The best will be what Superintendent

Wharton can arrange for you with the chief constable. You've been charged, and only a court can discharge you. But there are ways and means. There may even be an arranged escape—under surveillance of some sort; say my own. Still, that's all in the air. We're standing by you, and that ought to sound good enough."

"You sort of hold the string!"

Travers looked rather annoyed. "Was that . . . necessary?"

"Sorry! Unpardonable thing to say,"

"Right. . . . Later on, you'll get a fresh start, as the padre would say. You'll come to town and stay where Superintendent Wharton arranges—probably with me, while the scheme matures. If that escape stunt is worked, Braishe will be sure of your bona fides; then, to-morrow morning you'll begin a blackmail campaign—details to follow. Then, when everything's over, you can go to Kenya with some money in your pocket—but not Braishe's!"

Crashaw frowned. "Put the whole thing straight out. You want me to get Braishe for you. Is that it?"

"It is!" said Travers. "But I shouldn't put it like that if I were you."

"It's a job *I'm* not ashamed to do. Let me tell you in half a dozen sentences the sort of man Braishe was."

When he'd finished, Crashaw was looking the least bit ashamed of himself.

"Of course, it does make a difference . . . and anything I can do, I don't mind doing. All the same, I don't think I'd like to be paid. No offence and all that."

"Have it your own way," said Wharton. "Only I ought to tell you it wouldn't be government money!"

Crashaw flashed a look at Travers. Travers avoided it. "Don't you think," he said to Wharton, "it'd be a good idea if Crashaw rang up Braishe and announced his escape at once? It'd put you in a strong position—and it'd give Braishe his first shock."

"Very good idea!"

"Right-ho, then, Crashaw! Would you mind giving me that Bible on the shelf behind you? Rather grubby, by the look of it!"

Crashaw looked surprised. "You're not going to swear me in!"

"Good Lord, no! Just want to look something up for you—unless you know it."

Crashaw handed it over dubiously. "Know what?"

"Well, we'll leave it for the superintendent to decide. He's an authority on the Bible." He laughed. "What's it to be, George? The story of Uriah the Hittite ... or 'Had Zimri peace who slew his master?'"

CHAPTER XXIV
CRASHAW HAS THE LAST WORD

SOME DAYS LATER Travers was sitting in his room, waiting with extraordinary impatience for the arrival of Wharton. Not a great deal seemed to have happened since the morning when they left Levington. Wharton had been delighted with the results of that interview with Crashaw, but though most of the gaps in the evidence had been filled in, there were still sufficient holes for an astute counsel to stick his head clean through.

Events therefore had been largely governed by patience. Braishe had to be reduced to a state of desperation. He had to be brought to the condition of a bull, harassed by a dozen invisible matadors, so that his rush at the one visible adversary should be so blindly desperate as to be fatal. And there was just another chance—that he'd break down altogether. He might throw in the sponge and give himself up.

First, then, had come that cryptic telephone message, in a disguised voice, advising the reading of a certain chapter of Kings. "Who's that speaking?" came Braishe's voice with an unusual stammer. The chapter and its content had then been repeated; then the receiver had been hung up.

The following morning, in accordance with the prearranged plan, Crashaw had rung up again. This time he'd announced himself and had made an ironical inquiry about that house at Finchley, together with a comment on the folly of leaving ladders at the disposal of eavesdroppers. He had also requested a telephone conversation for the next day, and had received a number.

After that, Braishe was shadowed night and day. Wharton watched him like an angler with a trout. Crashaw was beginning to enjoy himself. His next disclosure was what had been seen by Ransome at the station—a perfectly safe guess. Then had come a demand for a further phone appointment for the following day. So things had gone on till Braishe must have wondered if Crashaw was the devil himself. How much he slept those three nights is problematic. Braishe had nerve—Travers knew that— but no man's nerve was proof against that sort of thing.

Then came the working up to the climax. Since Braishe had been shown that Crashaw apparently had occult knowledge, and that what he knew was easily proven fact, he could now be given merely hints that doings which he imagined even more hidden were just as well known. Finally Crashaw had come out into the open. He must have a personal interview with Braishe—and he must have three thousand pounds. He pledged his word, once the money was in his hands, not to return to England again or trouble Braishe from a distance. He must have cash in small notes, and Braishe was informed that any monkey tricks would be disastrous.

Thereupon Travers had let the strings drop from his fingers and had set to work in earnest. In the presence of Wharton there had been rehearsal after rehearsal, till every possible move of Braishe was forestalled and Crashaw was word perfect. As for the place of meeting, the Melton had been given the preference, since a private house, however secluded, might give rise to suspicions of a plant. The actual room was an end one, and Wharton had arranged for its one neighbour to be occupied—apparently—by a couple of girls who were to be on view at the time of Braishe's arrival. In that room, however, the dictaphone was installed, with an expert at hand.

What had happened, Travers was now waiting to hear. Wharton seemed to think that things couldn't go wrong, even though Crashaw was working on hypotheses rather than actual facts. Travers was not so sure. If one of those assumptions on which Crashaw was working was wrong, would Braishe see the chance to keep his mouth shut? And how would Crashaw stand the test?

Would his natural nimbleness of wit cope with a situation which was bound to arise out of something the rehearsed schedule had overlooked? Those were some of the problems that were worrying Travers and setting him to prowling about the room and squinting at the clock and going through all the other spasmodic restlessnesses of a man on tenterhooks.

And when Wharton did come in, he was all smiles. He even had a joke with the plain-clothes man who carried in the small suitcase. Somehow Travers felt he'd never see a case from the professional point of view. All that interested himself was the case itself; the actual arrest and the final hanging were as repulsive to him as the slaughter of the beast that provided his evening cutlet. Wharton, on the other hand, looked as ghoulishly delighted as an undertaker who has found the perfect corpse.

"Everything all right, then?" Travers asked.

Wharton beamed. "He stepped clean into it—and he ended with a *faux pas!*" He gave a peep into the case. "Better see these disks are in the right order. Your machine all right? Splendid! Get your earphones on, and we'll make a start!"

In a way it was like listening in to a wireless play, with the acting uncannily direct, gaunt, and yet curiously nervous. There was a tension that even the dictaphone hadn't missed. First, out of the buzzing, noises of the room could be picked up—shuffling, crinkling of papers, a low cough; then the faint sound of voices . . . and feet . . . then the opening of a door.

"Morning, Braishe! Rotten morning! . . . Come along in! Let me take your coat! . . . Have some beer!"

"No, thanks. . . . Why are you staying here?"

"Because I'm supposed to be an invalid who mustn't show his face out of doors. By the way, you haven't come here with any—er—lethal designs on me? If you have, you'll be remarkably sorry. I spent most of yesterday writing a couple of letters—details of what we're going to discuss. If I'm not alive in an hour's time, they'll be posted: one to Scotland Yard, the other to Tommy Wildernesse."

"What's Wildernesse got to do with it?"

"You'll hear that in a minute. The important thing just now is whether you're going to be sensible; I mean—if you don't mind me being crude—whether you've brought the money. . . . You look a bit peevish! Er—won't you take your coat off? It's a bit stuffy in here."

"I suppose you realize"—Braishe's voice was absurdly stilted—"that I haven't the least idea of complying with that damned impudent demand of yours. The law protects . . . anybody against blackmailers!"

"That's right! So it does! You mean you'll be described as Mr. A or Mr. B . . . and of course nobody in court will recognize you!"

"Exactly!"

"Of course you realize you'll have to say exactly *why* I tried to blackmail you. That'd be awkward . . . for *you!*"

(A pause.)

"What's beyond that wall?"

"Air, my dear chap—air! Have a look round the room. You surely didn't think I'd have a confederate! You're going to give me the chance of a lifetime. You're my Little Nugget gold mine. Do you think I'd let anybody in on the ground floor of a proposition like that?"

"Well . . . spill it, Crashaw . . . if that's your name. What do you think you've got hold of?"

"Ah! that's better! What have I got hold of? Well, you've had specimens! . . . You don't mind me referring to my notes? First of all—speaking to a man of genius like yourself—may I say that in my own line I'm a genius too? I'm an artist. Just as you've got to choose the likely out of a mass of very unlikely, so I've got the gift for summing up a situation. That's why I knew Little Levington Hall was a gold mine. That's why I've invested my time and my small capital in working this thing out. That's why I could afford to take my time while that rather humorous detective—the elongated Travers—was groping about in the dark. That's why I risked a short term of imprisonment by coming back to the Hall that morning, when I might have made a clear getaway. That's why I took steps—if I were taken to Levington jail—to have a friend on the spot. You'll pardon the boasting!"

"Get on with it!"

"Quite! Well, you'll admit that results haven't been any too bad. I've told you all the 'Ivydale' business. Would you like to hear any details—what you were talking about in the seclusion of the bedroom, for instance? That little bit about—"

"That'll do, Crashaw. Keep your filthy tongue—"

"You sit down! Try and lay your hands on me, and it's the last thing you'll do. . . . Then you'll take my word for all that? You'll agree that I *might* have been trying to break into that house when I overheard what I did? And I might have followed you back to town and later on to Levington as a consequence? And I might have kept an eye on the lady at the same time? You look rather incredulous! You don't see how I could have been in two places at the same time! . . . Well, suppose Ransome was a friend—confederate, if you like—of mine. That makes you think! ... You don't feel like talking about it? . . . What *shall* we talk about then? . . . Oh! I know—Charles!

"By the way, you mustn't ask me *how* I got to know all the things I do know. As far as you're concerned, the chief thing is that I know 'em! All sorts of people talked to me. Challis babbled away like anything. Travers and your uncle-in-law talked away at the tops of their voices, and so on. However, as I was saying, the thing is that I know what I'm talking about—and if you force my hand I'll say what I know, on oath."

"The oath of a burglar!"

"If you like. But a burglar who's not in danger of hanging! Now, where were we? Oh, yes, at Charles. As soon as his name was put up to you as the burglar—and because he had a foreign intonation—you began to think a bit. You wondered something that'd never occurred to you before. Was he genuine? or had he got himself planted in the house for the purpose of robbery? Then you were scared. Why? Because if he was a crook, then he might have opened the safe. And if he opened the safe, he saw something very remarkable in it! Not the siphon—oh, no! *There never was one.* What he might have seen was a toy balloon!"

"Rubbish! Sheer rubbish!"

"Then why were you so anxious to find out if he *could* open the safe? You offered him money—so I'm told."

(A longish pause—Braishe having apparently no answer.)

"That reminds me. If I were you, I wouldn't mention anything about doubting my word. You'd have been in queer street if I hadn't kept mine to you when the police collared me down there. And you'll take a note of something else. Everything I'm telling you now, is extra to that promise I made you. . . . However, we'll leave Charles and the safe. We'll go on to the time when that suspicious devil Travers wanted somebody to sleep in the pagoda. He had an idea—at least, I should say so—that whoever knew there was anything fishy about that pagoda would be the one to volunteer to pass the night there. I rather thought of volunteering myself, having an idea of what he was driving at—and naturally wanting to protect you who were shortly going to be a customer of mine! Then, like a fool, you fell straight into the trap. Not Travers's trap—because he hadn't sense enough to see why you did it—but into *my* trap. You see, I know just why you offered to sleep there!"

A laugh. "Really! Most amusing!"

"Isn't it! But before I tell you why, we'll go back to the time when you first devised the scheme—after Challis had outlined to you *his* ideas of a fancy-dress ball. We'll simply start at the night of the party. In the general confusion, after the guests had gone, you cut the phones and you got the servants away on various jobs. You also got that toy balloon out of the safe and took it— under your raincoat—to the drawing room. I was there, behind the settee. You then put out the light and went to the pagoda. . . . I was interested—professionally. . . . Shall I tell you what you did then? You threw the phones away over the snow, the receiver, as the lighter, going farthest. You didn't know it was going to stop snowing! . . . You don't see the point? Never mind. You *will* do! . . . Then you went inside the pagoda! Remember it? ... I see you do!

"I'll own up I couldn't *see* precisely what you did, but I *know* what you did. Fewne was sleeping on a low, camp sort of bed, with an old, wire mattress. You got down on the floor beside that bed. I don't know whether you bent the frayed wires yourself, or merely happened to know they *were* frayed, but the fact remains that two of the wires were frayed and their short, jagged ends were bent down. Beneath these you put the balloon—and kept it in position with a couple of dead matches. The lamp was *over* the bed. Everywhere underneath the bed was in deep shadow. Even if he'd seen the balloon, he'd merely have thought it a joke of some kind. Simple, wasn't it? As soon as he got into bed, *his weight sagged down the mattress* and the balloon automatically punctured!

"I said the scheme was *simple*. That's an understatement. It was a masterpiece. For instance, the mattress couldn't sag till Fewne got into bed. If he got into bed, it would be to go to sleep. Therefore he'd be found dead with his sleeping clothes on—and apparently of heart failure. If the balloon was found, the finder would shake his head and think it a melancholy souvenir of the ball—placed by Fewne in his pocket and then thrown on the floor. . . . That was how you worked it all out . . . only something went wrong! Fewne was found in a pretty ghastly state. He wasn't peacefully sleeping!

"Nothing to say? . . . Well, it takes a good man to know when he's beaten! But we'll go on. Next morning various other annoying things happened. Travers turned out to have a flair for inquiry work, so dear old uncle didn't have the sole say in the matter of the death of Fewne, as you'd anticipated! The horrible position of the body, I've already mentioned. Then there was the murder of Mirabel Quest, and that meant *police*—and Uncle George quite an unimportant person. Still, you had some luck. Travers didn't see all he might. You were able to move that balloon from under the bed. And Fewne had scattered balloons all over the room. And you slept in the pagoda and managed to hide the siphon—lucky you had an empty one at all!—and turn up or put right those frayed mattress ends.... That all right?"

(Pause. No answer from Braishe. Travers said afterwards he felt creepy at the sound of that *one* voice only!)

"Now Tommy Wildernesse. Where does he come in? That was *my* masterpiece. Travers wanted some help in the pagoda and happened to call him over. I should say Travers had an idea that you'd a private pipe of some sort which let the lethal gas into the room. At .any rate, he asked Wildernesse—being a young and active chap—to get down under the bed to examine the joint of floor and wall. Wildernesse nearly tore his head on those frayed wires—and he noticed them. Next morning, after you'd 'discovered' the siphon, Travers still wasn't satisfied. He had Wildernesse over to make another search, and once more he went under the bed. This time he went under face up so as to avoid those wires—*but they weren't there!* You wouldn't think him an observant or secretive sort of chap, but he noticed all that—and he didn't say a word to Travers about it. But he happened to let it all out to me—and there we are!"

"You mean Wildernesse has the same ridiculous ideas as you have?"

"Oh, dear, no! Tommy Wildernesse is one of my reserves! Didn't I tell you nobody was coming in on the ground floor? I know that he knows—and he'll remember that I know. I mean, when he gets that letter I've written him—if you make me send it, of course!—he'll be a useful sort of chap to have on one's side. Scotland Yard'll just *love* him!"

A sort of growl. "And you really expect me to take all this seriously?"

"Well—er—I do! . . . Oh, I see. You think because that pagoda's burnt down, and bed and balloon with it, you're going to be safe! Don't you see that was the worst day's work you ever did? It wasn't sentiment that made you destroy that pagoda. If that pagoda had vanished into thin air it'd be evidence against the person who made it vanish." (Travers here had to imagine the pretended horror of the thought.) "My God! I hope you weren't such a damn fool as to suggest to the police that you'd like to grub that place up by the roots! If so, you've probably torn it!"

There was the tiniest pause, then Braishe's voice came like a shot out of a gun.

"Who killed Mirabel Quest?"

There Crashaw must have shrugged his shoulders.

"I never take any interest in what doesn't concern my particular business!"

"And Ransome?"

"Ah! That's different! If you cut up awkward, I may have to bring that in as a sideline. . . . But talking generally, are you satisfied?"

There was a long pause, then what might have been the pushing back of a chair.

"I'm satisfied about one thing—that when you talked about writing letters to people you were putting up a bluff. You haven't got a confederate! You daren't have!"

"Daren't I? That remains to be seen."

"I don't think so. In any case, Crashaw, I'm prepared to talk sense—to you. I'm not going to lay myself open to this sort of thing from half a dozen people of your kidney. Here's your cash—on one condition. Own up frankly that you haven't got any confederates; that those letters were all bluff . . . that you're on your own in this game."

Travers gripped the arms of his chair. He saw the trap—and Crashaw falling clean into it. The pause here was very long, as Crashaw thought things over.

"Mind you," went on Braishe's voice, "I own up to nothing. If I care to spend this money to protect somebody's name, that's my business. It's no use your trying to make any conditions with *me*. . . . What's it going to be? . . . The cash—or not?"

"Pass it over! . . . I'll own up. I'm a freelance!"

What happened then was wild confusion. The two voices were intermingled: Crashaw's in alarm, Braishe's in rage. There was the movement of feet; what sounded like a scuffle; the voices again; a terrible cry—Crashaw's voice, surely!—the rush of feet . . . the slamming of a door. Travers gripped the arms of his chair and held on like death—his eyes staring. As the clamour of noises entered his ears and left no explanation his breath was coming in short gasps. Then the needle scratched ... a buzzing . . . another scratch, and the disk ended.

Travers leaned back weakly in the chair, then took off the phones. "My God, George! What was that?"

Wharton grunted. "Something we didn't anticipate. As soon as that young fool let on he was alone, Braishe seized his collar. Then he pulled out a siphon—like the other one. Crashaw yelled like hell and bolted like an eel, leaving Braishe holding the coat by the collar! He moves pretty quick at any time, but I should say he beat his own record. Soon as he got outside, he flopped. Lucky for him Braishe opened the window and went down by the fire escape. Norris was waiting for him at the bottom!"

"Crashaw all right?"

"Right as rain. Damn badly scared at the time."

"He'll be coming round here? He promised he would."

"He's coming all right—so he said. When I left him he was off to the bar—for what he called an emetic."

Travers smiled queerly. "He's a curious mixture! . . . Pity Braishe didn't have a sniff of his own dope!"

Wharton was horrified. "What! The case of the century—and you the big noise!"

Travers shook his head—and he looked uncommonly in earnest.

"If you bring me into that case, George, I'll let you down as clean as dammit! You've got a case without me." He cocked his ear. "Sounds as if he's coming!"

Out in the hall Palmer's pontifical voice was heard; then another voice which sounded rather like a mild reproach. The voices mingled; then came a tap at the door. Travers instinctively groped for his glasses. Wharton slewed round in his chair. The handle turned, and Crashaw appeared, his face slightly flushed and his expression one of questioning timidity. Wharton nodded at him.

"Come along in, young man! . . . Feeling better?"

"Er—yes . . . thanks!"

That was the Levington voice; the voice of the quiet little fellow who'd talked about nicknames. Travers smiled to himself as he fumbled in the pocket which held his check book.

THE END

Made in the USA
Monee, IL
08 December 2020